ROUGH AROUND
THE EDGES

ROUGH AROUND THE EDGES

SUSAN JOHNSON
Dee Holmes
Stephanie Laurens
Eileen Wilks

St. Martin's Paperbacks

ROUGH AROUND THE EDGES

ISBN: 0-312-96599-0

Printed in the United States of America

St. Martin's Paperbacks edition / June 1998

10 9 8 7 6 5 4 3 2 1

CONTENTS

PLAYING WITH FIRE

Susan Johnson

London, May 1785

"**A** h-hem." The Duke of Ware's valet cleared his throat. "You have a visitor, Your Grace." He kept his gaze respectfully averted from the figures sprawled nude on the bed, deep in sleep. The duke's latest paramour slumbering beside him was recognizable even unclothed as a fashionable countess of the Ton.

"They're dead drunk," the Duke's solicitor bluntly noted, unconcerned with politesse as he surveyed the young duke and his mistress. Quickly debating his options, he said, "Get the countess out of here. I don't want any of her hysteria when I wake him for his wedding."

With a cool equanimity that was one of his prime assets as legal advisor to the disreputable Duke of Ware, he watched the valet delicately cover and then carry the slumbering woman from the bedchamber. And a moment later, he picked up the pitcher of water from a nearby table and emptied it over the duke's head.

Coming awake sputtering and swearing, Rupert Marsh caught sight of his solicitor well out of arm's reach and in a dangerously soft voice said, "What the devil are you doing here?" No sign of drunkenness was evident in his piercing gaze.

"It's your wedding day."

"And if I don't choose to be wed?" the duke growled, shaking his wet hair out of his eyes.

"I don't have time for arguments, Your Grace. You know as well as I do what will happen if you don't marry Miss Overton. Your father saw to that." The late duke had dissipated the Marsh fortune.

"At least I didn't inherit his heavy hand with cards," the duke muttered, pulling the wet pillow from under his head.

"No, Your Grace, but even your gambling expertise can't support the estate *and* cover your father's debts."

Rupert softly swore. "It's Wednesday, then."

"Yes, sir."

"How much time do I have?"

"An hour."

The tenth Duke of Ware went very still. "Jesus, Tyerman." His dark gaze was accusatory. "You're actually *doing* this to me?"

"The marriage settlement is extremely generous, sir. Extraordinarily generous for a tightfisted merchant banker."

"But then Overton wants a dukedom for his daughter," Rupert churlishly muttered.

"Yes, sir. He does indeed."

"A shame my father didn't drink himself to death sooner."

"I believe your mother expressed those same sentiments, sir."

"Is Maman downstairs?"

"She's on her way to the church and she expects you on time, she said."

"So there's nothing for it." A halfhearted stab at escape.

"I'm afraid not."

"What does my bride look like?" The duke couldn't

precisely recall, having fortified himself with two bottles of brandy before their only meeting a month ago at which time they'd exchanged a few brief words. The lady's tone had been decidedly cool—icy, actually, he remembered.

"She's very pleasant looking."

"A dowd, you're saying." Ware briefly closed his eyes and cursed his father's ineptitude.

"No, sir, she's out of the ordinary, but not conventionally beautiful . . . not your usual style."

"That sounds ominous," Rupert murmured, rolling up into a seated position in a ripple of honed muscle. "You did your duty now, Tyerman. I'll see you at the church."

"I'm to accompany you, sir."

"So I don't bolt."

"Something like that, sir," the solicitor calmly replied.

And he didn't move from the room until the Duke of Ware was dressed for his wedding. He politely removed the brandy bottle from the duke's grasp, though, once his toilette was complete. "We don't have any more time," he quietly said.

An ominous thought, Rupert reflected as he exited the room, his bachelorhood ticking away. Lord, he wished he could make someone pay for this misery, he darkly thought.

The bride was equally reluctant; her wealthy father's wish for an advantageous marriage was a personal quest quite separate from her own. And her only meeting with the profligate Duke of Ware had only deepened her dislike of the man who was a byword for vice.

"I want you to hold your tongue until the ceremony is over," John Overton said, scrutinizing his daughter's wedding attire with a critical eye one last time as they stood in the entrance hall prior to their departure for the church. "You'd think for the prices Madame DeBlanc charges," he went on, ignoring his daughter's querulous mood, "she could have added some more embroidered pearls to that garment.''

''I told her not to.''

Her father's eyes narrowed and his mouth set in that grim, straight line so familiar to those who opposed him. ''Ware's going to have his hands full with you.''

''I'm obliged by law to do your bidding, Father, but I'm not obliged to do it gracefully.'' Olivia Overton's smile was cool. ''As for Ware, I hope to have very little to do with him.''

''I've bought a duke for you and you'll do whatever is required of a duchess.'' John Overton glared at the daughter who had never conformed to his notions of filial obedience.

''You overestimate your influence, Father. I'm no longer your chattel once the wedding is over. Have you considered that?''

''I've considered *everything*.'' The man who privately financed the Prince of Wales's extravagances was not a man of obtuse sensibilities; the intricacies of his daughter's marriage contract held considerable advantages for him. ''Don't underestimate me,'' he softly warned.

''I shall be out from under your roof at least,'' his daughter curtly replied. ''And for that I should be grateful to the Duke of Ware's neediness.'' She tipped her head toward the door. ''Shall we get this over with?''

Good God, she was tall, Rupert thought at the sight of his bride moving down the aisle toward him. How had he missed that at their meeting last month?

She'd been seated.

Deliberately, he guessed.

And beneath that veil he suspected was a horse-faced woman to match that startling height.

He drew in a deep breath and reminded himself he was

saving his estate from ruin. But a soft oath escaped under his breath.

Or not so soft an oath, for several guests in the front rows cast piercing glances his way and his best man whispered in a commiserating tone, "It'll be over soon and we can get drunk."

Could he stay drunk for the rest of his life? Rupert cynically mused. The thought of actually living with this stranger was inconceivable. But she was within ten paces of him now and moments later at his side. Further contemplation of their incompatibility gave way to the bishop's droning recitation of the marriage sacrament.

When the priest came to the point in the ceremony when he said, "Do you take this man for your lawfully wedded husband?" an awkward silence fell. The prelate gazed pointedly at the bride, nodding at her finally in an attempt to encourage her response.

Silence. She didn't move; not a muscle or an eyelash.

Rupert turned to look at her, a foolhardy dream of freedom appearing in his mind. Was it possible? Could this torture be over? As a man he couldn't refuse at this late date without dishonoring the lady. But if the lady refused, he would be free.

"She says, 'I do,'" her father barked from his front-row seat.

The priest's gaze shifted from the bride to her father and he wondered for a moment if Overton's recent generous contribution to the church coffers had been insurance against just this eventuality.

"She says, 'I do,' to all the questions," the merchant banker curtly added, glaring at the bishop.

The bishop coughed and cleared his throat, the devil's own dilemma before him—the new tower bell had already been ordered.

He glanced once more at Overton, indecisive. But moral

courage could not long survive the banker's black scowl.

He proceeded.

And Rupert's mirage of freedom disappeared.

The ceremony was blessedly brief after that, the bride and groom visibly aloof, careful never to touch, their voices inaudible as they gave the required responses. The wedding breakfast was abbreviated as well—the social mix of cits and aristocrats an uneasy blend, with the bride and groom seated at separate tables.

Despite the brevity of the nuptial repast, Rupert downed three bottles of champagne, a fact noted by not only his bride, but all the guests. And his request that a case of chilled champagne be loaded onto the bridal carriage added further spice to the buzz of gossip.

"Ware's not looking forward to his honeymoon," a society belle whispered to her companion, her gaze on the duke's set jaw as he motioned a lackey to refill his glass.

"He might miss it altogether if he doesn't slow down. If one were counting I'd say that's his fourth bottle."

"He can last all night, darling. Everyone knows that."

"Some know that better than others," her companion replied, his glance sardonic.

"He's *very* nice company," Countess Beresford said with a sly smile.

"All the ladies seem to agree on that," the elderly Baron Montague wryly noted. "Although his duchess doesn't appear the type to be easily charmed."

"She looks strangely bored." The countess's delicate brows lifted in quizzing scrutiny. Could the bride actually be indifferent to Ware when every female in the Ton wanted him in her bed?

"As though she can barely bear the tedium. A change for Ware. Would you care to wager on the outcome of the evening?" the elderly roue silkily inquired.

"Don't be ridiculous, Montague. The man's a legend."

"Miss Overton exudes a certain"—the baron lightly shrugged—"shall we say . . . determination."

The countess's trilling laughter rippled across the table. "You'd bet against Ware?"

The baron shrugged again, the merest equivocation in the gesture. "Only for tonight. He's not interested; he's halfway into his cups already and it's barely noon. The bride detests him . . . it's obvious. I'll wager a pony on the bride tonight."

"I'd be happy to take your money, Charles. You apparently don't know Rupert. But how can we confirm the outcome?"

"The coachman, her maid, his valet perhaps. Servants' gossip is always swift to reach the Ton."

"A pony then on Rupert." She smiled. "And if I weren't your friend, Charles, I'd take more of your money."

Within the hour, the bride and groom were escorted to their carriage in a shower of rose petals and cheers, the breakfast champagne having fueled everyone's enthusiasm. The bride was helped into the carriage by a groomsman while the duke checked that his supply of champagne was properly secured with the baggage. Accepting the congratulations showered on him with a grim smile as he pushed through the crowd surrounding the carriage, he entered the vehicle in a bound, pulled the door shut with a snap, and dropped into a sprawl on the seat opposite his bride.

"Thank God that's over with," he gruffly said, beginning to uncork the champagne bottle he held in his hand.

"And now we just have to tolerate each other for the rest of our lives."

His head came up, his dark gaze critical. "You're a duchess at least."

"And you have money again."

Startled by her bluntness, he looked at her for the first

time. Apricot-colored hair, oddly shaped winged brows, delicate teal-blue eyes . . . or were they gray? A straight nose, not delicate at all, but fine, he grudgingly admitted. Full, pouty lips—extremely seductive, he thought, surprised at his assessment. And a shrewish disposition he had no intention of abiding, seductive lips or no. "Kindly keep your observations to yourself, Madame. I have no wish to be apprised of your feelings."

"But then my father bought you for me, so if I wish to express my feelings, I shall."

"You're playing with fire, Madame," he softly murmured, sudden fury in his gaze. "Take care you don't get burned."

"Have they paid you in advance?" she coolly inquired, relatively unintimidated by male threats after eighteen years in her father's household. "I'd hardly suspect my father so inept. He always wants full value for his money. In which case my person should be well-protected until the final payment of your contract."

"Had I known of your petulance, Madame, I would have demanded a higher price for my title."

"Your solicitor apparently chose not to apprise you of my dislike for rakes. Your debts must be formidable."

"My father's debts." Disgust vibrated through the curt words.

"We have something in common then."

Her voice was so filled with repugnance that the champagne bottle he was lifting to his mouth lay arrested midpoint in its journey. "Pray tell, Madame. I'm consumed with curiosity as to what we have in common."

"Our fathers have ruined our lives."

A brief flicker of surprise showed in his eyes, quickly replaced by his former cool regard. "Amen to that," he murmured. Continuing the movement of the bottle and tipping it upward, he emptied a goodly portion into his mouth.

His mood darkened as the journey progressed, his consumption of champagne continuing apace, his glowering expression external evidence of his sullen mood. Conversation ceased, a relief for Olivia who wished nothing more than to be left alone. And she prayed the miles to Ware Hill would pass swiftly as if her wishes might lend wings to the horses' hooves.

She'd survive, she reminded herself, like she had in the years under her father's roof. And if Ware Hill was as decrepit as their solicitor had indicated, she could keep busy refurbishing it. Her horses had been shipped down already and she smiled faintly in anticipation of their company. Anton and Polly were like friends to her—although she took care never to mention her feelings of closeness to her mounts, lest they suffer for her affection. She'd learned that lesson early in childhood when her father had sold her favorite pony to punish her.

And her writing was a constant source of joy. All her books had been sent to her new home, along with fresh paper and quills and her favorite violet ink. So she'd manage quite well if her husband would play the conventional role in a marriage of convenience. He could live his life and she would live hers.

Optimistic by nature, she found her spirits slowly improving. Ware had plenty of women in his life. He also—obviously—had no interest in her. Surely they could muddle along without getting in each other's way.

While Olivia was concentrating on the brighter aspects of their life together, Rupert dwelt on the loss of his independence. Not literally, of course, for aristocratic males had enormous license to do as they pleased, but legally and conventionally and dammit in every other way because—he didn't *want* a wife! The fact that he was shackled with one relentlessly looped through his brain, a disagreeable, bitter thought so unforgivingly oppressive he found himself fantasizing about voyages to the Spice Islands, to Xanadu, to any distant location where he could ignore his marriage and wife and conjugal duties.

When they arrived at the inn where plans had been made to spend the night, he almost gave orders to drive on because he had no wish to talk to his wife or touch her. But the marriage contract had been quite specific regarding heirs and the sooner he fulfilled his obligations, the sooner he could return to London and his former life.

The innkeeper and his wife greeted them with beaming smiles, offering their congratulations to the newlyweds for whom their best chamber had been reserved. They were fussed over, addressed as lovebirds, and in general forced to endure a thoroughly awkward interval before they were left alone.

"Do oysters appeal to you?" Rupert inquired, shutting the door on their hostess's pealing promise to bring oysters up post haste.

"Not in the least, but the woman was insisting on feeding us a ten-course meal—none of which I could stomach. The oysters are a compromise."

"You had no need to compromise with her."

"It was harmless," Olivia said, dropping into a chair with a sigh.

"I'll cancel them."

"How long can it take?" she replied, relatively indifferent to the entire issue.

"Longer than I wish to wait."

"You needn't wait at all. I will."

"Suit yourself," Rupert murmured, beginning to untie his neckcloth. He was tired, damnably sober considering the number of bottles he'd emptied, and impatient to get over what needed to be gotten over.

"What are you doing?" She viewed him with a direct, open gaze.

"Undressing. You understand the gist of the addendum having to do with an heir, I presume," he added, tossing his neckcloth on the bureau. "Hopefully it won't take too long."

"Addendum?" Olivia's voice held a hint of belligerence.

"Once you're breeding, an added increment is paid to my solicitor and on the birth of a son, my father's debts are paid in full." He stripped his jacket off. "So I intend to bed you, my lady wife, with dutiful diligence—every day, twice or three times a day if necessary—until you find yourself with child."

"How dare you," she snapped, bristling at his languid tone, at the cold indifference in his voice.

"I needn't dare at all, Duchess. You're mine to do with as I wish." His smile was chill as he kicked off his shoes.

"I'll scream."

"And then?" He tugged his shirt loose from his breeches, his gaze bland.

"The innkeeper will come," she pettishly replied.

"And then?" His voice was muffled for a moment as he pulled his shirt over his head, but his casual tone was unchanged.

"He'll . . ."

"Save you from your husband?" the duke helpfully offered, slipping his silk stockings off.

"Yes."

"Not unless they've changed the laws since we left London."

"Damn you."

"The feeling is mutual, my lady. But you don't have a choice." He stood for a moment, clad only in his breeches, his powerful body taut with frustration, his dark eyes moody. And then he drew in a deep breath and exhaled it in a sigh. "I can make it pleasant. You won't suffer."

"You know that, do you?" Tart anger colored her voice.

"I know that," he softly said.

And then the sound of footsteps on the stairs indicated the returning landlady and his expression altered to something less benign. "Don't move or you'll regret it. I dislike public scenes."

He was right, of course, Olivia understood. She was his property as much as she'd once been her father's, so she refrained from drawing attention to her plight when no help was available. She realized, even while she might cavil, that a wedding night was required.

He cut the landlady short at the door, taking the platter from her hands with a graceful smile and a courteous thank you before closing the door firmly on her chatter. Walking over to Olivia, he offered her the oysters with a small bow, placing them on the table beside her chair. "Some claim aphrodisiac powers for the mollusks. Perhaps you'd like to fortify yourself for the ordeal," he noted with a fleeting smile.

"Thank you, no. I have a high threshold for pain."

He looked at her with minute attention and she noticed his eyes were tinged with lavender in their dark depths. Strangely, it personalized him.

"Are you expecting pain?"

"This entire day has been painful." She sat stiffly upright. "I only expect more."

"Acquit me, Duchess. I intend no such thing." She was trembling, and not from passion. A novel concept for a man whose capacity for pleasuring women was renowned.

"Then leave me alone."

"But your father expects an heir."

"Let him wait."

"If only," he murmured, "my father's debts would wait."

"This is all about money, isn't it?" she accused.

"Lack of money," he corrected. "Which unfortunately was my only inheritance other than the title your father purchased."

"So I'm to breed you a son and solvency."

"Apparently my solicitor and your father agreed on that plan."

"And you had no say?"

"Realistically, no. Did you?"

"Not when a dukedom was for sale."

"An earl no longer suited," he sardonically noted.

"Nor any other title. Father told me your handsomeness would make up for my plainness in our children."

"He was mistaken."

Her pained gaze held his for a moment. "You're not one whit plain, Duchess," he explained. "Thank God," he added with a small grin.

His compliment pleased her when it shouldn't—when she should hate him instead. "You didn't remember me did you?"

"I was three parts drunk when I met you. Tyerman had two men put me in the carriage. Although I recall your icy voice."

She recalled how his stark beauty had dazzled her when he'd strolled into the drawing room, his dark hair sleekly tied back with a black silk ribbon at the nape of his neck, his aquiline features so perfect she thought Adonis had come to life in her presence. And the breadth of his shoulders had stretched limitlessly before her eyes when he'd languidly bowed to kiss her hand. She'd decided then when his heavy-lidded gaze had lifted to hers that if she must be sold off for a title, he at least was worth the price in physical beauty.

"Look," he said, squatting down on his haunches so their eyes were level. "We're both forced into this durance vile." He lightly touched her fingers clasped in her lap. "So if we can put aside our anger for a time, maybe we can make this wedding night less objectionable.''

She took a small, steadying breath. ''I'd like that.''

He smiled again, a slow, delicious smile that promised pleasure and she understood why women followed him in droves.

''Are you charming me?''

''No, I'm too ill-tempered to charm.''

''I'm impressed nonetheless.''

''Good,'' he murmured so low she wasn't sure he'd spoken.

His skin was bronzed by the sun, his powerful musculature honed, sculpted. Like the body of a beautiful pagan god, she thought; athletic, virile and irresistibly . . . close enough to touch.

She clenched her fingers more tightly against the impulse and feeling the movement beneath his hand, he looked down for a second.

''You needn't be afraid. Here . . . relax,'' he gently offered, separating her hands, lifting first one, then the other to his mouth, brushing a light, warm kiss over her knuckles. ''Is that better?'' he murmured, gazing at her over her captured hands.

She nodded, but it was actually much worse. Her senses had suddenly become alert, and she realized that she was as susceptible to his potent charm as all the other ladies.

''I won't hurt you,'' he whispered, replacing her hands in her lap, rolling slightly forward so he could unfasten the bow at the neckline of her gown. ''We'll go very . . . slowly.'' The ribbon lay loose in his fingers. ''And if you're uncomfortable about anything . . .'' He unhooked the first hook at her bosom. ''Let me know . . .''

She should answer; she should speak, respond in some way other than this overwhelming rush of heat streaking through her senses. ''I'm warm,'' she said, artless and unsuave, her voice sounding oddly distant, as if the words had come from across the room.

"Good," he said again in that same low tone. He was pleasantly surprised at her precipitous response. His new duchess apparently had carnal urges. Although the next cynical question was whether they were virginal urges or not.

He'd find out soon enough.

He undressed her in a slow, measured way while she sat silent before him, her flesh warming to his touch, a rose blush coloring the paleness of her skin. And he kissed her lightly from time to time on her neck and ears, her cheek, on the gentle curve of her bare shoulder.

Until her breathing changed and she trembled when he touched her. Until, bared to the waist and eyes shut, she moaned softly as he cupped her plump breast in the palm of his hand and kissed its taut crest.

He sucked gently, her whimpers erratic, small sounds in the quiet room, and when he slipped his hand beneath the muslin froth of her skirt and touched the silken warmth between her thighs, she gasped.

He smiled faintly. His bride was slippery wet with desire. Sliding his fingers forward, they met resistance.

His *virgin* bride, he observed.

The thought perversely aroused him although he'd never had a taste for virgins. Perhaps one needed a virgin of one's own, he derisively thought. But the seduction took on a new and irrepressible excitement. A novel sense of possession gripped his senses.

She was his alone, he licentiously reflected, as if he owned that tantalizing, heated portion of her anatomy to the exclusion of all other males.

And unsated, she waited for him to satisfy her desires.

He was suddenly in the mood to accommodate her, his aversion to his new bride, he discovered, was subject to the volatility of carnal lust and the more curious variable of ownership.

He kissed her for the first time on her full, seductive lips and her mouth opened slowly beneath the inexorable pressure of his kiss. Tantalized, touched with elusive longing, her mind was filled with sweet possibility, her body pulsing in new and strange ways.

Then he moved his hand between her thighs and inexplicably a chill shuddered down her spine, suddenly reminding her that she was face-to-face with the ultimate barter.

Jerking her head away, every muscle in her body stiffened and she said, curtly and low, "Don't touch me."

He was touching her of course—intimately—which added a taut incredulity to the moment.

"Too late."

"I mean it," she hotly insisted. "I'm not a commodity."

"Yes, you are," he softly said. "You're here and I'm here because we have a function to fulfill. You're a biddable miss—or supposed to be," he added, a touch of grimness in his voice. "And I'm the means of seeing that you're biddable."

"And I'm the means of discouraging such arrogance. Move your damned hand."

He did, shifting back on his haunches. Curbing his temper with difficulty, he quietly said, "Look, we can't avoid this if we argue till doomsday. Consummation is a requirement . . . if not tonight, tomorrow or the next day. What's the point in delaying the inevitable?"

"Because I wish to," she flatly said.

He abruptly rose to his feet in a flaring, brusque anger, and stalked across the room, distancing himself as far as possible in the limited space. Standing at the window, he gazed down on the scene below, the yard a frenzy of activity, wondering exasperatedly how his life had come to this abysmal point. If it weren't the most ungodly oppression to be married, now his bride refused to be *touched*. And forcing women wasn't in his repertoire. At the ludicrous thought, a smile formed on his mouth, his experience to date more a matter of fending off pursuing females. Ironic retribution, he sardonically reflected.

Surveying her husband's rigid posture, Olivia realized he loathed this mandated wedding night as much as she and, at base, his response was eminently practical and sensible. It didn't matter one whit in the endless years of this marriage whether consummation occurred now or later. But occur it must. Drawing in a sustaining breath, she steeled herself for the distasteful inevitability of a wedding night with this stranger.

Her gaze took in the large tester bed draped in a hideous crimson velvet, lingered for a moment on her husband's clothes lying in disarray on the floor, and moved irrelevantly to her perfectly manicured nails—as if it mattered that her nails were buffed for this occasion. So much for the profundities of life, she silently derided and then, resolution firm in her voice, she said, "I'm ready now."

A remnant of Rupert's smile still lingered as he turned from the window.

"You find this amusing?"

"Not in the least." Resting his hands on the windowsill, he leaned against them. "I'm glad you changed your mind," he politely remarked, wishing he could change *his* mind and ride back to London.

"Then we might as well get it over with," Olivia tautly said, as though she were about to step into the jaws of hell. Rising from her chair, she unhooked the remaining fastenings on her gown. The white muslin tumbled to the floor, gown and petticoats and chemise. "Where would you like me?'' she curtly inquired, standing nude before him, her brows raised in gelid query.

Back in London, in your father's house, unknown to me, Rupert briefly thought. ''Why don't we try the bed,'' he said instead, courteously holding out his hand.

Her eyes were tightly shut at first, her muscles tense as she lay on the bed, but the duke's amorous reputation was well-grounded in fact and unimpeachable. He also was intent on *never* having to go through another wedding night. So he caressed and stroked, kissed and petted, and in due time her lashes fluttered open, her limbs relaxed and she said in a dreamy whisper, ''That's ever . . . so nice . . .''

He knew, but he looked up from the vicinity of her mons where he was presently ensconced and said, ''I thought you'd like it.''

''I'm hot and . . . shivery, too.'' Her gaze was half-lidded, heated. ''Everything . . . tingles.''

''Here?'' he gently asked, licking the swollen flesh of her labia.

She groaned, an exquisite pulsing accelerating deep inside her.

''Or here?'' he murmured inserting his tongue into her heated cleft.

A small, muffled cry escaped her and she lifted her hips, reaching for elusive sensation.

He'd tantalized every inch of her body, with gentle hands, with gentle kisses, with an expertise acquired and cultivated in boudoirs from Stamboul to Land's End. And she was ready now; more than ready—ravenous.

Moving upward, he settled between her thighs. ''Touch me,'' he whispered.

Her eyes widened at the shocking notion, but a second later her hands slipped downward between their bodies and she touched his velvety skin, her fingers closing over his erection.

"That goes *here*," he softly said, stroking her throbbing flesh.

Impatient now, almost greedy, she shifted the position of her hands and he helped her, guiding her hands with his, carefully placing the engorged head at precisely the right point.

She didn't know how to ask for surcease, but a breathless eagerness impelled her and she clung to him, lifting to meet him.

He plunged forward in a swift, sure thrust and her fingers dug into his back for a brief moment of shock. Then he slipped inside her luscious warmth and Olivia Overton's denouement was complete.

"Are you all right?" he whispered, gazing down at her.

"Oh, *yes*," she whispered back, waves of rapture beginning to inundate her brain. "Please—don't stop . . ." Sliding her hands down his spine, she held him more securely, not wanting to lose the precious feeling.

"Does this hurt?" he gently asked, driving deeper with a carefully controlled momentum.

"Oh, God, no," she breathed, pure pleasure melting through her body, the feel of him inside her exquisite, riveting. "Do it again," she gasped.

He did, over and over again, penetrating and withdrawing slowly, gently, performing with an unselfish, virtuoso proficiency until the new Duchess of Ware expired in a trembling orgasm.

And then the Duke of Ware discharged his duty and semen, and the first transaction toward securing the dukedom was complete.

Later that night a second, third, and fourth pleasurable mating further assured the conception of an heir. And duty no longer motivated the duke, only raw lust.

His new bride tempted and aroused him, her ingenuous desire both innocent and gratifyingly torrid. And during the long, heated hours of the night, while Olivia learned the tempestuous allure of sexual desire and Rupert pleasantly tested his stamina and zeal, he momentarily forgot the onerous burdens of marriage.

But he was gone when she woke, the morning sunshine streaming in through the casement windows and it took her a moment to sort the tumult of her feelings. Her husband deserved his reputation for giving pleasure; she couldn't fault him on that. He was the consummate lover, gentle when gentleness was required and tantalizingly wild when it was not. She felt a streaking heat rush through her body as she recalled their wedding night. But she quickly reminded herself that making love was his specialty and she would only be hurt if she read too much into a night of physical gratification.

Although, she thought, a smile forming on her lips, she now realized there were raptures beyond those she experienced writing sonnets and prose—until now, her most intense emotions. And while her marriage was of a certainty not made in heaven, it gave promise of at least an occasional glimpse into paradise. However, she was a practical woman—a necessity when raised by a father immune to human feeling. She understood the perimeters of her role as wife. But if there was more in terms of intimacy with her husband, she would consider it a bonus.

Rupert held himself aloof after their wedding night, sending up a groom with a message concerning the time of departure. Riding ahead on one of his thoroughbreds that had been brought to Bainbridge instead of keeping her company in the carriage. His initial conjugal responsibilities performed, he had no intention of befriending his wife.

When Ware Hill hove into view that afternoon, the sight was impressive even to a wealthy banker's daughter. Visible from a great distance, the baroque mansion sprawled atop a gentle rise, framed by acres of gardens in full bloom. The scent of roses was heady as the carriage bowled along the miles-long drive, hedges of rosa mundi and damask rose bordering the cobbled road.

Rupert helped her down from the carriage before a towering Van Brugh portico. When she'd alighted, he waved a hand in the direction of the servants lined up in rows in the courtyard, and casually said, ''Duchess, I'd like you to meet the staff.''

She smiled at the countless faces. So many, she thought, suddenly daunted by the extent of the household.

''You'll get to know their names in time. Mrs. Hodges is quite capable. Maman preferred not involving herself in the day-to-day activities. Feel free to suit yourself on that count. Now if you'll excuse me,'' he politely said, as though he were not abandoning her before acres of mansion and an army of retainers. ''My stud manager tells me two new foals arrived yesterday. Mrs. Hodges,'' he called, motioning forward a short, rotund woman.

And with a bow he walked away, already in conversation with two of his stable staff before he was five paces distant.

She was on her own, Olivia realized, an intimidating thought even for a woman who had spent a solitary existence in her father's household. But the duke was offering her a degree of freedom as well, and for that she was grateful. The housekeeper smiled at her and she smiled back.

It was a start.

''Ware Hill can use a new mistress,'' Mrs. Hodges said, gazing up at the new duchess. ''Welcome to your home.''

''Thank you. I'm sure I'll be relying on your expertise to see that I don't make too many faux pas.''

''You needn't worry, my dear. The dowager duchess didn't lift a finger and we're no worse off for it. Let me show you your rooms.''

And on the lengthy walk through corridors on the first and second levels, Mrs. Hodges kept up a pleasant chatter having to do with the location of rooms, their decor, and the need for renovation. "Poor Rupert was left in terrible straits by his scoundrel father. Everyone breathed a sigh of relief when the ninth duke died."

Olivia took note of the familiar use of her husband's name, and decided Rupert's household was several degrees less punctilious than her father's. "Is the dowager in residence?"

"No, dear, she has no intention of interfering, she said, after having to endure her nasty mother-in-law for ten years."

"I see," Olivia said on an astonished breath. Apparently no bit of family history was sacred to Mrs. Hodges. "Is the duke often in residence?" she asked next, knowing her best source of information on her husband was walking at her side.

"Not often, although he told his manager Gordan, that he would be here through the summer. The staff is pleased because they don't see enough of him. He's loved by all."

"I see," Olivia repeated, surprised anew. Rupert Marsh had the reputation in London of spending his days and nights in gambling clubs or bordellos. She hadn't thought him well-acquainted with those on his country estate.

"Now don't be alarmed by the sight of your rooms. The dowager duchess collected Meissen figurines and she thought you might like them as well. She took her best ones with her, of course, but there's a tumble of them still left."

An understatement, Olivia discovered when she entered her suite of rooms. Glass cabinets lined the walls, filled to overflowing with delicate porcelain figures. Tabletops were aclutter with them as well as the mantel and bedstand. "Oh, dear," she murmured, unable to control her shock.

"I told her to take them out, but Melanie isn't one to

be told much,'' Mrs. Hodges said in an affectionate tone. ''And Rupert likes them because his mother likes them. He adores his mother.''

A small sadness transiently overwhelmed Olivia as she thought of her own lonely childhood without a mother. ''They're fine for now,'' she said, surveying the colorful collection. And she didn't know if she was delaying her decision or pleasing her husband, an untidy chaos distorting the normal functioning of her mind. Her preconceived notions about the Duke of Ware were being swiftly altered.

She didn't see her husband the rest of the day until he slipped into place opposite her in the dining room very late that evening. He was out of breath and had hastily dressed for dinner—his hair was still wet. ''Pardon my lateness. Hodges told me I had to be here for dinner.'' He smiled. ''And I almost made it.'' Taking note of the food on Olivia's plate, he spoke to the butler hovering at his shoulder. ''I'll have some beef with my dessert, Boyd. And a bottle of claret.''

He was polite and gracious before the servants, talking more to them than his wife, at home in his surroundings. And when Mrs. Hodges came in a short time later and announced, ''Tea is ready in the Canaletto salon,'' with a significant look at the duke, he grinned at her.

''Am I behaving properly, Hodges?''

''Hmph,'' she snorted. ''As if someone should have to be telling you what to do.''

''I always thought it was your job. Since Maman never learned to give orders.''

''Which accounts for your wildness,'' she muttered. ''Now take the duchess to the salon before the tea gets cold.''

''I hope you wish for tea,'' he said to Olivia with a smile as he rose from his chair, ''because there's no way out of it.''

"Tea would be most pleasant," Olivia replied, earning herself a warm smile from the housekeeper.

He offered her his hand a moment later and she thought looking up at him that he was much too handsome for his own good. Or more pertinently for *her* good. A sudden shiver ran down her spine as their fingers met, his hand hot to her touch. And she was reminded how hot he could be, how lustful and passionate, how zealous a lover.

"Your hands are cold," he said, immune to the heady sensations she was feeling. "Tea will warm you up."

A cogent reminder, she thought, to resist romantical notions apropos her husband.

He didn't drink tea, of course, but he drank a good share of the cognac Mrs. Hodges had had the good sense to put on the tea tray. And he spoke to Olivia of the new foals, the dredging of the wetlands to the east of the house, and the villagers' appreciation for the new roofs on their cottages.

"You were busy since I saw you last."

"Your money is reclaiming Ware Hill from decay." And while his words were courteous, his tone was touched with bitterness.

"My father's money."

"Has no one told you you're an heiress?" he coolly remarked, refilling his glass. Surely she wasn't so naive.

"If I am, it does me no good. Had someone asked me, I might have preferred donating my money to a needy charity rather than be sold away for my father's aristocratic aspirations."

"So we're both in bondage."

"Luxurious bondage," she noted, surveying the magnificent salon decorated by Canaletto three decades ago.

"Which brings to mind my responsibilities for servicing you."

"How rude you are."

"How beholden I am."

"And I'm to pay for your resentment?"

"Someone has to," he said with a chill smile.

"Kindly focus your servicing functions on someone else."

"I don't think your father would like muddied bloodlines in his grandson. Are you so gracious a wife as to offer me my amorous freedom?"

"I doubt I could dictate to a man of such licentious repute. Or are you saying I could? That you would be faithful?"

He laughed. "Men aren't faithful."

"Apparently many women aren't as well." She'd heard all the stories of his various lovers.

"As long as you are."

"Is that an order?"

His gaze was piercing. "Damn right it is."

"Perhaps heiresses are less submissive than other women." If he could be resentful, she could as well.

"But submissive nevertheless," he softly growled, setting his glass down.

"Are you threatening me?"

"Simply stating a fact. Now if you'd kindly go to your bedchamber, I'll be up shortly."

"I have no intention of going to my bedchamber. I prefer having tea."

He leaned across the small tea table separating them and took the cup from her hand with such swiftness she hadn't time to react. His eyes had turned predatory. "Will you go of your own accord or must I carry you?"

"I most certainly will not." She clasped the chair arms.

His eyes narrowed. "I'm not in the mood tonight to play the polite suitor."

"And I'm not in the mood to respond to your boorishness."

"Too bad." He rose.

"Will you embarrass me in front of the servants?"

"Without a qualm." In two strides he was beside her, her hands were pried free, and a second later she was scooped up into his arms in a flurry of rustling silk. "I can't resist my young bride," he sardonically murmured, striding toward the door. "The staff will find it quite romantic unless you scream." He smiled. "Although they might find that romantic as well."

"I'll make you pay for this," she hissed as he swung open the door.

"You already have, Duchess, more than you know." He nodded at the lackey at the base of the stairs. "The duchess is feeling faint," he pleasantly said. "Have some hartshorn sent up."

Olivia had to bite her lip to keep from screaming, damn his insolence.

"There, there, darling," he consoled in a voice that carried through the halls. "You'll feel better soon."

"I'll feel better when I give you a good swift kick," she muttered.

"You're not strong enough."

"I'm stronger than you think."

"I didn't know you had such gumption."

"My father was careful to deceive you on that point."

"You interest me, Duchess," he murmured, his gaze unabashedly sensual.

"Apart from my money, you mean."

"You *are* a little bitch, aren't you?"

"They didn't tell you that either?"

"They told me what they had to to sell you off," he brusquely said.

"I, on the other hand, was only told to order my wedding gown."

"Perhaps at some later time we could argue the inequities of life," he said, cheeky and rude. "Right now," he went on, "my function in this marriage contract is yet to be performed. I must get you with child."

"I hope it happens soon," she snapped, "so I'm rid of you."

"The faster the better," he muttered, kicking open the door to the duchess's suite. "Get out," he growled at the startled lady's maid. At her fearful expression, he added a slightly less surly, "Please," his smile tight. "The duchess will be sleeping late. Don't disturb her until called for."

The young woman scurried from the room.

"She'll tell everyone," Olivia accused, wriggling in his arms, struggling to free herself.

"Good," he muttered, tightening his grip, restraining her. "Maybe next time you'll behave."

"I don't intend to behave." Her hot gaze was inches from his. "*Particularly* for you."

"You'll learn," he grimly said, tossing her on the bed.

She rolled off the bed in a flash and, holding her skirts high, she raced toward the dressing-room door. With the bed separating them, she almost managed to escape before Rupert caught up to her, his hand sliding between the jamb and the dressing-room door just as it was closing.

She pushed hard.

He grunted at the sharp pain and then swore, stiff-arming the door open with such force, she was wedged between the door and wall. Keeping her pinioned there, he examined his throbbing fingers.

"You're hurting me," she muttered, her voice muted through the heavy oak.

Easing his hold, he held up his purpling fingers. "You're damned dangerous," he said, his voice unnaturally restrained, his temper barely in check.

"You'll heal," she acidly retorted, moving away from the wall.

"Not so fast." He clamped his good hand around her wrist.

"Let me go," she snapped.

He shook his head.

"I *despise* you." She tried to shake his hand off.

"Tell me something I don't know," he brusquely replied, his hold crushing. Propelling her toward a small upholstered chair, he abruptly pushed her facedown over the chair back, lifted her skirts with a sweep of his hand and said, low and taut, "Luckily this doesn't require cordiality."

"You bastard!" She struggled to rise. "Release me!"

Her pink bottom was provocatively raised as he held her firmly in place, his hand hard on her back. "In a minute," he murmured, perversely aroused by her submissive pose, by her blatantly exposed labia. "I'm going to screw you first." And the pain he was presently suffering as he unbuttoned his breeches with his injured hand gave him added license to indulge his whims—retaliation as it were.

Exerting sufficient pressure to restrain her, he moved against her tantalizing bottom, guided his erection to her enticing cleft, and penetrated her.

"Damn you!" she cried, arching away, trying to elude his invasion. But he held her securely, his uninjured hand braced against her back, his bruised fingers lightly placed on her hip as he plunged deeper, her squirming attempts to dislodge him only opening her pliant flesh further to his thrusting strokes.

Until fully impaled, she felt the first traitorous ripple of pleasure.

Swearing a plague on his head, she renewed her efforts to escape.

But he knew better; he'd felt it too—her rigid muscles had unclenched beneath his hand and the tiny whimper she'd tried to conceal was a familiar sound to a man of his libertine habits.

She was wet for him—or more pragmatically, he noted—for sex. "If I had more time," he drawled, rude and impudent, "I'd let you climax, too." Unfortunately, he wasn't in the frame of mind to be generous. She was flowing wet around him and in a swift rhythm of penetration and withdrawal, he quickly came to orgasm. Immediately he withdrew from her, she lunged upright, spun around and slapped him so hard, he was jolted briefly off balance.

"Cur! Knave! Villain!" she screamed, her fists pummeling him wildly, tears running down her cheeks, hating him for what he'd just done to her, deeply shaken by her unwonted response. "I hate you! I hate you! I hate you!"

He stood unresisting under her fierce attack, roughly putting his clothes in order, warding off the blows as best he could, his own temper at tinder point, not sure how long he could restrain himself from striking back. Damn her and damn her father and damn his own ill-fortune! Angry, frustrated, bleeding, he bitterly noted—his wife's nails having gouged deep scratches down his face—all because a fuck wasn't a fuck wasn't a fuck. In his case, unfortunately, it was a damned command performance.

He swiftly took the offensive though when Olivia swept up a Meissen figurine from the table beside the chair and raised it over her head. "Not my mother's Pierrot," he snapped, capturing her hand before she could hurl the object. Easing her grip from around the fragile porcelain, he replaced it on the table.

"That's enough," he grimly said. "I think we're about even in terms of damage."

"Don't delude yourself. I'd kill you if I could."

"But you can't." His grasp on her hand was just short of bone-breaking.

"Don't be so sure."

"Jesus," he softly breathed, startled by her malevolence. "How the hell did we get to this point?"

"You acted like an animal. That's how!" Flushed, disheveled, her face tear-streaked, she glared at him.

"*Merde,*" he softly swore, releasing his grip, the degree of enmity in her tone, her stance, her heated gaze like a punch in the gut.

"Is that an apology?" she caustically inquired.

"Do you want an apology?"

"I want you out of my life."

"And I you," he quietly replied. "But it's not an option. If it helps, I'm sorry." A rueful grimace marred his handsome face. "Look, it's punishing to us both—this obligatory sex. And I truly beg your pardon."

Shocked by his apology, still breathless from her assault, Olivia stood wide-eyed, silent. Was this some ruse or was he genuinely sorry?

In the charged hush, Rupert looked at his wife for perhaps the first time that evening, his gaze taking in her dishabille, her tousled hair and pink cheeks, her rucked-up skirt and disarranged decolletage. And suddenly, he felt an unconscionable jolt of desire. Abruptly stepping back, he said in a tone of chill politesse, "I'll bid you good night," forcing himself to act the gentleman in his wife's bedchamber.

When carnal urges flooded his mind.

He'd missed a button on his breeches, Olivia thought, when she shouldn't be looking at his breeches at all. But she had, for inexplicable reasons, and she saw his erection swell beneath the fine black silk. "You missed a button," she whispered.

His gaze snapped downward, his erection swelled further and when his eyes met hers a moment later, irresolution flickered for a brief second. Prey to carnal impulse—a powerful motive in his life—*and* to the small heat beginning to shimmer in his wife's eyes, Rupert said very low, "Do you suppose . . . we could try this again—differently?" His smile, charming, genial, and suggestive of mutually agreeable pleasures, had been perfected in the course of his youthful apprenticeship in the Countess Boulonger's Parisian boudoir. "Your rules," he softly added. When she didn't respond, he equivocated, "It's just a thought." His own impulses highly ambiguous, he questioned how he could allow himself to feel interest in a woman who was anathema to him.

Temptation warring with reason, her fickle body capricious with unsated need, Olivia murmured, "I don't . . . know . . ."

His brows quirked—in understanding or query, even he wasn't sure in this minefield of emotions.

"My feelings are—indecisive . . . in turmoil actually," she confessed, looking chaste and virtuous in her rumpled silk gown, like the ruined child/women Greuze portrayed with such erotic innocence.

"I regret my actions," he said with exemplary courtesy. "Perhaps this marriage is too new for us both."

"And miserable."

His mouth curved into an almost-smile. "Last night wasn't completely miserable."

"The sex, you mean?"

His dark brows raised infinitesimally. "It's a start." His smile this time warmed the depths of his eyes.

And suddenly she couldn't resist smiling back. "That always works, doesn't it?"

He shrugged, not about to get into a new argument. "I can keep you up all night again if you like," he offered instead.

"Such assurance, Ware." Mildly piqued, she challenged, "What if I want two nights?"

"Then we have more in common than I thought," he replied with a wicked grin. "And I'd be happy to oblige you."

"I should hate you."

"Hate me later. Let me indulge you now." My God, she was rosy and pink and so damnably fresh, she should have dew on her skin.

"So selfless," she sarcastically murmured.

His brows rose again. "Hardly." He held out his hand. And after the briefest hesitation, she placed her hand in his.

He undressed her so slowly, she was panting with need before he obliged her the first time, placing her arms around his neck, lifting her bodily, wrapping her legs around his waist, and entering her in such breath-held, languid degrees that she was begging him at the last. His erection swelled at her ravenous desire and he gave her what she wanted—what he wanted—and she sighed away brief moments later, going limp in his arms.

He carried her to the bed in her half-swoon, laid her gently down and began undressing himself. The air felt like velvet on her skin and a kind of contentment she'd never experienced shimmered through her senses. How beautiful he was, she thought, watching him—even more beautiful unclothed, his lithe power and grace, his untrammeled virility every woman's dream. Fascinated, she watched him discard his coat, then, in quick succession, his shoes and stockings. His neckcloth came free and his white silk shirt was tugged off with swift masculine efficiency and she felt the heat between her legs rekindle and anticipation strum through her brain. "Let me," she whispered when he began sliding his snug-fitting breeches down his hips, the throbbing deep inside her palpable now.

He stood perfectly still and waited for her, the engorged veins of his penis visibly pulsing, the flaunting length of his erection increasing, expectation taut in every sleek muscle of his body.

Sliding from the bed, Olivia padded barefoot across the Aubusson carpet, her plump breasts quivering, her long slender legs and the moist apex between them drawing his gaze.

When she touched him, he felt a sudden need to plunge inside her, but he restrained such gauche impulses, drew in a deep breath of constraint and watched her lower herself to her knees before him to slide off his breeches.

As he stepped free from the garment, he slipped his fingers through her glossy red-gold hair, holding her head lightly between his palms.

Gazing up at him, heated passion in her eyes, she ran her fingertips up his erection as if measuring the extent of her pleasure. "You're very tempting."

"I'm glad," he said on a suffocated breath, her mouth only a hair's breath away, every nerve in his body acutely sensitive to the matter of distance.

A knock on the door crashed through the stifled hush.

"The duchess's hartshorn, your grace!"

"Go away!" the duke shouted. "If you don't mind," he added, glancing down at Olivia.

"I don't think I need hartshorn," she murmured, her upturned gaze teasing. "I'm rather wide-awake."

"Aren't we all?" he whispered, tightening his hold.

Her fingers closed around him, her tongue touched him, then her mouth opened and she drew him in and within seconds Rupert's entire concentration was focused on the gratifying bliss of friction and tempo. He stroked her throat in an inadvertent gesture of possession—dominant male to yielding female. And then he felt the sensational small bite and he groaned softly, each tender nibble agonizing, intoxicating.

A short time later, he held her immobile for a brief moment and said, "Are you sure?"

Her glance lifted, she nodded, a wanton heat in her eyes and her teeth lightly closed on him.

"Oh, God," he breathed, his fingers flexing in her hair.

She swallowed, drew in a hasty breath, swallowed again and then took care to suckle more delicately. And after offering a last tender nibble, she rose to her feet. "I think it's my turn now," she said smiling up at him.

"Give me a minute," he murmured, his breath still ragged, his gaze only marginally focused.

"You *look* ready," she playfully said, taking note of his arousal, still splendidly upthrust. "I just adore *this*," she softly added, running her fingertip lightly up his erection.

He sucked in his breath.

"Now look at *that*," she said with delight.

Much, much later, tucked into the curve of his arm, she turned her head, gazed up at him and whispered, "I've lost count."

"No one's counting," he murmured, pulling her closer, but he smiled into the darkness.

"Stay with me," she whispered, drowsy, sated, content. And if she hadn't been so tired, she would have noticed his lack of reply.

It wasn't anything personal, Rupert thought, carefully easing himself from the bed after her breathing had settled into the hushed rhythm of deep sleep. It was simply a matter of freedom. He stood for a moment, taking in the enchanting sight of her curled up like a small child in the vastness of the bed.

The sex was exceptional, flagrant yet oddly joyful.

But he didn't want a wife.

Not now or ever.

In the following days, the duke continued to live up to his husbandly duties in a gentlemanly and at times even warm-hearted manner. Hopefully his wife would be pregnant in a month—surely before the end of the summer, he told himself because he needed a limit to his mandatory duties. And once she was pregnant—freedom.

Fortunately, there was much to be done to put the estate to rights, and in the uneasy days and weeks of their honeymoon, Rupert and Olivia both worked long hours. Rupert was an efficient estate manager, Olivia came to realize. His capabilities surprised her; she'd thought him a profligate wastrel. He woke early each morning and spent the day with his manager: implementing programs to restore the productivity of the land, having advanced equipment brought in to farm the thousands of acres, seeing that new crops were introduced that wouldn't deplete the soil. Irrigation and drainage ditches were dug, bridges repaired, and the village square was refurbished with a small folly, benches, and flowers. Rupert's stud was augmented by new blood stock. Even in his relative poverty, he'd won most of the prestigious races each season. Now he had an opportunity to breed bloodlines that would assure him a place in racing history.

But each purchase, each outlay of money that improved Ware Hill was bought at great cost to his pride, his sense of obligation profound.

And as Olivia began renovating the house, even though it was badly in need of repairs, his resentments accumulated. Each new curtain or carpet, chair or sofa seemed to remind him of her remark on their wedding day about his being for sale.

Over dinner one night—the only meal they took together, and she suspected Mrs. Hodges was instrumental in that—Olivia said, "I was thinking about having the drapes pulled down in the library tomorrow. Would you be averse to having your desk and files put under dustcovers for a day or so?"

"Don't feel you have to ask me. It's your money."

"But it's your desk."

"I'll have it moved out."

"Why must you be disagreeable? Other people manage this sort of living arrangement, don't they?"

"How the hell should I know what other people do?"

he retorted, although he did know—the bulk of his acquaintances lived in marriages no different than his.

"I'll leave the drapes."

"Good."

And they ate in silence for some time, both exasperated, nettled, feeling aggrieved. Until Rupert drank another half bottle and Olivia finished her chocolate dessert and they happened to both look up at the same time.

He smiled first. "Take the damned drapes down."

"You're sure now?" And she wondered at the small warmth that invaded her soul, amazed at how easily she was won over by his smile.

"Of course I'm not sure, but how can it matter?" He shrugged. "Although I wish a thousand times a day that my father hadn't been such an ass and lost all his money."

"My father's an ass *with* money," she offered.

Her smile seemed particularly beautiful in the candlelight, he thought. She had an innocence and warmth he found refreshing. "There's no guarantee then."

"None." She'd decided that long ago, when she'd understood her father couldn't be trusted.

"I don't want to be a father like that."

"You'll be a fine father," she kindly said.

His dark gaze narrowed. "You're insufferably optimistic."

"A product of my origins. It was a matter of survival."

"I turned to dissipation instead." He gazed at her over the rim of his wineglass.

"I'd heard." Her voice was without inflection, a moderate, careful tone.

"And you don't approve."

"Not particularly," she said in the same circumspect way.

"If I didn't know you better, I'd say you're prudish.

But," he went on in a lazy drawl, "we both know you're not in the least."

She glanced at the footmen standing at attention by the door.

He followed her gaze and when their eyes met once again down the length of the table, his grin was wicked. "They don't hear; they don't see."

"Don't embarrass me."

"You're blushing like a young maid."

"I didn't realize you knew any," she remarked with a touch of sarcasm.

"I didn't until I married you. That will be all," he said in another tone of voice, nodding his head in the direction of the servants.

A moment later, they were alone in the vast dining room.

"Is this less embarrassing?" His eyes were amused.

"Now you can't embarrass me at all," she calmly replied, relieved their audience was gone.

"Is that a challenge? Perhaps I should take you up on it," he murmured, preparing to rise from his chair.

"No, no." She quickly waved him back with a flutter of her hands. "I know better than to challenge you."

He settled back in his chair and smiled at the memory she'd evoked. "The laundry maids never saw us that morning."

"They *could* have if they'd looked up."

"But they didn't. And you seemed to be enjoying yourself." He'd found her once in the orchard and half-teasing made love to her within sight of the laundry maids hanging wash in the adjacent yard.

"I'm not arguing enjoyment, Ware, only the venue. I almost had an apoplexy." Her gaze was pointed. "So don't get any more outrageous ideas."

"What's outrageous to some isn't to others," he softly remarked.

"Just don't get any ideas at all then," she briskly retorted. "Eat your dessert."

"I would if I liked chocolate. You must have ordered the menu."

"Mrs. Hodges didn't say anything."

"She loves you, that's why. I should be jealous," he added with a lopsided grin.

"At least someone loves me," she sardonically noted and then realizing the implication of such a sentiment, immediately apologized. "Forgive my gaffe. I must have had too much wine."

"You never have too much wine."

"Apparently too much for me," she drily remarked.

"Maybe we should talk about love. Come here," he murmured, holding out his hand.

"Talk about love or making love?" she equivocated, not moving.

"About making love."

"And if I don't want to?" Constraint vibrated in every syllable.

"Then I'll have to convince you." Rising from his chair, he strolled toward her. "It's never very difficult."

He *was* very convincing, as she well knew from past experience. Resist or not, protest and rebuff, he was eventually so convincing the servants had considerable grist for their gossip mill when they came in later that evening to clear the disarranged table.

"Mrs. Hodges and Martha say the new duchess will be breeding in a month," one of the footmen said, surveying the spilled dishes and debris scattered over the carpet.

"And I think they're right," another murmured, straightening an overturned chair.

"The duke's had plenty of practice," a third footman

remarked with a faint leer. "He'll service her right fine."

"When an heir's born," a maidservant piped up, "Martha says the duke will have all his debts paid off."

"And the duchess won't never see him again."

The maidservant turned a baleful eye on the young footman. "Mrs. Hodges says it could turn into a love match."

"Women," the footman deprecatingly muttered. "They always see love everywhere. It ain't that way with a man."

Those belowstairs saw life with blunt reality.

And married life went on for the master and mistress of Ware Hill in a continuing emotional turmoil—their feelings untidy, moody; resentments and frustrations a constant in both their lives. But kinder emotions came to prevail in the carnal interludes that had begun as duty and day by day altered into something more. Desire intervened: sexual attraction, memories of erotic pleasures they'd shared.

A sense of anticipation, restless and irrepressible simmered in their consciousness when they were apart. Rupert found himself thinking of his wife when he should have been concentrating on estate business—a sudden salacious image of Olivia would appear in his mind and he'd recall when he'd last seen her like that. And immediately want her. An unnerving impulse for a man who had always viewed women as a pleasant vice but never a necessity.

For her part, Olivia suppressed her urges when memories of their past pleasures filled her mind. She refused to follow in the footsteps of all the other women in her husband's life. How familiar it must be to him—females who wanted him for his sexual prowess.

But the begetting of an heir took on a provocative new dynamic.

One morning, Olivia was in the rose arbor writing an essay on female independence—a subject much debated among the bluestocking literati and of acute personal interest to her, when a footman brought her a letter from London. Addressed to the Duchess of Ware, it took her a moment to realize she was the recipient. On opening it, she found a disagreeable message from her father. He was planning a visit the following week and in his usual fashion, he made his wishes clear: *I want a room facing the front, not the back,* he ordered; *a carriage at my disposal to view the estate; my meals at normal times without any Frenchified fluff*—his menu was included. *Expect me on the tenth.*

Her immediate reaction was anger as always when dealing with her father's demands, but this time, as chatelaine of her own home, she felt in a strong position to refuse him. If Ware agreed, of course, she reflected a second later, since Ware Hill was his.

Uncertain of his relationship to her father, however—not having been privy to any of the negotiations over the marriage contract—she hesitated briefly. Would he support her decision? But still hot-tempered a second later, she rose from her shaded nook and took herself to the horse track where her husband could often be found, to put the question to him.

He saw her coming from a distance and he found himself watching her, fascinated despite all rationale to the contrary. Gordan spoke to him twice before he heard the question and even then he gave a distracted answer, intrigued by his wife's delicious image in her frothy summer frock. She seemed to be floating down the grassy incline, a light breeze ruffling the white muslin of her gown, her hair golden flame under the summer sun and he suddenly recalled how the scent of it filled his nostrils when he bedded her, how soft it felt. Like she did, all lush and willing and hot for the feel of him.

He wondered if other men lusted after their wives, and how aberrant his own carnal sensations were. "I'll come back to your office later," he vaguely said, handing Gordan the timing watch.

"Very good, sir," his manager replied, exiting diplomatically, inclined to agree with Mrs. Hodges's perceptive view of the duke and duchess's future.

His wife's breasts bounced gently as she walked, Rupert noted, his libido responding predictably. Her very large breasts, he pleasantly recalled. With the morning sun behind her, the shapely contour of her legs were tantalizingly revealed through the muslin of her gown. He shifted in his stance to accommodate his rising erection and wondered what brought her searching him out.

"Could I have a moment of your time?" She spoke before she'd fully reached him, a restless tremor in her voice.

"As many moments as you wish," he murmured, intrigued by her visit, her palpable sensuality, the possibilities inherent in both.

"Look!" she heatedly said, waving her father's letter at him. "He wants to come here!"

"Who?" Rupert's fingers lightly closed around her wrist, stilling her arm.

"My father!"

About to pluck the letter from her fingers, his hands dropped away. "Impossible! I won't have him."

"You won't?" she exclaimed, and at the firm shake of his head, a wild happiness infused her spirit. Overjoyed at the prospect of filial liberation, she impulsively threw herself at his chest and hugged him. "You dear, sweet man!" Her eyes were alight, her smile blissful. "I wasn't sure, you see, if you might rather *favor* his company, seeing how you and he had come to agreement on the money and—"

He stopped her rush of words with a gentle finger on her mouth. "Let me make this clear. I *never* want to see him."

"Oh Lord, I love you, *vastly*, Ware! I *really* do!"

His shock registered on his face for a second and she realized her blunder. Quickly stepping away, she said, "Please . . . forgive me. My enthusiasm—how embarrassing for you."

His composure restored, Rupert smiled faintly. "No need to apologize."

"It's just that I dislike him so," she softly explained.

"Something else we have in common," Rupert murmured.

"Something *else*?"

"Besides sex," he said pleasantly.

She blushed.

He laughed and they both smiled at each other for a small moment of rare companionship outside the bedchamber.

"Your father's not welcome at Ware Hill," Rupert declared, speaking to cover his discomfort at this new form of intimacy. "I'll write and tell him myself."

"Would you really?"

"With pleasure."

She beamed. "I shall be eternally grateful."

His mouth quirked. "A lady obliged to me. How appealing."

"Must everything be sexual with you?" she repudiated, but her voice was teasing.

"I find myself in rut more than not with you. It must be your very large breasts among other things," he murmured, brushing his fingers lightly over the delicious curve of one breast, more comfortable in the role of gallant than congenial husband.

"Write the letter," she insisted, brushing his hand away, refusing to lose sight of her objective, regardless the tiny shiver sliding down her spine.

"We could write it together," he softly said, holding

her hands captive in his large grasp, touching the hardening tip of her nipple through the muslin of her gown, *his* objective purely physical.

"Right now." And for a moment she wasn't quite sure whether she meant the letter or something else entirely.

Her meaning was ambivalent to him as well, but selfishly carnal, he went on instinct. "We'll compose it in the summerhouse." It was close and conveniently furnished with a large chaise. He gently squeezed her taut nipple.

"Don't do that." Her voice trembled.

"This?" His fingers tightened again.

"Damn you, write the letter," she whispered. "Hurry."

Another of those ambiguous words.

But she suddenly jerked away and, turning swiftly, began moving toward the small Palladian structure. He didn't long debate ambiguity with the graceful sway of her hips before him.

"I can't thank you enough for your cooperation," she said as he caught up to her, her passions forcibly in hand, her voice once more conversational.

"I'm sure you'll be able to."

She glanced sideways at him.

And his innocent gaze met hers.

"You fascinate me, Ware," she sardonically murmured. "Such an unvarying focus."

Years of practice, he thought but said instead, "While you fascinate *me*, my lady. You're so easily aroused."

"You can't touch me," she ordered, "until the letter is finished."

"Your servant, ma'am," he drawled, all courtesy and charm, when he could touch her in a hundred ways if he wished. But they had all the time in the world this fine summer day; he could afford to be gracious.

After they entered the coolness of the summerhouse, he pulled a small table up to the chaise, brought over writing materials from the cupboard in the corner and, patting the olive silk tussah upholstery, said, "Sit down and tell me what you want me to write."

"Burn in hell," she declared, smiling as she sat down beside him.

"Perhaps something more diplomatic," he suggested, grinning. "Why don't we say, it would be inconvenient at this time for your visit." He wrote the words in a casual scrawl across the fine vellum, paused for a moment and turning to Olivia, said, "That should be sufficient."

"I think several degrees more bluntness is necessary with father."

Neither Olivia nor myself choose to see you at present, he added.

"Or ever."

"He's your father," he remarked, one brow lifted at her vehemence.

"Would you like yours back?"

Or ever, he wrote. "Is that enough?" His dark gaze held hers.

"Short of expletives, yes."

"You shock me, Duchess."

"Do I really?"

He smiled at her sweet naivete. "In countless ways, my lady," he smoothly said, her artlessness a continuous source of surprise to him. He signed his name, including his title and set the note aside to dry. "I'll have a servant deliver it tomorrow."

"Why not today?"

"Later today," he agreed.

"Thank you, thank you, thank you," she said with a sigh, leaning back against the striped silk. "I'm deeply in your debt. For the letter," and then more softly she added, "and for the degree of freedom you allow me."

"Freedom?" His gaze was quizzical. "I have no impulse to own you. Aside,'' he added with a slight grimace, aware of the legalities governing wives, ''from the requirements of the marriage contract. And if I could have raised the money some other way . . .'' He shrugged; every possibility short of marriage had been scrutinized.

''I understand your need for money. It would have been unthinkable to lose Ware Hill.''

''Marshes have lived here since William the Conqueror's time,'' he quietly said. ''I couldn't let my father's ineptitude destroy that.'' His gaze held hers and for the first time he felt a degree of gratitude for her sacrifice. ''I've never thanked you for all you've contributed to my home, although,'' he said with a grin, ''your father sold you too cheaply.''

''But then a dukedom isn't often available,'' she pointed out, cautious not to read too much in his admission of gratitude.

''Most peers aren't as stupid as my father.''

''While *my* father capitalizes on ruined men. He takes pleasure in his acquisitions.''

''I hope he had pleasure enough; he won't get more at our expense.''

She felt a sudden tenderness at his companionable use of the adjective our, as if they were partners in an enterprise, co-conspirators against her father. ''Will an heir make you completely solvent?''

''I'm nearly solvent now.'' He smiled. ''Your dowry and my race winnings have seen Ware Hill back to productivity. If you give me an heir, the remainder of my father's debts will be paid.''

He was asking kindly, she thought, no longer making demands or threats and she found herself enchanted by such benevolence.

''After that I could repay you for your dowry in installments," he went on. "I'm very good at the gaming tables."

"You needn't repay me. The law is quite specific."

"I need to repay you for my peace of mind."

"You can start with a kiss. I'll deduct a guinea," she laughingly said.

"You're paying me then—for pleasuring you?" His voice was teasing, too, but he was briefly uncomfortable.

"I *should* pay you for your ingenuity and finesse—and for . . . your stamina," she finished in a purr.

"We'll exchange guineas then because a libido like yours always offers me fresh inspiration."

"We're a perfect match," she provocatively whispered, reaching for the buttons on his breeches. "Come into my body . . ."

He needed no coaxing and the chaise was put to good use that morning. First he rode her and then she him and then they lay in each other's arms and marveled at the degree of lust still strumming through their senses.

"I can never have enough of you," Olivia whispered, reaching up to stroke the broad sweep of his shoulder.

"Obsession has become a constant in my life, my dear sweet bride," he softly murmured, running his warm palm over the juncture of her thighs, exerting an exact, precise pressure.

She gasped as though she'd not climaxed short moments ago and her hips rose to meet his hand. Slipping two fingers inside her, he gently explored the hot, earthly paradise that lured his senses and lust. And in the coolness of the summerhouse that morning, they pressed the exquisite boundaries of sensation and discovered in the zealous and tantalizing pursuit that landscapes opened to them beyond the finite limits of sensual pleasure.

Soft green meadows of tenderness.

Distant horizons reminiscent of love.

And a wild, rare happiness.

But John Overton came despite Rupert's letter, arriving early on the morning of the tenth as if he'd never received the duke's reply. And when Olivia was informed that her father was in the Chinese drawing room, shock and a brief, mindless terror like that felt in childhood overcame her. "Find the duke," she instructed Martha, throwing aside her bedcovers, marshalling her faculties to oppose her father. "And quickly!"

"The duke rode over to Lord Barlow's after the training runs."

"Send someone to fetch him."

"Boyd says Mr. Overton is in a temper, my lady," Martha warned.

"I'll deal with my father," Olivia asserted, beginning to unbutton her sleeping gown. "Take out the yellow silk for me to wear and have Jenny bring me up some chocolate and brioche," she briskly added.

A half hour later, she descended the staircase, fed, dressed, coiffed, and additionally fortified by her temper, which had risen to fever pitch during her toilette. The sight of her father's luggage in the entrance hall added further degrees of heat to her anger. Damn his presumption! A footman opened the door as she approached the Chinese drawing room and throwing it wide, announced in carrying tones, "The Duchess of Ware."

"It's about time," her father snapped, turning from the window. "I've been cooling my heels for an hour."

"Not an hour, Father, a half hour. And you shouldn't be here at all. Thank you, Jem, that will be all," she added, nodding her dismissal. Although he'd listen at the door, she knew. "Did you not receive the duke's letter?" she tartly asked.

"Don't take that tone with me, my fine lady. I put you in this position."

"Did you receive the letter?" she repeated, her voice tight with constraint.

"No letter is going to stop me from visiting the house I bought and paid for. I'll come anytime I want."

"You're not welcome."

"Then you'll have to see that I am welcome."

"The duke is clear in his wishes."

"The duke can go to hell. I own every inch of this pile of stone. See that my luggage is brought up to my room."

"You don't understand, Father. You will not be staying. Your luggage will not be brought anywhere and if you don't leave soon, the duke will personally see that you do."

"He told you that, did he?" John Overton had made his fortune in the India trade and his early years had been spent in the rough-and-tumble seaports of the east. He wasn't easily intimidated.

"He made that clear to me."

"You don't look like you're breeding yet," he observed, ignoring her warning, his rude gaze traveling down her body. "Let's hope you're not a weak vessel like your mother with barely the strength to birth one child. I'm counting on an heir and a spare or two for my investment."

"You presume too much," she snapped, sick to death of his authority.

"I presume you'll do your duty."

"My duty is not to you."

"Your duty is always first to me."

"You're unrealistic," she coldly said. "As a married woman the legalities aren't in your favor."

"You *owe* me for putting you in this marriage," he decreed.

Lifting her chin, she gazed up at him with hatred. "I don't recall signing any such agreement. Now if you'll see yourself out." She turned to go.

"Haven't we become the hoity-toity lady," he sneered,

moving swiftly for a man of his size and bulk, placing himself directly in her path. "Now listen, missy, I'm here and I intend to stay here." It was inconceivable to him that he'd lost control of his daughter. "I'll expect to be given a tour of this estate tomorrow so I can see the grand piece of property I bought from this man who spends his days in gambling dens and brothels." His smile was cruel. "Someone has to keep an eye on my property."

"I don't intend to argue with you. I've sent for the duke. Kindly step out of my way."

"Sit down," he snarled, taking her by the arm and dragging her to a nearby chair.

"Take your hands off my wife," a cool voice interjected.

John Overton spun around, Olivia still in his grasp.

"Take your hands off my wife," Rupert repeated, his voice scarcely more than a whisper this time, his powerful form filling the threshold.

"She's my daughter first."

"Then take your hands off your daughter." Rupert shut the door on the hovering footmen.

"So territorial, Ware. I'm surprised. Has the honeymoon changed your taste in women?"

"My taste in women is none of your concern. You have two minutes to leave my house."

"Or?" Overton's fingers tightened on Olivia's arm.

"Or I'll see that you do."

"Is this the thanks I get for saving your lands and title?"

"Were you expecting thanks? I thought you were expecting payment in human flesh," Rupert coolly said. "Did I read the wrong contract?"

"You won't get another penny if you throw me out."

"I'm assuming my solicitor is more competent than that. Now get out."

"Will you make me? A fine gentleman like you? You'll soil that fine linen."

"A small price to pay for my privacy," Rupert murmured, pushing away from the door.

At his approach John Overton shoved Olivia aside and, furious at being thwarted, prepared to teach his new son-in-law a lesson he wouldn't soon forget. He'd ruled supreme in his small portion of the financial world for more than twenty years, and he'd continue to order his life to his liking for twenty more. "No moneyless blue-blood is going to tell me what to do," he snarled, lunging at Rupert.

Bristling at the slur, Rupert ducked under his flailing arms and landed a vicious right to his father-in-law's nose.

"Damn your hide!" Overton bellowed, shaking his head, spraying droplets of blood over the carpet. "Damn your whoremongering hide!" Hurtling forward like a maddened bull, he caught Rupert with a glancing blow to his jaw.

Why was he engaged in this brawl? Rupert thought, leaping back, pain stabbing his senses. This distasteful scene in his drawing room was like a bad farce, this annoying man forcing himself into his house. Moving swiftly to put an end to the disagreeable encounter, he called on all the expertise he'd acquired over the years at Jim Sheridan's gym. In a blur, he slammed a hard right to Overton's chin, then a left, another right, and, as his father-in-law began to stagger backward, he connected with an undercut that heaved Overton off his feet and dropped him in a heap on the floor.

Breathing hard, Rupert stalked to the door, pulled it open and said to the footmen who'd been eavesdropping outside, "It's over. Carry him out to his carriage."

Moving back into the room, he helped Olivia to a small settee. Dropping into the chair opposite her, he gruffly said, "Christ, that was ridiculous."

Glancing briefly at her father's motionless form being

carried away by four footmen, still partially stunned by the conflict, Olivia murmured, "I feel as though I should apologize for him."

"Someone damn well should," Rupert muttered, nursing his bruised jaw.

Smarting at his churlish retort, Olivia debated for a moment whether she might be responsible for her father's actions. "Actually," she said, her decision made, "he's not my responsibility."

"Thank you for your understanding," Rupert coolly said. "Maybe you would have preferred he stay with us for a month."

"Direct your anger elsewhere. As you saw, I have no control over his actions."

"Your kind always has an excuse."

"*My* kind?"

"Yes, your kind. You're his damned daughter, aren't you?"

"And you're his damned debtor. Let's not forget the reasons for our—" she couldn't bring herself to say the word marriage when theirs was such a travesty—"cohabitation."

"At the moment," he said, glaring at her, "'I feel a great need for respite from this wretched—" he spat the word "—*cohabitation*. You can reach me in London if you have need of me."

"I have no *need* of you."

"How convenient," he said, clipped and curt. "We agree. I wish you pleasure in the country, madame," he derisively offered, rising precipitously from his chair. "And if all goes well, we might never meet again."

"I'll *buy* a child if necessary—if that will keep you away. Perhaps you have some suitable by-blows in the neighborhood."

His expression went grim. "Your sense of humor fails

to amuse me. The next duke is mine and yours, madame. Make no mistake," he brusquely murmured. "And if it requires having you locked in your rooms, that can be arranged."

"Everything suddenly has a familiar ring. From one tyrant to another. The life of a woman is to be envied," she retorted, sarcasm heavy in her voice.

"I'll leave orders with Mrs. Hodges," he declared, as if she'd not spoken. "You're to keep to the parkland and estate," he commanded. "You will receive no visitors in private."

"Would you like to put me in a nunnery?" she inquired, overly sweet and malevolently.

His smile was chill. "It's a thought."

"And you will be equally celibate, I presume?" she murmured, ill-intent in every word.

"I do as I please, madame," he curtly said.

"Then your whores will appreciate your return. Especially now that you have money to entertain them in style."

"How I entertain my whores isn't your concern," he softly replied, "nor will it ever be." His gaze narrowed. "One last warning. Any child you bear will resemble me or I'll divorce you and take that child from you. Understood?"

"I don't answer to you."

"Understood?" he growled.

"I'll think about it," she said, recklessly defiant.

Incensed, he made to strike her and only stopped when she met his gaze with such fierceness, he had to admire her courage. "Damn you to hell for ruining my life," he said through clenched teeth and, spinning around, he stalked from the room.

"Damn your father for ruining both our lives," she whispered into the stillness.

*   *   *

The Duke of Ware reached London late that afternoon and immediately made a call on his solicitor.

"Forgive the dust of the road," he said, entering Tyerman's office, "but I told Overton to go to blazes this morning. And now," he said, throwing himself onto the sofa Tyerman kept for his late nights at the office, "I need you to tell me the settlement is airtight."

"You could murder him and still collect your money, Your Grace," Tyerman calmly replied.

Smiling, Rupert stripped off his gloves. "That must be why I pay you so well."

"Begging your pardon, Your Grace," Tyerman said, returning the duke's smile, "but with your propensity for—er—adventure, you need to pay us well."

"Well, rest easy, I didn't murder him," Rupert said, adjusting his dusty boots comfortably on the arm of the sofa. "But I may have . . . damaged his corpulent body in some small way."

"How much damage?" Tyerman quietly inquired, watching his client for nuances of expression that might indicate the degree of litigation in the offing.

"Nothing much. A broken nose, bruises; he'll probably have a lump on his head for a time. He hit the floor damned hard. He started it, Tyerman, so don't look at me like that. The bastard wouldn't leave my house."

The solicitor leaned forward in his chair. "He was there against your wishes?"

"Damned right. I asked him to leave at least twice. As did the duchess."

"In that case," Tyerman said, relaxing against his chair back, "he'll be hard-pressed to convince any barrister to take on his case. Not that he would under any circumstances—a peer has certain advantages after all. But Overton's fortune can't be overlooked."

"I don't need much more of his money anyway. Did Gordan write you?"

"He did, sir. I understand your finances are much improved since the race meet at Donchester."

"*Much* improved, Tyerman. I wish I could tell the old bastard to keep his money."

"I wouldn't recommend that, sir. After all, you married for that money. A step you didn't take lightly."

Rupert sighed, his dark brows settled into a frown. "This marriage isn't working out, Tyerman. Not one damned bit."

There wasn't a betting man in town that would have taken odds on Ware's happy marriage, Tyerman knew, nor had his own instincts suggested this arrangement was ever anything more than a marriage of convenience. "I believe most couples in circumstances like this adapt in some businesslike fashion."

"For the rest of my life? Jesus, Tyerman, that's a helluva long time."

"You need not be in company together often."

The duke cast his solicitor a critical look. "Unfortunately, I like Ware Hill."

"Perhaps the duchess could be persuaded to move to one of your lesser estates."

"I'm not so sure," Rupert murmured, remembering his wife's defiance.

"She has few legal rights, sir."

"Make her move, you mean."

"It would be within your rights."

"*Merde,*" Rupert softly swore, not sure he had the ruthlessness to do such a thing. He traced a small pattern in the dusty surface of one boot with his quirt while a small silence fell. "To hell with it," he finally said. "I'm in town to forget all that." Swinging his feet onto the floor, he sat up and smiled. "I'm sure the festivities at Brooks will soon efface all these problematic concerns." Coming to his feet, he said, "Wish me luck at the gaming tables and maybe I won't need Overton at all."

"Don't be rash, sir." Tyerman's voice was always moderate. "Overton's money is yours by right. There's no sense in giving it up, regardless of your luck tonight."

"Sensible as always, Tyerman. What would I do without you?"

"You'd be married to that actress you met at Brighton when you were seventeen, sir."

"By God, you're right. What was her name?"

"Molly Kelly, sir."

He smiled faintly, her image recalled. "She was a beauty, wasn't she?"

"She was indeed."

"How much did that cost me?"

"Five thousand. She was more than pleased, no offense, Your Grace. She never expected the marriage was legal anyway. I believe she went back to Dublin and opened a very nice hotel."

"Lord, that was a long time ago," Rupert murmured, standing silent for a moment as he remembered that carefree summer.

"Ten years, sir," Tyerman gently said.

"You've been keeping me in line for a long time, haven't you?"

"It's been a pleasure, Your Grace."

"I don't suppose I say thank you very often."

"Often enough, sir," the solicitor replied with a genuine fondness. A friend of the dowager duchess, William Tyerman had always considered the duke much more than a client.

"Well, thank you again, Tyerman. And while I didn't murder Overton," he said, grinning, "it's comforting to know I could if I wished."

"I'd caution you, sir, against anything so rash."

"Duly noted. Don't worry, Tyerman, the only pleasures I plan on enjoying are those having to do with women and cards."

"Very good, sir. I'll see that the London house is fully staffed for your stay."

"It's good to be back," Rupert said.

Two hours later, bathed, dressed, and pleasantly cheered by a bottle of brandy, Rupert strolled into Brooks. The company was thin so early in the evening but there were always members willing to sit down for a game. Charles Fox and Carlisle spent more time at Brooks than at home. And the Marquis of Newstead was always willing to lose some of his father's fortune.

"Honeymoon over?" Charles Fox murmured as Rupert seated himself at their table. Although already half drunk, Fox's smile was as charming as ever. "It didn't last very long."

"Long enough." Rupert shrugged out of his coat and handed it to a footman.

"Here for the night, are we?" Carlisle remarked, lounging back in his chair, his gaze speculative.

"Why not?" The duke smiled round the table at his friends. "I like the company."

"In contrast to domestic tranquility?" the marquis sardonically queried. He and his wife had agreed to disagree years ago.

"Surprised you lasted a month," Fox said, his own liaisons rarely long-lasting. "Can't imagine having a wife."

"Does she bore you already?" Carlisle languidly inquired.

The question struck a nerve, for Olivia was anything but boring, and Rupert suddenly thought of her wild, easily aroused passions, her intoxicating way of making him want her. "Is it whist or faro tonight?" he murmured, taking a fresh pack of cards from the tray held out to him.

"Do I detect a *tendre* for the duchess?" Charles significantly queried when Rupert failed to rise to the bait.

"Do I ask you about your private life?"

"Constantly."

"The duchess is all one would wish for in a wife," Rupert said with cool precision.

"Far away, you mean."

What *was* she doing? Rupert suddenly wondered, the thought of his wife alone at Ware Hill not necessarily a tranquil reflection. Would she be as hot-blooded for another man? A woman so easily aroused might have urges. Had he been a fool not to leave orders for Olivia's confinement?

"Are you going to deal or fall asleep?"

Forcibly putting aside his uneasy thoughts, Rupert dealt the hands for whist. The play was high, the stakes extravagant enough to soon gather the attention of a crowd. And before long, a mass of spectators followed the game. Rupert's winnings were piled before him; Charles Fox had won his share as well. And the stakes on the table for the next hand were twenty thousand guineas. Everyone was three parts drunk by now or the Marquis of Newstead would have had more sense than to ask such a personal question. "So, Ware, how's work going on the addendum?" he jovially inquired.

Rupert's brows rose in cool query.

"Old man Overton is crowing about your diligence," the marquis cheerfully went on, disregarding Rupert's warning look. His smile over his hand of cards was wicked. "Apparently he has spies. Says he'll have a new duke in the family soon."

"And is your wife breeding again?" Rupert said, his voice cutting. "Who's the father this time?"

A collective gasp rose from the crowd.

The marquis's smile vanished. "Damn you, Ware. Name your seconds."

"Now, now," Charles Fox quickly interjected. "Rupert, apologize, for Christ's sake. Bucky didn't mean any harm."

Gazes swung to the Duke of Ware.

"My marriage is none of his damned business," Rupert softly said, his expression unyielding.

"Apologize, Bucky," Fox ordered, his role of mediator familiar after two decades of friendship with the men. "Didn't Rupert save your ass at Wandsworth?"

"So what if he did? He can't say that about my wife."

"You wouldn't be here to have a wife if Rupert hadn't beat Algerton into a pulp for you. Apologize."

"If *he* will," the marquis sullenly muttered.

"Ware?" Fox interposed.

A sudden silence fell, everyone's breath in abeyance.

"Your wife is a fine woman," Rupert said, his voice tight with restraint.

"Overton's an ass," Bucky replied and then smiled sheepishly. "Didn't mean to offend you."

The crowd's breathing resumed and the buzz of conversation rose afresh.

"Now we can finish this game," Charles remarked, a duel Bucky didn't stand a chance of winning averted. "I could use the money with my losses lately."

"Sorry, Charles," Rupert gently said, playing his card, placing his ace of spades face up on the green baize.

"Damn you, Ware. I had a queen," Fox grumbled, tossing his cards down.

"I need it more than you do, Charles. I don't have a *pére* who left me half a million."

"I'm done then," Fox gruffly said, pushing away from the table. "Let's see what the Abbess Rogers has on the block tonight."

"Last time I was there she had a pretty young miss just off the mail coach from Bedford," Bucky noted. "Fresh new goods," he added with a sly wink.

"What say, Ware?" Charles inquired, slipping into his coat. "Have enough energy for a fuck?"

"When doesn't he?" Carlisle interposed, a touch of humor in his voice.

"I could be persuaded," Rupert drawled, rolling down his shirtsleeves. "I haven't seen Dolly for a month."

While her husband was enjoying London's nightlife, Olivia was sequestered in her bedchamber, writing furiously, railing against men in general and her husband in particular. A fire burned low in the grate despite the summer night, fragments of paper curled in the flames. The first to be consigned to ash had been a calendar page with a red heart drawn around the date when they'd made love so tenderly in the summerhouse. She'd been so in love since then.

Or more realistically, she'd fallen under her husband's practiced charm, she thought, disgruntled, scribbling vengeance with every word.

That treacherous calendar page had burned in a flash and the additional pages with which she was stoking the fire were an attempt to eradicate the memory of her perfidious lapse. She wrote in a boiling rage, reminding herself of her betrayal by men, of fathers and husbands who used her as though she had no feelings. Vengeful, hurt, bursting with anger, she vowed to never again be so naive, so gullible. Never, she wrote in a thousand variations. Never again.

She stayed up all night because she couldn't sleep with the turbulence in her brain. When dawn began coloring the sky, she finally rose from her desk, threw open the window and watched the sun rise.

The morning light seemed to drench the new day in glory, everything before her golden-bright and fresh. And as if the dark bitterness in her heart was touched by the splendor as well, her mood began to alter. Perhaps the cathartic writing had drained away her anger. Or perhaps no degree of fury could be so long maintained. Or maybe simple exhaustion had blurred all the sharp edges.

What was done was done, she thought with a kind of weary resignation. She was his wife after all and ten thousand burned pages would never change that. Taking a deep breath, she gazed at the garden below her window, sparkling with dew, bright with color, the fragrance of rose faint in the still morning air—a sense of renewal delicate, subtle— transmuting her perceptions.

She was young, she reflected.

And capable.

And wealthy.

She'd make a life for herself *without* the Duke of Ware.

The Abbess Rogers's elegant home was crowded so late at night, but she greeted Rupert and his friends with the cordial smile she reserved for her best clients. "Let me show you upstairs, gentlemen," she pleasantly said, moving toward her gilded staircase. "I hear the play went high at Brooks tonight."

"Ware's luck never fails," Charles Fox grumbled. "Damn him."

Turning to Rupert, she said, "Congratulations, Your Grace. Ware Hill prospers, too, rumor has it."

"It does. With enough from Brooks tonight to build a new dairy and alehouse."

"Lord, Ware, you sound like a farmer," Bucky noted as they climbed the stairs.

"I *am* a farmer."

"He's lost his head, Abbess, as you can see," Carlisle drawled. "With the grace of God we may yet save him."

"And put him back on the path to dissipation," Charles Fox genially added.

"The ladies have missed you, Your Grace," the abbess remarked, leading them down a candlelit hall.

"And I them," Rupert pleasantly noted, keeping pace with her. "Is Dolly here tonight?"

"In the back, my lord. You know the way. Gentlemen." Indicating the other men with a small bow, she stopped at a set of doors flanked by two footmen. "Please make yourself at home." At her nod, the doors were opened and the brilliant light from Venetian chandeliers shone over a room filled with comely women.

She stood for a moment in the quiet corridor after Ware's friends had gone inside and watched the tall figure of the duke stroll to the very end of the lengthy hall. He opened a door and went inside. Another aristocratic marriage dispatched, she thought, surprised at her twinge of distaste when she made a fortune on those infelicitous marriages. He hadn't been gone very long, she reflected. What was the extent of Ware's sojourn in the country? Three weeks?

"Rupert!" Dolly Jordan cried at the sight of him. Quickly rising from her chair, she moved toward the door, her arms outstretched, her smile dazzling. "I'm so glad you came."

"You look stunning as usual," Rupert murmured, taking in the voluptuous platinum blonde wafting toward him in a cloud of mimosa scent and ruffled silk.

"I've been pining away," she cheerfully replied and a moment later she slid her arms around his waist and hugged him.

"You *feel* damned healthy," Rupert whispered, his hands sliding down her back, pulling her close.

"And you feel as good as you look," she breathed, slipping her hands to his waistcoat buttons, beginning to undo them. "I heard you were at Brooks. I've been wait-ing."

"The stakes were worth staying for," he said, shrug-ging out of his coat.

"Are you back?" she softly inquired, their friendship a long-standing one.

He nodded, untying his neckcloth.

"Good. I missed you."

"Fitzroy didn't entertain you in my absence?"

"He bores me, darling. You know that." As a partner in the fashionable bordello, Dolly indulged her own tastes. "Are you at your house or apartment?"

"The house," he said as she slipped the last button free and eased his waistcoat off.

"How convenient," she murmured, tugging his shirt loose from his breeches. Her townhouse was scarcely a block away.

He pulled his own shirt off and lifted her into his arms in a flurry of rustling silk and familiar scent. "I'd know you in the dark," he said with a smile, her personal fragrance filling his nostrils and senses as he walked toward the bed.

"You bought the perfume for me in Florence."

"A long time ago."

She smiled up at him as he placed her on the bed. "We were both a lot poorer then."

He laughed. "And younger."

"Are you rich again?" she cheerfully inquired, untying the ribbons at the neckline of her peignoir.

Seated on the side of the bed, about to pull off his boots, he turned to look at her. "Near enough." But Ware Hill came into his mind and the woman lying before him sud-denly had the wrong hair and face and voice.

"I'll take you sailing tomorrow."

Shaking off the uncomfortable sensation, Rupert pulled

his second boot free and said, "After the auction at Tatter-sall's."

"I'll go with you. You can pick out a new racer for me."

Her talk of horses reminded him of the time Olivia had come to him at his training track, the sudden memory unnerving. When they'd made love that afternoon in the summerhouse, he'd felt ... His gaze swiftly surveyed the elegant room, decorated in primrose silk and peach damask, deliberately avoiding recall of his feelings. He didn't want to think of Ware Hill; he didn't want to remember *anything* about his wife. Of how their lovemaking had changed that day. And altered the balance of his life. Brushing aside such seditious thoughts, he quickly slid over Dolly, slowly lowered his body over hers, gently kissed her.

"You're eager," she teased a moment later. "Do you think it might be better if we took all our clothes off?"

Disturbed by his utter lack of feeling when he'd kissed her, Rupert kissed her again.

When his mouth lifted from hers that time, she said, "What's wrong?"

Rolling away, he exhaled a great sigh, obviously discomposed. "Talk to me," he murmured, his mind in turmoil.

Sitting up, she gazed at him. "Are you sick?"

"No."

But she'd never seen him so grave. "What would you like me to talk about?"

He shrugged.

"Do you remember the time we took a picnic to Richmond and never even saw—"

"She's not like you and me, Dolly."

It wasn't necessary to be clairvoyant. "She's very tall I hear?"

"She has this ... self-possession," he murmured, as if

he were thinking aloud. "And a curious innocence . . ."

"And you miss her."

His gaze swung around, piercing and black. "No."

"But she's on your mind."

He sighed. "Unfortunately."

"Does she love you?"

He laughed bitterly. "She hates me."

Dolly's brows rose. She doubted there was a woman alive who could hate Rupert. "Is she with child yet?" Everyone knew of the settlement terms.

He shrugged. "I don't know."

"Maybe you shouldn't be in London until you do know." She'd become wealthy in the course of her career and she well understood financial prudence.

"She threatened to buy a child so she didn't have to see me again." His gaze was on the shirred canopy above his head.

"People say things in anger."

"She meant it."

"And you can't bear a woman not to love you."

He shook his head and turning, his dark eyes held hers. "You know me better than that."

She did. He was without vanity despite his glorious looks. "You can't bear for *her* not to love you," she amended.

He shook his head again.

"You don't know *what* you want."

Rolling over on his side, he propped his head on his hand. "I thought I'd just walk away and return to my former life."

"Not such an easy course at times. Have you been cruel to her? Is she afraid of you?"

He laughed. "Hardly."

"I mean in bed. Is she virginal and prudish?"

"She's astonishing," he breathed, lust and covetousness in the simple phrase.

She'd lost a lover, Dolly suddenly realized, the duke's partiality clear. If she didn't care to lose a friend she would have to be unselfish. "Go home to her," she gently urged.

"I don't want to."

"You do."

He went very still.

"It's not so terrible," she encouraged.

He smiled faintly. "Easy for you to say."

She talked to him of her own long-ago marriage then, her memories never before disclosed. Of the man she'd loved, of their child—both lost to her. She was the only one to survive the fever that summer, she explained, and for months after, she'd wanted to die herself.

But she'd been blessed, she told him, to have once known such love.

"If you care about her, Ware," she said, "or think you may love her; if you value the child you may have sired, you have to go back. Give her a chance."

He didn't answer for a lengthy interval and then eased upward into a seated position. "I didn't expect this," he said, his voice low.

"Love's elusive, darling—odd and bewildering. It doesn't respond to calculation."

"I need a drink," he gruffly said, rolling off the bed.

Seated beside him on her settee a short time later, cognacs in hand, she listened while he talked of his new wife: the scent of her hair; the beauty of her smile; her frankness and artless ways; the astonishing number of books she'd brought to Ware Hill; her renovation of the house; her superb horsemanship. He smiled when he spoke of that. "She rides like a man," he proudly said.

And when Rupert finally left Dolly's apartment, he said

with a gentle smile, "Thank you for all the years of friendship."

"You're welcome," she murmured, knowing she wouldn't see him again, smiling because he wouldn't care to see her tears.

His kiss was tender, lingering—a farewell kiss.

And he walked away from the fashionable brothel and the old familiar pattern of his life. But after returning home, a moody restlessness pervaded his mind, his uncertainties profound. And he drank into the night, trying to find resolution to his disordered thoughts.

Tyerman found him in his study in the morning. "You look like hell for a man who won thirty thousand last night." News traveled fast in the Ton.

"I feel worse," Rupert murmured, his eyes half-lidded, dark stubble shadowing his face. "Hand me that bottle."

"Overton is back in London and resting quietly at home," Tyerman offered, pushing the bottle toward him before sitting down. "I wanted to let you know."

Olivia was free of him, Rupert thought, gratified, or he was free of him; they were both free of him. "I don't want the rest of his money," he bluntly decreed, a decision made on that at least in the small hours of the night—regardless all else was still in limbo.

"I'd caution you against that."

"I understand." The duke's brows arched briefly in wry acknowledgment. "Have the papers drawn up anyway and send them to Overton."

"You're turning down a great deal of money."

"I find the bondage galling."

"Your Grace, marriage settlements are by definition about controlling money."

Rupert smiled. "But then I so dislike controls . . . as you well know. I believe you had to intervene on several occasions for me when it came to that—beginning at Eton."

"You're sure now."

"I know that look, Tyerman. You mean am I drunk? I am, but not that drunk. I don't *want* any more of Overton's money. I'm quite lucid on that point." He set his glass down, pushed away the brandy bottle, another discovery suddenly clear as well.

He missed his wife.

"I'm going back to Ware Hill, by the way, if you have any commissions you'd like me to perform."

Tyerman didn't often smile but he did now. "Very good, sir. If you'd be so kind, I do have several books for the duchess. She particularly likes Mrs. Burney."

Rupert's dark gaze lifted, languid with fatigue and drink. "How the hell do you know that?"

"She corresponds with me, sir, on various matters having to do with the house."

"She does, does she?"

"Yes, sir. She's most astute in her purchases, always demanding the very best quality, Your Grace."

Sliding upward from the depths of his chair, Rupert asked, "Do you suppose she'd like emeralds?"

"I wouldn't know, sir. We generally speak of domestic items. Although Howell and James has some very good emeralds."

"No lectures on extravagant spending this morning?" Rupert sardonically inquired.

"The duchess deserves them, sir. Might I suggest pearls and emeralds?"

"Perfect," Rupert said, rising to his feet, the consideration of pearls against Olivia's lush flesh, strong incentive for a swift departure. "I'll sign a blank page before I leave; you fill in the details for Overton later. Have Howell and James bring over some pearl-and-emerald necklaces. I'm off to bathe. A half hour?" he briskly queried.

"Done, sir," Tyerman replied, delighted with the

duke's change of heart. His dear friend, the dowager duchess would be equally pleased. She was looking forward to her son's growing family.

There was considerable time on the journey home for Rupert to have second thoughts, third thoughts, and twentieth thoughts. But the pearls lying warm against his heart in his inside pocket, together with the vivid, at times graphic, images of Olivia and those pearls gave him sufficient, increasingly lustful motive to go on. Beyond that he wouldn't allow himself to contemplate the intricacies of his feelings. But when he entered the house, a mild apprehension overcame him—unique for a man of his repute.

In the time he'd been gone, Olivia had fretted and fumed, although she'd sharply chided herself for her unreasoning anger. How could it matter, why did it matter in a marriage such as theirs if he resumed his rakish pursuits? She knew the rules; she understood the requirements of such a union. It was ludicrous to expect anything more than civility.

But when she received word of the duke's arrival and his summons to join him in the Gibbons drawing room, she steeled herself for the meeting.

He was dozing on the sofa when she entered the room and he came to a seated position slowly, as if it pained him to rise.

"Would you prefer sleeping?" she coolly inquired, his dissipation emblazoned in his weariness, in the dark circles beneath his eyes. "I could come back later."

"No, please," he quickly replied, coming to his feet, looking elegantly disheveled in buff breeches and black coat, tailored to the inch, his neckcloth loose. "Please, sit down. Would you like tea?"

Shaking her head no, she cast him a curious look before

sitting, his politesse mannered like a young boy going
through his paces.

"I brought you something," he said with that same ear-
nestness she found so disconcerting. Pulling a small silk-
wrapped article from his pocket, he handed it to her before
dropping back down on the sofa.

With heedful caution, she unwrapped the silk to find a
magnificent pearl-and-emerald necklace. Too much had
passed between them though, to view his gesture with anything but suspicion and resentment. Did he think all was
resolved with his usual gift to a female? Taking umbrage,
she wondered how often he'd employed this conciliatory
device—how many women had received expensive jewels?
How many women had succumbed to his generosity. "You
needn't bother wooing me," she said, her voice chill. "Martha tells me I'm most assuredly with child," she added, the
words sounding alien, the startling fact disclosed only this
morning when she'd vomited her breakfast all over her bed
tray. "So you're absolved from any further duty."

"I may *prefer* wooing you," he softly said, his gaze
transiently flickering over her trim stomach.

"Are you drunk, Ware?"

"Not in the least. Would you find my wooing distasteful?" For the first time he pondered the possibility that a
woman might not want him and he waited for her answer
with a keen sense of awareness. He could sense the rhythm
of his own breathing and he noticed that her eyes were more
green than blue this morning.

"What if I said yes?"

It took him a moment to answer. "I'd respect your
wishes, of course."

"When you never have to date."

"I have many times to date," he said, a half-smile
forming on his mouth at recall of the particular sexual variations she preferred.

"Must everything be sex with you?"

"It's the only common ground we have, Duchess."

"We're having a child."

"Another area of friendship then."

"*Can* we be friends?"

"We can be anything you'd like us to be," he quietly replied.

"You're much too accommodating."

"I missed you in London."

"Even with all the women?"

"I've never missed anyone before," he said as though she'd not spoken. "It's a startling epiphany."

"Do you love me?" she suddenly asked, knowing she shouldn't with a man of his reputation, when she didn't understand herself why it mattered.

He looked at her for a breath-held moment. "Is this love, do you think?"

"I don't know. Why did you come back?"

"I wanted to see you again."

"I need more than that." Perhaps she had some of her father's blood after all, she thought—wanting so much.

"Such as?" he cautiously queried, very new at this bargaining for love.

"My feelings returned."

A flicker of surprise showed on his face. "Last I heard, you never wanted to see me again."

"Now that I see you again . . . I feel—differently."

"How differently?"

It was her turn to resort to caution, not sure she was capable of exposing her vulnerability to him. "Love interests me," she carefully said.

"Love love or sex love?"

"Love love."

He went silent for a moment. "I didn't see any women in London," he said, as if in answer to her remark. Which wasn't precisely true, but he'd walked away from a lady who'd been the most desirable woman in his life for years so it was near enough the truth to count.

"Thank you."

"Thank you for this child. It pleases me."

"Do *I* please you?"

"Very much. I found myself wanting to talk to you a score of times while I was gone. You please me in a thousand ways, Duchess mine."

She liked the gentle sound of the word mine, wanting to belong to someone perhaps more than others who'd not had such a lonely childhood, "If I'm yours," she said, still not tactful and obliging when any sensible woman would be at this point, "are you *mine*?"

The Duke of Ware had spent the entirety of his adulthood evading that female question. He slumped lower into the soft cushions of the sofa and when he gazed at her, his eyes were half hidden behind his dark lashes. "Isn't it enough that I'm here?"

"And you're staying?"

He nodded.

She smiled at his patent discomfort. "It's enough for now. Would you like tea?"

His grin was instant, his dilemma forestalled. "Just for the record, darling, I would *never* like tea."

With the word "darling" ringing in her ears, she softly said, "Is there something else you'd prefer?"

His smile turned wicked. "Oh, yes."

A frisson of pleasure warmed her senses. "I should send Martha away." She glanced toward the closed doors. "She's listening, I'm sure."

Rising from his chair, Rupert shouted, "Go away, Martha. That's an order! Now then, darling" he said in an altogether different voice, crossing the small distance between them, lifting the necklace from her grasp and setting it on a marquetry table. "Let me show you another present I brought from London," he murmured, pulling her to her feet.

"I need kisses first." She twined her arms around his neck.

"I have kisses," he whispered, his mouth brushing hers. "We *could* just kiss if you like," he added, his breath warm on her lips.

Tipping her head back, she stared at him, incredulity in her gaze.

"Or we could do something else," he amended, grinning.

"Don't tease." Her mouth pursed into a seductive, pouty moue. "You've been gone twenty-four hours."

"Am I behind schedule?"

"Way behind," she replied in a breathy purr, her body accustomed to the sensual extravagance of Rupert's unrestrained quest for an heir.

"I've work to do then to come up to quota," he said with a grin, his hands splayed across her bottom, holding her hard against his erection.

"Ummm." Swaying her hips in a gentle rhythm, she whispered, "I remember that . . ." Her body opening, as if it recognized the touch and feel of him, understood the approaching splendor.

"I'm glad I wasn't away a week," he murmured, amusement in his voice.

"You *can't* be gone a week." Impatient, she tugged at his coat.

"I can see that," he laughingly replied, helping her pull off his coat.

"I'm serious." She began unbuttoning his waistcoat.

"Lucky for me," he pleasantly said. And he moved then with the precipitous speed required of a *lengthy* absence such as his, stripping off his clothes in record time, disposing of his wife's garments with equal dispatch, offering her the kisses she craved in the process. And in short order the duke and duchess were about to engage in marital intercourse on the sea-green damask sofa when Olivia, said, sharply, "The drapes."

Poised as he was about to enter her, his expression indicated his shock.

"Close them," she nervously said.

"We're ten feet above the ground, darling," he replied, resuming his rather critical progress.

"Someone might see." A degree of panic trembled in her voice.

He briefly shut his eyes, took a steadying breath and, withdrawing from the incipient stages of penetration, said, "I'll close them." Which he did with the speed of a man on the cusp of orgasmic union.

"Thank you," she sweetly said upon his return.

"You're welcome." A touch of strain colored his voice.

But in terms of sexual compatibility, the duke and duchess had always been in accord and the duke's homecoming went on to be entirely satisfying, indeed so satisfying it was some time later before either noticed the room had become entirely dark.

"We should light some candles," Olivia murmured. "What will the servants think?"

"They'll think we're fucking in the dark, darling." He lay over her, his weight supported on his elbows, his smile white in the dim light.

"I wish I could be so cavalier."

He resisted saying she had been for quite some time now, not wishing to engage in an argument with their reunion so ideal. "I'll be cavalier for both of us," he said instead.

"I suppose we should dress."

"Don't if you don't want to."

"I'm hungry."

"You don't need clothes to eat."

"Rupert!"

"You don't," he repeated, shifting his weight off the sofa, walking to a window and throwing back the drape to reveal a twilight sky. "What do you want to eat? I'm famished."

"Why didn't you say something?"

"Because you were intent on reaching your quota, darling and I much preferred that to eating. I'll ring for a servant and you tell him what you want."

"I couldn't."

"Of course you can. I pay them well; they can look the other way."

But she wasn't able to so easily embrace the duke's *laissez faire* attitude, so he relayed the menu to a footman outside the door, received the food on a wheeled table when it was prepared and played *garçon* for his blushing wife.

"You should put clothes on," she said to him, seating herself at the table, re-dressed in a minimal way.

"I'm too hot," he simply said, reaching for his wine goblet.

And while he couldn't convince her initially to dine sans clothes, by the dessert course, he found her more amenable.

An hour had transpired by then.

And his wife's libido, charmingly needy, was ravenous again.

"Take your gown off and I'll be happy to oblige," Rupert murmured.

"I couldn't."

He smiled and shrugged.

"I really couldn't."

"I understand."

"I'd be terribly uncomfortable eating like that."

"Suit yourself, darling."

"You're very annoying."

"Really?" He smiled. "I'm sorry."

"This is blackmail, you know." Carnal longing filled her senses.

When he stood up to refill her goblet, his enormous erection was revealed and a spasm of lustful longing coursed through her body. "Damn you," she whispered, clenching her legs together against her urgent desire.

"You're not eating," the duke said, casually stroking his upthrust arousal, the spectacular length stretching from his groin to his waist. "I thought you liked creme brulee."

She shivered, his erection further swelling before her eyes. "You're much too dissolute," she said, sulky and restless with gratification so near.

"And you have your temperate moments I see," he lightly mocked. "There's no one here to see if you eat clothed or nude, darling. Indulge me."

"And you'll indulge me in turn," she murmured on a considered note.

"Of course."

"This is a negotiated settlement."

"I'd say so," he murmured, indulgent in all things, unthreatened by her need for independence.

"And you'll do something for me then if I ask?"

He had been for quite some time, but charmingly refrained from mentioning it. "Without question," he politely replied. "How many times would you like to come?"

The pulsing inside her responded in a hard, steady rhythm to his lascivious query, her gaze on the tantalizing size of his erection.

"Why don't I help you with your dessert," he murmured, picking up the small dish of custard, pulling his chair closer and sitting down. "Take your gown off, come sit on me and I'll feed you this,'' he softly said, selecting a spoon from the table.

She couldn't resist—how *could* she resist—and when she approached him brief moments later, he set the dessert aside to help her onto the chair.

He cupped her breasts in his hands as she settled onto his lap. "These are larger..." he whispered, squeezing them lightly.

"For the baby." Her eyes were already half-closed, her voice the merest breath.

"And for me," he murmured, lifting them so they mounded in pale, firm globes, so she felt a throbbing ache at the very center of her body spiral upwards, fill her with feverish longing. His mouth closed warmly on one nipple and she absorbed the flaring rush of pleasure with a breathy moan. Holding his dark head between her hands while he sucked and teased her nipples, nibbled in little tingling bites, she wondered how she'd ever lived without this ravishing delight.

But greedy for more, the orgasmic ecstasy he'd introduced her to now a craving, she gently moved away. "I can't wait," she breathed, rising to her knees, grasping his rigid length in her hands. Adjusting the engorged head between her pulsing tissue, she swiftly slid down his erection.

"Take your time," he softly admonished, curtailing her equally rapid ascent, his hands constraining her.

"I don't want to; I want to come." Her breathing was agitated, her gaze heated.

"You will," he promised, allowing her to move upward slowly. "You can come as many times as you like. For hours or days—for a week," he whispered, sliding her down again, exerting pressure with his splayed fingers, driving her further, stretching her. "I'm here to service you, to make love to you—" he raised her again, drawing her up until only the pulsing head of his penis lay inside her "—to bring you to orgasm," he murmured, slipping back into her sleek flesh. "You don't have to do anything else."

She was trembling in near-orgasmic rapture, his words stirring her lust, her body, her mind overwhelmed with carnal desire.

"You can lie abed each day, ripe and nude and wait for me to pleasure you. Would you like that?"

She was panting, her eyes clenched shut.

"Answer," he softly ordered, holding her body immobile.

"Yes, yes," she whispered, the images he evoked lasciviously sensual, her role both submissive and in command, utterly sexual. "Oh, yes," she added on a languorous sigh as he forced her down so hard she was totally subject to wild sensation. Gasping, she cried out at the irrepressible hot rush and, whimpering in a sobbing frenzy, she died away in his arms.

He held her close while she drifted back into the twilight world of the Gibbons drawing room and when her head lifted from his shoulder and she languidly purred against his neck, he murmured, "You forgot to eat your dessert."

She bit him and he yelped. Rubbing the reddening circle of teeth marks on his neck, he said with a smile, "Maybe you want to climax a few more times to work up an appetite."

"Maybe I do," she retorted. "Is that a problem?"

"It hasn't been so far," he pleasantly said.

"How reassuring."

"Consider me at your disposal for *reassurance* anytime."

"You please me, Ware."

"And you me."

"So are we going to manage this matter of love after all?"

He looked startled. "You make it undeniably attractive," he finally said.

"Tell me." She was a brave woman.

A short pause ensued and then he said very, very softly, "I love you."

"Is the disreputable Duke of Ware actually caught?" she asked, her smile dazzling. "What will the gossips say?"

"They will say that Overton girl must be exceptional in bed," he replied, his gaze amused. "And they'll be right." He chuckled. "We'll be the talk of the Ton."

"Do you mind?"

He knew what she was asking and it had nothing to do with the Ton. "I don't mind," he quietly said.

"Good."

"Now that that's all settled," he went on, his grin unabashedly sensual, "would you like—say . . . a bit more—ah—reassurance?"

"You read my mind."

His lashes lowered fractionally. "It's not that difficult."

"Are you complaining?" she quizzed.

"I would never be so foolish," he murmured. "Now Duchess mine," he proposed, his voice silky, the small portion of creme brulee he raised to her mouth quivering on the spoon, "open wide for a little sustenance to maintain your strength and we'll see if we can break some new records tonight . . ."

SIMPLE SINS

Eileen Wilks

To Gayle, Liz, Laura and Jim:
Live long and prosper.

◆ONE

Felicity was not used to standing around in the rain. She wasn't used to trespassing either, or being out alone so late at night.

It sure was dark. Between the storm and the forested slopes surrounding the old Reed place, not a speck of light made it from nearby Cross Creek to the old frame house on Cross's Mountain. Thank goodness for her penlight. If it weren't for that, Felicity's world would have been as dark as the inside of a tomb.

Though a good deal noisier.

Lightning flared. Thunder crashed—and Felicity jumped. Unfortunately, she'd been standing tippy-toed on an upended bucket, so when she jumped she fell, dropping her penlight and stubbing her big toe. The metal pail made quite a racket, too. But the storm was making even more noise, she assured herself as she retrieved the tiny flashlight, still bravely glowing. *He* wouldn't have heard her. The only lighted window she'd seen when she drove by earlier had been at the front of the house. She was at the back. And it was a very big house.

Felicity set the metal bucket back in place next to the house and stepped up on it. Her right toe throbbed in rhythm with her left shin, which she'd barked against a tree stump while trying to cross the inky-dark yard without using her light.

She frowned as she went up, painfully, on tiptoe again. There was no excuse for putting utility boxes so high up on the side of the house. Not everyone was six feet tall. Why, her friend Becka Lynn, who worked as a repair person for the phone company, was only a couple of inches taller than she was.

She pulled the door of the metal box open, shined her light inside and sighed with relief. At least one thing was going according to plan. Two things, really, she reminded herself, mentally thanking the forecaster for being right about the weather. Storms stranded travelers in the mountains from time to time, so this one would provide just the excuse she needed. If only the weather would keep it up for another hour or so, she would be well on her way to getting what she'd come here for.

Now she just had to make sure she couldn't call for help once she got in the house. Everything inside the utility box looked just the way Becka Lynn had described it to her. Her penlight went between her teeth so she could use both hands, and she tipped her head back to direct the beam at the box.

Her hat fell off. Cold rain washed her face and runneled down her front, sneaking beneath her yellow slicker.

Adventures, she reminded herself, were not supposed to be comfortable.

The bright color of her slicker bothered her more than the rain did. Hollywood spies and burglars always dressed sensibly in black when going about their business, but Felicity didn't own anything black. No decently dark navy or gray, either, except for the silk shirtwaist dress she wore to funerals. Her closet was stuffed with the light, bright colors she loved.

Since she didn't think a thin silk dress was appropriate

for her activities tonight, she'd settled for wearing her new cropped shirt and matching slacks. They were, at least, green rather than orange or yellow. She'd reassured herself that the night was too stormy and dark for *him* to see her, anyway, no matter what she wore.

In Felicity's opinion, the awkward location of the telephone switch box was typical of the house's former occupant. Gertrude Reed had been mean-spirited all eighty-one years of her life. She was probably just as difficult in death, too. By stretching as high as her five-feet-two-and-one-half-inches could go, Felicity could just reach the green wire looped around the farthest lug. She pulled it off.

Lightning cut a ragged gash in the sky. Thunder boomed about two feet above her head. She flinched, pulled off the orange wire and decided not to contemplate old Mrs. Reed's current status.

The last two wires came off easily. She stepped off her bucket and picked up her rain hat. It was sopping wet, but so was her head, so she pulled it back on. She set the bucket by the back porch where she'd found it and started around the house, using her penlight sparingly in an attempt to avoid any more stumps, rakes, holes, or other hazards.

It was a cold, drenching rain. Even in the summer, a big storm tended to be cold in the mountains. Her sneakers were soaked. So were her pant legs, her hair, and far more of her body than the rain should have been able to get to. By the time she rounded the corner of the big old frame house, Felicity was wet, cold, and limping slightly. And smiling.

She was having a wonderful time.

There was still just one lighted window at the front of the house—the big, square window to the left of the front door. Not that she could see in. The drapes were drawn. Felicity squished up the steps and across the wooden porch

to the door, took a deep breath, and knocked. Hard. And
waited.

Several strands of her shoulder-length hair were trapped
beneath her collar. They dripped wetly down her back. She
shivered, knocked again, and waited some more. Finally the
porch light came on, the door opened, and there *he* stood,
darker than her dreams and twice as scary.

Damon Reed.

He stood in shadow. The porch light didn't reach his
face, and he hadn't bothered to turn on the hall light. His
body was long and lean, his jeans were tight, and his
midnight-blue shirt wasn't buttoned. He had dark eyes, dark
hair and, if local rumor and Hollywood gossip columns
could be believed, a sin-darkened soul.

It had been thirteen years since Felicity had seen Damon in the flesh, but she would have known him anywhere.

She swallowed, smiled, and spoke her lines brightly.
"Hi! My name is Lily. Lily Smith. My car broke down a
little ways down the road. May I use your phone?"

He didn't speak. He just stood there in the doorway and
looked her up and down. At last he smiled a slow, knowing
sort of smile and stepped back, holding the door open wide.
"Come on in . . . Lily."

Apprehension shivered up her spine at the way he
looked at her, the way he spoke the name she'd picked
out—but that was nonsense, she told herself briskly. There
was no way Damon would recognize her after so many
years. Good grief, she'd been a runty little thirteen-year-old
the day the police released him and he left Cross Creek.
He'd never come back. Not for a visit, not for his grandmother's funeral two months ago. No, he wouldn't remember her.

When she started forward, her rubber-soled shoes made
wet, squishy noises. She paused in the doorway. "I'll just
leave these outside." Maybe she was lying to Damon and

planning to trick him, but she couldn't just track mud in on his floor. She toed one sneaker off, but the laces were knotted on the other one. Standing on one foot, she bent to remove it.

This time the lightning and thunder came at the same instant. It was like being right inside a pair of cymbals as they crashed together. The lights went out. Felicity lost her balance and hopped madly on one foot.

She landed against his chest.

He grabbed her elbows, steadying her up against him. "That's funny," he said, much too close to her ear in the sudden darkness. "You look just like this funny little kid who used to follow me around. Her name was . . . damn. Give me a minute," he said. One of his hands moved to her waist, where it slid back and forth in a restless, irritatingly warm caress. "It will come to me."

She couldn't see him, but she could feel the heat of his body . . . and smell the liquor on his breath. She cleared her throat. "I don't think—"

"Felicity," he said. "Yes, that's it. Felicity Armstrong. You look just like her." His roving hand slid right on down her hip until it rested on her fanny. "Except you're all grown up, aren't you?" He squeezed.

She yelped and backed up, and to heck with whether she got mud on his floor. "I—I—people call me Lily nowadays."

"Do they?" His voice was as slinky and sexy as temptation, and it sounded like he was following her.

"Oh, yes. Well, sometimes." She took another step back and bumped into the door. It swung shut, trapping her there in the darkness with him.

The lights flickered, then came back on. Damon stood several feet away, near the open archway that led to the one lighted room in the house. When she'd first seen him standing in the shadows, he'd been dark, mysterious, a bit scary.

Now, with his shirt hanging open and the light falling directly on his unshaven cheeks, he looked like a fallen angel. "Little Felicity," he said, smiling with unholy amusement. "Still following me around?"

"My car broke down," she repeated desperately. "I need to use your phone."

"But of course." He turned and went into the living room.

He moved as gracefully as she remembered, but the grace struck her as deliberate now, probably because of the limp. Felicity bit her lip. Reading about his accident wasn't the same as seeing such a magnificently physical creature damaged.

She limped, too, when she headed for the coat rack that held a black leather jacket, but her lopsided gait came from having only one shoe on. She hung her yellow vinyl so it wouldn't drip on Damon's black leather and bent to tug her sneaker off, then hunted up its mate and set them both near the door.

With the necessities attended to, she snuck a look inside the darkened doorway across from the living room, and grinned. She'd gotten inside the house, and she'd found the study. Everything was going as planned.

Two steps inside the living room, she stopped and stared.

Felicity had never been inside the house before. She'd heard descriptions, so she was expecting antiques, but the reality far outpaced her imagination. This was definitely not a room for muddy sneakers. It was a Victorian wonderland of bric-a-brac and overstuffed furniture. And everything was *red*, from the flocked wallpaper to the velvet that covered everything that could be swaddled, draped, upholstered, or swagged.

Dark red. Bright red. All shades of red, clashing and competing.

"Good heavens," she said faintly.

"Ugly as hell, isn't it?" Damon stood beside a table swathed in gold-fringed burgundy. A bottle of cheap whiskey sat amid the ceramic animals capering on the tabletop. He picked up the bottle. "You will join me, won't you? I'm sure we can hunt up another glass somewhere."

She realized then that his oddly deliberate movements came from more than his injury. "You're drunk!"

"Not yet," he said pleasantly, "but I'm working on it."

She frowned. Now that she knew what to listen for, she could hear the slight slurring of some of his consonants. In the old days, drink was the one vice that hadn't interested Damon. He hadn't wanted to lose his edge, whether he was racing, fighting . . . or doing things a thirteen-year-old girl wasn't supposed to think about.

"Don't worry. Your trip out here won't go to waste. The essentials," he said with a little bow, "are unimpaired."

"What are you talking about?"

"Use your imagination." He sipped at his drink.

It bothered her to see him drink. It bothered her that he didn't button his shirt. There was a small patch of dark, curly hair right in the center of his chest. "I don't see the phone."

"Perhaps it's on the desk."

The magnificent old rolltop desk was so cluttered it took her a moment to find the old-fashioned black telephone. She picked up the receiver. Sure enough, there was no dial tone. Felicity took a moment to savor the glow of accomplishment before saying, "Oh, dear. I think the phone lines must be down."

"Do you?"

She pushed the switchhook a few times for effect. "Yes, I'm afraid so."

"Then I suppose you're stuck here. Unless you'd like me to run you into town?" he asked politely.

Courtesy from Damon was the one contingency she'd hadn't planned for. "I'd hate to get you out on such a night. And, uh, no offense, but I'm not sure you should be driving."

He smiled as sweetly as the choirboy he'd never been. "I can't help wondering what you are doing out on such a night yourself, though. Particularly on this road. There's not much out this way—unless things have changed changed since I left . . . ?"

"Not exactly." She thought frantically. This was why she'd wanted to be a stranger named "Lily Smith"—well, one reason, anyway. People who didn't know the area sometimes missed the turnoff and ended up on the dead-end road that ran by the old Reed house, but no native would have made that mistake. "No, the road still stops at the old quarry," she said. "I was heading out there to, ah . . . do some thinking. I hadn't realized quite how bad the weather was until it was too late."

"And then you had car trouble."

She nodded hopefully.

"I suppose it might be simpler for you to just stay until morning," he said. "Since the phone line is down."

Good. He was finally reacting the way he was supposed to. "If you're sure you wouldn't mind—"

"Not at all. There are plenty of beds in this old place. Though I hope you're not fastidious about where you lay your head." Something about his smile made her stomach clench nervously. "I'm not sure how long it's been since any of the sheets were changed."

Felicity made a mental note to sleep in her clothes. "I'm not picky," she assured him.

"Good," he said, and set his glass down on the desk. "Do you do a lot of thinking out at the old quarry at night?"

"Not really." It would have been so much better if he'd let her go on being Lily, she thought, vexed. A woman named Lily might be able to handle Damon Reed. "I, ah, had some personal problems to work out."

"You were feeling sentimental, perhaps?" He started toward her. "I suppose your current lover let you down. Men are such cads, aren't we? Perhaps you wanted to reminisce over your first experience of love."

The old quarry was the traditional place for many of Cross Creek's girls to lose their virginity. Not Felicity, of course. She'd waited until she was off at college, out from under her mother's eye, to take that rather disappointing step into adulthood.

"Really," she said in the repressive voice that worked well on her third-graders. "I don't think that's any of your business."

"You're entitled to your opinion, of course." He came to a stop, and his eyes drifted lazily over her. "You know, I don't think that first, delightful flush of lust was so very long ago for you, was it? There's a certain freshness—"

"That's just about enough." More than enough, in fact. Felicity had never been looked at in such a way before. It was terrible. It made her palms tingle, and gave her the oddest curling sensation in the pit of her stomach.

He continued to look her over, his eyes lingering in places he really shouldn't be staring at. "Very nice," he murmured. "Would you mind turning around?"

"What?"

"I'd like to look at your ass now," he said pleasantly.

She blinked. He was more drunk than she'd realized. "I'm going to bed," she said and turned around so she could get out of there.

His hands on her shoulders stopped her. "So hasty," he said. "So impetuous. Not that I'm complaining, mind you. I love fast women."

"Let go." Her heartbeat was the only thing about her that was fast. The rest of her was scared.

Instead, he pulled her up against him, her back to his front, and bent to nibble on the side of her neck, sending horrid little ripples of sensation through her. She tried to push his head away. "Don't do that!"

"Where would you rather have my mouth?"

"I—nowhere! That isn't what I came here for!"

"Isn't it?" His breath was hot against her skin as he murmured, "You don't have to pretend with me, sweetheart. If you want me, all you have to do is say so. Pull your pants down and bend over, and I'll—"

She yelped. Shock gave her the adrenaline boost she needed to pull away. Or maybe he let her go. When she spun around, she saw his wicked expression. He was *laughing*. At her.

It was all a joke to him. What he'd said, what he'd done—a joke.

She closed her fingers into a fist and swung.

But Damon hadn't lost the reflexes that had kept him alive on the drag race circuit, and later made him one of Hollywood's top stunt drivers. He grabbed her fist as easily as a big league catcher plucks a baseball from the air. "Temper, temper," he chided. He wrapped both of his hands around her right hand, pulled it to his mouth, and forced her fingers open, those devilish eyes laughing at her the whole time.

She felt his tongue, hot and wet, in the palm of her hand—and damn him, it made her blood leap and her heartbeat go crazy.

So she smacked his face with her left hand.

The blow startled him, at least. He dropped her hand.

Felicity stepped back, angry tears hazing her vision. "I am going upstairs," she said. "*Alone*. You stay down here and finish drinking yourself into oblivion. With any luck, when you pass out you'll hit your head and bleed. A *lot*."

She blinked the tears away, turned, and marched off, her head high.

Two

Damon's cheek stung. Felicity packed a surprising wallop . . . in more ways than one. He smiled and followed her.

She was heading up the stairs as fast as her sock-clad feet could carry her. He leaned against the wall and enjoyed the view. She had a tiny waist, which set off her shapely rear delightfully. He might have wished for a tighter pair of pants on that pretty bottom . . . or for nothing at all.

He watched her heart-shaped fanny as she hurried up the stairs and thought about what she would look like in that green top and nothing else. In seconds, he went from very interested to stiff as a board.

Little Felicity. Felicity Jane Armstrong. Odd that he'd recognized her after so many years. Yet even through the haze of alcohol and lust, he remembered a skinny kid with freckles and braces, and smiled. She'd had quite a crush on him.

Maybe she'd stuck in his mind because of who she was. Just as he was the last of the Reeds, she represented the tail end of the other two "founding families" of Cross Creek— a subject of paramount importance to his grandmother. Felicity's mother had been the last of the Sheffields. She'd married the Armstrong boy, who had died soon after that.

That was one thing, the only thing, he'd had in common with little Felicity—they'd both been raised without a father.

Damon had been working at Mowbry's gas station that last summer in Cross Creek. His eighteenth summer. He remembered Felicity showing up at least twice a week that summer to buy soft drinks or gum and stare at him when she thought he wasn't looking. He'd thought she was a cute enough kid, in a stringy sort of way. And those eyes . . .

She wasn't stringy anymore, and the braces and the freckles were gone. Almost gone, at least. He'd noticed that she still had four freckles, three on her right cheek, one on her left. And in spite of all the delightful changes growing up had wrought on her, he'd recognized her eyes. Such solemn eyes, the blue as pure as an angel's prayers.

He thought of the tears he'd put in those big, blue eyes a few minutes ago. He really was a bastard, wasn't he?

Well, yes, he answered himself as he wandered back into the living room. He was undeniably a bastard, by right of birth as well as his own efforts. His dear grandmother had made that clear enough when he was growing up in this house.

But if he was a bastard, sweet Felicity was a liar.

So people called her Lily nowadays, did they? He chuckled and reached for the glass he'd left on the desk.

If he'd had any doubts about her story, she'd dispelled them when she went upstairs to escape him, instead of back out to the car that supposedly had broken down nearby. No good girl would have willingly stayed here after his behavior. The weather was nasty, but not dangerous. She could have spent the night in her car if she'd really wanted to get away from him.

No, Miss Felicity Jane Armstrong had some overriding reason to stay here in the house.

Damon wanted to know what it was. He wanted quite

a few things from her. Both the lust and the curiosity came as a surprise after being numb for so long.

He picked up the shot glass he'd left on the desk and wondered if Felicity might actually *be* a virgin. He contemplated how he might go about finding out. Amazingly, the idea aroused him. It was surely a sign of degeneracy, he thought as he took a healthy swallow, that the idea of having a virgin excited him.

The liquor went down rough, like the rotgut it was. He enjoyed the burn, but paused before taking another drink.

No, he decided, setting the glass down. He had more interesting things to do than finish getting drunk. He'd given that activity too much of his attention lately, anyway. He was still letting the old bat get to him, even after her death, or he wouldn't have felt the need to anesthetize himself against this place.

Enough of that. He had better things to do now. He was, temporarily, leading a simple, rural life, wasn't he? A simple life called for simple entertainments. Simple sins.

Like seduction.

He grinned and started for the servants' quarters at the back of the house, where he was staying. A shower and a cup of coffee would go a long ways toward restoring him. He intended to be awake and alert. Whatever sweet little Felicity had in mind, she'd gone to a great deal of trouble to get inside the house to do it. He doubted she intended to hang around tomorrow, which meant she would act tonight.

Damon didn't begrudge his guest whatever it was she planned to steal. He just didn't want her to leave before he uncovered her secrets.

Among other things.

The third stair squeaked.

Felicity froze. In the past couple of hours, the storm had settled into a steady rain too quiet to conceal any noises she made, but around her the old house creaked and groaned constantly, like an arthritic old woman. One squeaky stair shouldn't disturb Damon.

She made a face at the darkness. It would probably take an elephant stampede to disturb Damon by now.

After Felicity had escaped to the second floor, she'd explored a bit while waiting for him to go to sleep or pass out. She wasn't good at waiting, though, or at sitting still. So she'd done what she usually did when she was upset or needed to think. She'd cleaned.

Scrubbing the hall bathroom had worked off most of her hurt and anger. Those feelings still jabbed at her a bit, rather like sore muscles will, but mostly she felt sad now— sad for him, because of the drinking. Sad for herself, too.

People just didn't always turn out the way you thought they would.

The Damon she remembered had been wild and sometimes selfish, true, but he'd been capable of kindness. A lot of eighteen-year-old studs would have been cruel to a geeky thirteen-year-old admirer. A few might even have tried to take advantage of her infatuation. Damon had been patient and tolerant and, well, *nice*. "Nice" wasn't a quality that anyone she knew would associate with the rebellious grandson of old Mrs. Reed, but she didn't know a better way to describe the way he'd treated her back then.

He sure had changed.

It doesn't matter, she told herself as she resumed her stealthy progress, carrying her penlight and the blanket she'd appropriated from one of the bedrooms. She wasn't here to contemplate her first big crush or to get to know Damon better. She was here to save her mother.

Felicity was used to saving her mother, but in the past that had always involved avoiding adventures, rather than seeking one out. Ann Armstrong was a devoted mother. Maybe a little too devoted. Felicity did understand, though.

Ann had lost her husband shortly before Felicity's birth. Then she'd learned that her newborn daughter had a heart problem. What woman wouldn't worry?

Of course, Felicity had outgrown the heart murmur before she entered school. But once Ann Armstrong took up the habit of worrying, she'd been unable to put it down again. There were so many things to worry about, from broken bones and stitches to the thousand and one social and moral choices that had loomed like a rock-strewn rapids as Felicity moved into adolescence. The possibilities for disaster had always seemed endless to Ann.

But tonight, Ann Armstrong was out of town. Out of the state. Felicity had persuaded her to take the cruise she'd talked about for years, leaving Felicity free to accomplish her mother's rescue in her own way. The old house was dark and spooky, and as she crept downstairs her heart beat as quickly as it did when she read a Stephen King novel late at night.

She gave a delighted little sigh.

At the bottom of the stairs she used her penlight to guide her across the dark hallway to the study doorway. It occurred to her that Damon must not have been completely drunk when he went up to bed. He'd remembered to turn off the lights.

She frowned. She did not want him to wake up and find her snooping. Not this new, unpredictable Damon. That would be a little more adventure than a novice like her was ready for.

Once inside the study, she closed the door and used the blanket to muffle the crack between the door and the floor. When she didn't find a light switch on the wall, she pointed her penlight around the room, searching for a lamp. The narrow beam skimmed over a love seat, shelves of books, a desk, a face—

She yelped and dropped the light.

Leather creaked. A lamp on the desk came on.

Damon sat behind that desk. "Change your mind?" he asked, smiling.

THREE

"My bedroom is at the back of the house," Damon said to her, "but I don't mind improvising if you prefer the ambience in here. You always did like books, as I recall. That love seat is hard as hell, I'm afraid—but then, so is the desk, and the floor—"

"Oh, shut up." Felicity felt a mortifying urge to burst into tears. Everything had gone wrong.

"I'm afraid I'm not the strong, silent type," he apologized as he stood in a smooth, flowing motion and started out from behind the desk. "But I'll try to put my mouth to better use."

"Would you cut it out?" Because her knees felt suddenly uncertain about holding her up, she walked over to the love seat. It was upholstered in a dark, brooding maroon, and Damon was right, she discovered as she sat down. It was very hard. "You don't mean any of that."

"I don't?" He stopped in front of the desk and leaned against it. "I wonder why I'm saying it, then."

The dratted man still hadn't buttoned his shirt. Felicity had to admit that the way his chest muscles flexed when he crossed his arms was rather interesting. "You probably think you're teaching me a lesson or paying me back or something."

"You know, I believe you're right. That may be part of it. But only part."

"And your perverted sense of humor is the other part." She'd seen the laughter in his eyes when he pretended to want her, and she'd still reacted just the way he'd wanted her to—by running like a scared rabbit. She gave him a dirty look. "I'll bet you weren't even drunk."

"Now, now, I never claimed to be drunk, just well on my way. I was honest enough . . . for the company."

She flushed. "Maybe I lied about who I was, but—"

"You lied, all right. About pretty much everything. Not that I have anything against lying, you understand. Some of my best friends are liars. And I can certainly understand that you might prefer me to be drunk—easier to take advantage of me that way, isn't it? Just what is it," he asked curiously, "you intend to steal?"

Felicity straightened indignantly. "I was not going to steal anything! And I didn't know ahead of time that you'd be drunk, so I couldn't have come here to take advantage of your condition." Though a sneaky part of her rather liked the idea. Taking advantage of Damon Reed sounded exceptionally daring.

"What would you rather call it? Borrowing?"

"If I'd known you were going to be like this, I would have come here earlier, before you showed up." Damon had arrived unexpectedly two days ago and delighted the town's gossips by dismissing the house sitter hired by his grandmother's lawyer.

Of course, two days ago her mother hadn't left. She sighed. "I wasn't going to take anything that belonged to you. Just something that shouldn't have been here anyway."

"And that something would be—?"

"No," she said, "I'm not telling you anything else." It wasn't her secret.

"Perhaps you'd prefer to explain your position to the police."

The police? She couldn't keep from chuckling. "Maybe you've forgotten that Charlie Witherspoon is my godfather. Do you really think he'd believe I came out here to rob you?"

"I think that you would rather not have your godfather—and the rest of Cross Creek—know you've been out here with me at night. Alone. All night. Especially since when you go home in the morning, you'll never see me again."

As threats went, that one had a bit more teeth. They took a painful little nip out of her. "Still," she said, "even if everyone did believe I came up here for a one-night stand, that would have its upside."

"It would?" He abandoned the desk to come sit beside her on the love seat. His arm rested along the back of the little couch, not quite touching her.

The muscles in her legs twitched with the urge to jump up and run, but she refused to give herself away like that. "Sure. I mean, it might make everyone think I'd lost all sense of decency, but at least they'd have to admit I'm an indecent *adult*."

The corners of his mouth turned up. His gaze slid over her as snugly as last year's swimsuit. "I don't see how that can be in doubt."

She looked at him suspiciously. "Are you trying to flirt with me?"

"I was thinking more in terms of a seduction than a flirtation."

She pushed to her feet. "I wish you'd quit that."

"Quit mentioning that I plan to seduce you, or quit doing it?"

"You don't mean it," she assured him, taking a few

steps away and turning. "You're just saying it because it bothers me."

He leaned against the back of the love seat. The movement spread the edges of his shirt, giving her an excellent view of his chest. "Good," he said. "At least I know I'm bothering you. I think we should make a deal."

Midnight blue was a good color on him. The contrast between the dark silk of his shirt and the warm flesh of his chest was . . . interesting. She really wished he would button that shirt. "What kind of a deal?"

"I'll let you get whatever it is you came here for, in exchange for two things."

She dragged her eyes up to his face. "What two things?"

"First, I have to see whatever you take with you."

"No way," she said promptly.

His eyebrow lifted. "You expect me to let you waltz out of here without me even knowing what you're taking?"

Put that way, it didn't sound realistic. She chewed on her lip. Her hands automatically sought something to do. Since she was standing by the desk, she started tidying it. "It isn't my secret," she said, straightening a small pile of papers, picking up a few stray paper clips. "You have to promise me you won't use what I tell you against anyone."

"I know I'm a bastard, but I'm not interested in blackmailing a woman into my bed."

As if he'd ever needed to. Felicity had never believed that all of the Cross Creek girls who'd claimed to have succumbed to Damon's charms had really been given the opportunity, but plenty had, and plenty more had wanted to. And he was, if anything, even more appealing now. "That isn't what I meant," she said. "I'm looking for something that belongs to my mother. Some papers."

"Your mother?" A grin tugged at his mouth. "I'm sure

she's an attractive lady, but I think I can promise that she's safe from me.''

''She wasn't safe from your grandmother. Gertrude Reed blackmailed Mom for years.''

''You'll have to do better than that. Grandmother was vicious enough for blackmail, but she had too much pride and too much money to bother with it.''

''Oh, it wasn't about money.'' There was nothing more to straighten on the desk. Restless, she moved to the built-in bookshelves. The books were neat enough, but dusty. ''It was about things like the Harvest Dance.'' With the cowed support of Ann Armstrong, old Mrs. Reed had been able to run the annual dance, and the rest of Cross Creek's society, to suit herself.

''I have no idea what you're talking about.''

''You don't have to,'' she said, looking around for something to dust with. ''You just have to agree to let me have the papers when I find them.''

''What kind of papers? I might feel a touch of reluctance to let you walk out with the deed to this place, you understand.'' He paused. ''Not a good example, I suppose, since I've been trying to decide whether to remove a few things before I burn the house down, or let it all go up together.''

She looked at him, shocked. He'd sounded like he meant it.

His lips twisted wryly. ''Don't worry. I'm having a great deal of trouble making up my mind about things lately. I think I can promise to restrain any arsonist urges while you're here.''

''You really hated it here, didn't you?'' She hesitated before asking, ''Did you hate your grandmother, too?''

He stood in that single, graceful motion she'd noticed before. ''Aren't you curious about my other condition?''

His expression made her wary. It reminded her of the

way her mother's cat watched a bird or butterfly just before pouncing. "Well—no, I don't think so."

He started toward her. "I suppose the word 'condition' is misleading. 'Warning' might be more accurate." Now his smile reminded her of her mother's cat *after* it caught the bird, and was playing with the poor thing. He stopped in front of her. "Don't mistake my honesty for chivalry. The game is more fun if you're on your guard, that's all."

"You have an odd notion of fun," she muttered and stepped back, only to come up against the bookshelves. "Not that I know what you're talking about."

"I'm talking about seduction," he said, raising his hand to her cheek. "About sex. Hot, messy, mindless sex." His fingertips barely touched her as they skimmed from her cheekbone to her jaw. "I hope it will take you several days for you to find your mysterious papers, Felicity Jane Armstrong."

She was astonished. "You really *are* trying to seduce me!"

"Yes, I really am." His fingers glided down her throat, trailing goose bumps. "Shall we make a bet about whether or not I succeed?"

She shook her head, confused. "You don't know me. And I don't know you, not really, not anymore."

"Men and women don't have to know each other to enjoy each other. Have you never fantasized about sex with a stranger?"

His words shocked her. So did the way she stood there and listened to him. Why didn't she move?

Those lazy fingers of his had drifted again. Now they brushed her skin next to the square neckline of her shirt. It was so nearly innocent, that touch. He wasn't near any forbidden areas. He was touching her collarbone, for heaven's sake. Surely no one would call a collarbone erotic.

Yet her lips had parted. Her breathing was shallow. Her

skin tingled along the path his fingertips traced. "This is not a good idea."

"Probably not, for you," he agreed. "But I think it will be very good indeed for me."

Involuntarily, she glanced down. Her body still looked the same. Ordinary. She was, at best, cute. Her chin was too pointed, her face too round, legs too short, and her eyes too big. Yet Damon wanted to seduce her. He made her wish she could be wild and wicked, but she was in over her head. One small adventure hadn't transformed her into a woman capable of dealing with Damon Reed.

"I'm going to kiss you now," he said. His hand dropped to his side.

"No." She told him that, but she was staring at his mouth. He had very sensual lips for a man. Extravagant lips. They looked capable of a great deal, those lips.

Yes, she thought as his mouth brushed hers once, light as a butterfly's kiss. They were very capable lips.

Her eyelids felt so heavy. When her eyes started to close, she forced them open and watched, wary and fascinated, as he skimmed her mouth with another whisper-soft kiss.

His lashes were thick and lowered, but his eyes weren't completely closed. Behind those thick lashes she saw the dark-blue crescents of his irises. He was watching her watch him.

His lips lingered, nibbling gently at hers. Her breath sucked in as a long, languorous wave of heat rolled through her. She was so close to him she could see the shadow of his beard, the pores of his skin. With every breath she breathed in his scent—which was, she realized, free of the sweetish stink of bourbon she'd smelled earlier.

He was sober now. And he still wanted her. It was heady knowledge.

When he said her name, she felt it on her own lips in

puffs of warm, moist air. She felt the rest of him, too. Though they weren't touching, he'd moved closer, close enough that she felt the warmth of his body all up and down hers.

She wanted to rest her hand on his chest and see what that little patch of hair felt like. She clenched her hands into fists at her sides to keep from reaching for him.

"Sweet Felicity," he murmured. "Such big blue eyes. So solemn. Close those pretty eyes, sweetheart."

She couldn't speak, but managed to shake her head.

Those capable lips turned up in a wicked curve. "You like being persuaded, do you? All right." And his mouth feathered a string of downy kisses along her cheek.

Her eyelids drifted down. When his tongue traced the curve of her eyelid, her fists went lax with surprise. And pleasure. This man knew everything there was to know about pleasure, that was obvious. More than she knew how to guard against.

How could she have known that excitement could be so lazy, though? She was floating. Muscles that had always worked perfectly well turned to butter just because his tongue flicked out to dampen her skin. He slid a hand up beneath her shirt. Not far. It rested on her side, and she had never felt such a *naked* hand before, so warm and bare and compelling.

She made a great effort, and opened her eyes. He was watching her, calculating her pleasure with dark, knowing eyes. The contrast between the control with which he used his hands and mouth and the heat she saw in his eyes made her sigh with pleasure.

And step away.

Felicity's whole body pulsed, slow and steady, with the desire he'd awakened in her. "That was wonderful," she said, smiling at him mistily. "Thank you."

She'd surprised him. He forgot, for a moment, to wear

any of his masks, and what she saw on his face was honest confusion. "I hate to tell you this, sweetheart, but that isn't all. If you'd like to express your gratitude in the morning, though—"

"In the morning I'll be gone." It was a pity, but Felicity wasn't stupid, and she wasn't up to playing sexual games with Damon. "I used to daydream about kissing you, you know." She gave another little sigh, half pleasure, half regret, then shook her head. "Well. It's late and I found a bedroom with a lock on the door, so I'm going upstairs."

She walked quickly to the door. Damon still looked more puzzled than predatory, but that could change at any second. And she wasn't fooling herself that he had much in the way of conscience. She wasn't safe yet. She picked up the blanket she'd used to muffle the crack beneath the door, then opened the door.

"Felicity."

Uncertainty was a mistake with this man. She knew that, but she couldn't keep from looking back. He hadn't moved. He looked dangerously sexy standing there with his shirt undone and his eyes all sleepy with desire, making her wish she were just a little less sensible.

"I didn't kiss you so you could live out some damned teenaged fantasy of yours," he said. "I did it for the same reason I do most things. Because I wanted to."

"I know," she said softly. "That's what made it so special. Good night, Damon."

FOUR

"What do you mean, the road is out?" Felicity exclaimed.

Damon sat on one of the benches in the breakfast nook. The sun shone down outside on an exuberantly green and dripping world. Here in the big, old-fashioned kitchen, the rich smell of coffee filled the air while the radio sang about a little old lady from Pasadena.

Damon observed Felicity's dismay with satisfaction. "Sit down," he said. "Have some coffee. The news will be on again in a few minutes, and you can hear it for yourself."

She looked drowsy and disgruntled as she glanced at the radio that sat on the counter. The music switched to the Supremes. A smile twitched at one corner of her mouth. "I doubt this is the sort of music you usually listen to."

"Not usually." He smiled back. There was something about Felicity that made him want to smile almost as much as he wanted to drag her pants down, put her up on the table, and push inside her. He didn't understand either urge. She was cute this morning, dammit. Rumpled, wrinkled, and wary, but *cute*. He'd never been drawn to cute before. "FMIX hasn't changed, has it?"

The local radio station was the only one that many Cross Creek residents could get in easily, because of the mountains. The management tried hard to please everyone by playing oldies in the mornings, country western in the afternoon, and hard rock at night. The compromise, naturally, created more bickering than goodwill.

"Not a bit." She headed for the bread box. "Not much changes around here. Agatha Littleton still gets up a petition every year, trying to ban every song written after Elvis died. You want some toast?"

"Sure." He enjoyed watching her move around the kitchen, her pretty little rear swaying enticingly as she found the butter and lit the broiler. Her eyebrows were drawn together in a thoughtful frown. His news might have thrown her for a moment, but she bounced back quickly.

He thought about bouncing with her on the double bed in the servant's quarters. *Soon*, he promised his demanding body.

The news came on. When the deejay confirmed, amid other bits of local news, that the rising river had once again flooded the intersection of Highway 97 and the old quarry road, she nodded once.

Curious, he asked, "Resigned to your fate, are you?"

"The flooded road is a nuisance, but it won't keep me here. I'll drive as far as I can after I've eaten and had some coffee." She slid a cookie sheet filled with buttered bread beneath the broiler.

"You expect your car to have healed itself overnight, do you?"

Her frown chided him for referring to last night's lies. She poured a cup of coffee. "It probably just got some water in the carburetor or something," she said airily. "In a pinch, I can walk to the crossing. I'll call Meg or Andrea to wait for me on the other side of the intersection and drive me into town."

Damon remembered the young Felicity as rather timid and frail. The contrast between his vague memories and the self-possessed woman he saw now increased his curiosity. "You know, it strikes me that if the crossing isn't safe for a car, which is made out of metal and weighs a couple thousand pounds, it may not be safe for a flesh-and-blood woman who weighs about a hundred pounds."

"One-ten. I'll be fine. The water never rises very high, just high enough to drown out a car." She sipped at the coffee. Her eyes widened in surprise. "This is good."

"My one culinary skill. You've forgotten about the phone lines being out."

Her guilty expression pleased him. "Well, I, uh—I may be able to fix that."

"I already have. Do you suppose the toast is ready?"

While she grabbed a hot pad and opened the broiler, Damon reached down to the seat beside him and retrieved the little surprise he'd gotten her early that morning. He set it on the table where she couldn't miss it.

She busied herself with getting the toast onto two plates, her back to him. "So you fixed the phone line, did you?"

"Mm-hmm." He sipped his coffee.

She sighed and started toward the breakfast nook with the plates. "I'm sure you figured out how all the wires came to be off—" She stopped two feet away, her mouth hanging open.

A tangle of wires sat on the table. Green, yellow, red, blue—a foot or two of each of the wires that she'd so carefully slipped from their connections had been cut off. It would be no simple thing to restore phone service now.

He smiled. "Like I said. I fixed the phone line."

Felicity tried not to panic. She nibbled at her toast and reminded herself that she'd walked away from Damon last night. It hadn't been easy, but she'd done it, and she could just keep doing it until the river went down and she could leave. She couldn't believe he'd force her, so she should be safe as long as she kept her head.

When she picked up her coffee cup, her eyes accidentally met Damon's. He smiled, and her whole body went on alert.

It was horribly unfair. No woman should have to face her darkest middle-of-the-night fantasy at the breakfast table. Felicity's hormones started making a nuisance of themselves, humming in gleeful anticipation of what that sinful smile of his promised. Her mind stayed sleep-fuzzy, but her body insisted that it, at least, was wide awake.

When she made herself look away, her heart was pounding merrily.

She was in trouble.

Felicity didn't want to look at the man seated across from her. For one thing, she was trying to pretend he wasn't there. For another, she wasn't really awake yet, regardless of what her body thought. Waking up took all her attention in the first hour after getting up, and at least two cups of coffee. At twenty-seven Felicity still slept as hard as she had as a child, so deeply that her anxious mother used to wake her up sometimes just to make sure she could.

While not looking at Damon, she checked out the kitchen. This, she decided, was the pleasantest room in the house. The big windows and glass-fronted cabinets gave the kitchen an open, uncluttered feeling. And it was white in here, not red. White linoleum floor. Old white appliances. Worn white countertops on solid pine cabinets.

As soon as he'd finished eating, Damon stood. "More coffee?"

She nodded. He had some virtues, she conceded. He made darned good coffee, he didn't talk at breakfast, and he didn't expect her to jump up and wait on him.

"I offered you a deal last night," he said, bringing the pot over to the table. "I'm in an even better bargaining position now, but I hate to take advantage of that.'' He smiled like the gorgeous snake he was.

''Sure you do,'' she muttered and reached for the mug he'd refilled.

''It's probably simplest if you just tell me what my grandmother was blackmailing your mother about.''

''I thought you didn't believe me about the blackmail.''

''I was hasty.'' He set his coffee on the table, but didn't sit. ''I automatically thought of blackmail as involving money, but money wasn't what mattered to Grandmother, was it? Our illustrious name, and her position in this fly-speck of a town—those were the altars she worshipped at. And, of course, she loved to bully anyone weaker than her.''

Felicity thought of the pale, quiet woman who had been Damon's mother. Elissa Reed had seemed to wither away in the shadow cast by her domineering mother, much the way a sapling rooted too near the oak that spawned it might slowly starve for want of sunlight. She'd died before Damon turned eighteen. ''Mrs. Reed was a bully,'' Felicity agreed. ''And Mama—well, she isn't very good at standing up for herself.''

''How did you find out about Grandmother's little foray into blackmail?''

When Felicity met his eyes this time, she didn't look away. She saw curiosity there, a hint of anger, but none of the seductiveness or cynical humor she expected.

She could trust him with this, she realized. Damon wasn't like his grandmother. He wouldn't prey on the weak or the fragile. Her mother was safe from him, just as he'd said. ''After your grandmother's funeral I found Mama in tears, which surprised me. I had thought she'd just gone to the funeral because that was the proper thing to do. They'd sat on a lot of committees and things together, you know. Mama has always placed a lot of importance on being a lady,'' she added wistfully, thinking of all the things ladies don't do.

"Tried to cram you into the same mold she'd been forced into, did she?"

The sympathy in his voice unsettled her. She nodded. "Anyway, I went to see Mama that day and found her crying, and she told me everything. Or almost everything. She was upset because she wasn't upset, if you get what I mean."

"Funny," he murmured. "You mother was upset because she couldn't grieve for an old woman who'd tormented her, while I . . ."

"Did you grieve for your grandmother, then?" she asked gently.

"No. But I'd expected to feel a good deal more relief than I did. Are you going to tell me what your mother's deep, dark secret is?"

"I don't know exactly." She'd speculated plenty, though she suspected it wasn't much of a secret. Ann Armstrong had lived such an anxiously upright life. "She was scared the lawyer would find out when he went through the papers, so I know there's some kind of document involved. I thought it might be a love letter." Mixed in with Felicity's need to ease her mother's worry about the whereabouts of that document was a dash of purely selfish curiosity. Just who might her mother have written an indiscreet letter to, and when?

"And you only found out about all this two months ago, when my grandmother died."

"Of course. I would have taken care of things earlier if I'd known."

"Would you, now?" He looked amused. "Well, let me assure you I won't stand in your way. You may search to your heart's content. I'll help."

Now that sounded like a bad idea. Definitely a bad idea. "No."

He ignored her. "We might start with Grandmother's bedroom. I've already been through the study, and I'm sure I would have noticed if there were any scandalous papers there connected to your mother."

"You've searched the study?" Her brow wrinkled in perplexity. "Surely you didn't get up before dawn to search for—well, you wouldn't have known what you were looking for."

"I wasn't looking for naughty love letters. I started searching as soon as I got here, you see, and the study was a logical place to begin."

"What were you looking for?"

"The will."

"But your grandmother died intestate." Everyone in Cross Creek knew that. Mrs. Reed's lawyer, Harold Stimmons, had been drawing up a new will for her when she died, but she hadn't signed it yet and no copies of the old will had been found.

"Oh, there's a will. That bungling lawyer of hers may not have found it, but I'm sure the old bat kept a copy around here someplace."

"But if you find a will—" Felicity stopped a split second short of repeating another bit of common knowledge. Everyone knew Mrs. Reed had cut her grandson out of her will years ago, when he left town.

He nodded as if she'd finished the thought. "Exactly. Grandmother never wanted me to have a dime of her money. She told me so often enough before I left. So there's a will around someplace. She wouldn't have taken a chance on dying and having me inherit just because the law foolishly considers me her next-of-kin. Once I find it, I'm free of this place for good."

* * *

It started raining again shortly before noon. The road was going to stay flooded for at least another day, Felicity thought glumly. Probably more. She sighed.

She sat on the floor beside one of the ceiling-high bookcases in the library, a narrow room with a dark, gloomy carpet and no chairs. An empty coffee mug sat beside her. The single window, high on the west wall, looked like it hadn't been cleaned in years.

Damon wasn't there. He had been, though. He'd stayed in the library with her most of the morning, helping her look through the books. He'd flirted and he'd flattered and he'd said all sorts of things that he shouldn't, but he hadn't touched her. She suspected he was trying to get her to relax. To trust him.

Unfortunately, it was working. Felicity didn't know how to stay on her guard with someone she liked.

She took down the last volume of the encyclopedia and flipped through the pages, making sure there were no secret papers tucked in between ''Xenocrates'' and ''xenogenesis.'' She didn't trust Damon—no, she wasn't that far gone. But she had relaxed with him. She was very much afraid she liked him.

How could she not, though, when he made her laugh? He'd told her such funny stories about Hollywood people. And he'd laughed at her stories, too. He ought to be an actor, she thought as she felt the cover of volume twenty-two, checking for suspicious bulges. He'd had her convinced he really enjoyed hearing about her third-graders.

Then he'd left. Twenty minutes ago he'd said he had some business to take care of, and out the door he went. What business could he possibly take care of in a house with no phones? No connection to the outside world at all?

What an odd man he was. She wasn't going to think about him anymore. She reached for the next book.

He wanted her. It amazed her, but it did seem to be

true. Maybe he had the wrong idea about her, though. She paused, frowning. Maybe he thought she was a *real* risk-taker, like he was. After all, he'd encountered her on her one big adventure, and that could have given him the wrong impression.

Of course, he probably wasn't thinking about her at all right now. She'd undoubtedly left his mind as soon as he left the room. Just like she'd stopped thinking about him.

When Felicity pulled out the next book, she smiled. It was a thin book with an elephant on the cover. Dr. Seuss. She'd loved Seuss's books when she was little. Shoot, she still did, as much for their integrity and idealism as for their nonsense. She read them to her class sometimes, even though some of the kids pretended to be too sophisticated for the antics of cats in hats.

Had Damon's mother read this book to him when she tucked him in? How odd to think of him as a little boy someone had read bedtime stories to.

Not that she was going to think about him at all, of course.

She opened the book and smiled at Horton the elephant, who knew that a person was a person, no matter how small.

FIVE

Damon headed back downstairs, satisfied with the conversation he'd just had with his agent on his cellular phone. Nothing was solid yet, but if everything went well, Damon would coordinate the stunts for an upcoming action-adventure flick.

He just wished he could feel some enthusiasm. His career had meant everything to him for so long, yet he couldn't summon much excitement over moving up to Stunt Coordinator. But his lack of enthusiasm, surely, was because of this business with the house. Once he unloaded his unwanted inheritance and broke that last tie with his past, he'd be able to move forward.

Of course, something *had* broken through the numbness. Someone. That's why he'd called Phil—to make sure the man didn't call him. It wouldn't do for Felicity to hear his cellular phone ringing.

He smiled as he started down the hall. Beneath Felicity's sober surface, he suspected, there lurked a respectable temper. He didn't object to inciting it; he just didn't intend to let her use his phone to escape ahead of schedule. *His* schedule.

The library was at the back of the house. That cramped little room didn't really rate the title of ''library,'' of course, but he'd grown up calling it that. Old habits died hard . . . and some of them never seemed to die at all. The past was a Hydra-headed beast, he thought. Lop off one jeering memory and two more loomed it its place.

At the door to the library he paused.

It was a dismal room, especially on a rainy day. The carpet was old and drab, and the dark wood of the bookcases and panelling made the walls of the narrow room seem much too close. Everything was drab and faded, from the covers on the books to the dusty drapes that Felicity had insisted on opening.

All the color in the little room belonged to the woman sitting on that dingy carpet, her head bent over a book. Her shoulder-length hair was a light, sun-striped brown with just enough wave to soften it. Her clothes were wrinkled, her feet were bare and her skin was as flawless as a baby's bottom. Except for those freckles, of course. Three on her right cheek. One on her left.

"What does a schoolteacher do," he said softly as he stepped inside, "to get such sun-streaked hair, yet so few freckles?"

She looked up and smiled. She had a pixie's face, wide at the temples and narrow at the chin. "Wear sunscreen, of course."

"You must spend a fair amount of time outside instead of cooped up in the classroom. Are you a gardener, or an athlete?"

"I like to swim." She said it almost shyly, as if she were admitting to a questionable activity. "I spend a lot of time in the pool during the summer."

"You swim?" A drifting piece of memory fell into place, bringing a quick, irrational alarm. "But your heart . . . don't you have a heart problem?"

She grimaced. "I had a *mother* problem when I was growing up. I was born with a heart murmur, but I was one of the lucky ones. The hole was small, and it closed up before I started school. Only nothing has ever persuaded my mother I'm not frail. It took me years," she admitted, "to believe it myself."

"But you succeeded." He walked over and joined her. Lowering himself to the floor took more concentration than it would have before the accident. The muscles in his right leg still wouldn't obey him properly, which bothered him more than the pain. According to the doctors, the damage was permanent.

But then, the doctors hadn't expected him to walk without a cane, either. "That's rare, you know."

"What do you mean?" Her lips remained parted slightly. Her eyes took on the softened look of a woman who wants a man, her pupils growing large, the lids heavy. Yet he could have sworn he was more aware of the signs of her arousal than she was.

She was so innocent. It was almost enough to make him pull back. But for the first time in his life, he was as aroused by innocence as he was by a woman's body. "Very few of us are able to discard whatever image we had of ourselves as a child." Her sun-kissed hair drew him, so that's what he touched first, taking one strand between his fingers. "Your hair looks like you've been swimming quite a bit this summer."

"Quite a bit," she echoed, then cleared her throat. "Don't do that." She reached up to remove his hand.

He took her hand in his instead, threading his fingers through hers. "Don't do what?"

"Don't touch." She tried to tug her hand away.

He chuckled. She sounded so much like the grade-school teacher that she was. "It's difficult to seduce a woman without touching."

"I hadn't planned to make it easy." She blinked, then

blushed. "I didn't mean—that is, I'm not trying to make it either easy *or* hard—"

"Yet you've definitely made something hard."

Her flush deepened. She stood, pulling her hand free. The book in her lap fell to the floor.

He picked up the book and stood. "Dr. Seuss." His eyebrows went up in surprise. "Maybe she didn't know it was here," he murmured.

"What do you mean?"

He frowned. It wasn't like him to speak his thoughts aloud. "Nothing important. I'm just surprised the old bat didn't get rid of this when she had the bonfire."

When she flushed, he knew she'd heard about that portion of the events surrounding his departure thirteen years ago. "It was a terrible thing to do," she said. "Burning all your things when you were in jail for—"

"For stealing from her?" Her unexpected defense amused him. "I did, you know. Just as she claimed."

"So why did you do it?"

"For spite, mostly." He shrugged. "It was a stupid thing to do. I'd saved enough to leave town without using a penny of hers, but that wasn't . . . satisfying. I stole from her because I knew it would infuriate her. I was right, too. I just hadn't realized how far she would go to retaliate." He should have, though. His grandmother had never been able to give up or back down.

Just like him. He sighed. "Don't try to paint either one of us in softer colors than we deserve, Felicity. She was a vicious old woman, but I've done my best to live up to her expectations of me."

She frowned. "Your grandmother dropped the charges, though. She may have had a change of heart."

"She agreed to drop the charges when I gave her my word I'd never show my face in this town again."

Her eyes went wide and shocked.

Such gentle blue eyes, he thought. Only a bastard would take advantage of her sympathetic distress to arouse other sentiments in her pretty breast. He smiled and reached up to stroke her cheek. "Don't feel sorry for me," he said softly. "I'm not worth it."

"At least find an original line," she snapped, and pushed his hand away.

He laughed, grabbed her hand and carried it to his lips so he could nibble at her fingers. "Do, please, keep resisting me. I love a challenge." He drew her fingertip into his mouth and sucked lightly.

Her pretty blue eyes looked appallingly innocent, all wide and wary, even as the pupils dilated with pleasure. He wondered which bothered her the most—his action, or her response to it.

She pulled her hand away. "I'm not resisting in order to titillate you."

"Titillate?" He smiled, delighted with her. "Such a prim, civilized word. Crude creature that I am, I'd probably have said something a bit earthier, like—"

"Never mind!"

She looked so funny and flustered and flushed. Damon forgot that he was seducing her. He forgot to plan his actions, to study her reactions, and did what he wanted to do. He put his arms around her and kissed her.

She went as still and stiff as a startled kitten. Then her hands pushed against his chest. He ignored that to court her mouth with his tongue, asking her to open for him.

She felt so good, impossibly good. He wanted her to move. Yes, he needed that, needed to know how it felt for her to move against him. He ran his hands down her stiff back to cup that enticing little ass of hers. He cupped her cheeks and slid his leg between hers. While his hands kneaded her bottom, he pressed up with his thigh.

She gasped. It left her mouth open and undefended, so

he swept inside. She tasted like sunshine and coffee. She felt like everything soft and female. And slowly, tentatively, she kissed him back. One at a time, her hands crept around his neck.

The feel of her fingers, shy and eager—one on the nape of his neck, the other sneaking up into his hair—made Damon's head spin. He'd known she wanted him. He'd known, yet that first uncertain response sent heat shimmering through his blood as if he were a boy with his first girl.

He lifted his head so he could see the lips he'd been kissing. They were wet and swollen. Irresistible. He tilted his head to try a new angle.

"Damon," she whispered.

He liked the way she said his name. He wanted to hear it again, but he couldn't keep his mouth away from hers. He slid one hand up her hip to her waist, then under her shirt. Her bra surprised him. It was very feminine and a little bit naughty. The cups were lacy and dipped low over the small, warm breast he cupped.

Her nipple was already hard. When he kneaded her breast, she moaned.

Every muscle in his body went on alert. He would have her here, right here. Now. He wanted her on the floor. On her back. He started to urge her down.

She made a small, distressed sound.

"It's all right," he murmured against her mouth. "I'll be careful, sweetheart, so careful." He plucked at her nipple through the thin lace of her bra. She shivered and pressed against him. Her response ignited him, overwhelming his senses and his sense. "You're so hot and sweet . . . so damned hot, and so innocent."

She stopped moving.

Damon knew something was wrong, but he'd become caught in his own trap. He couldn't step back, couldn't think, couldn't find her weakness and use it. Instead he searched mindlessly for the yielding heat she'd given him a moment ago, caressing her breast, kissing her throat.

Two small hands pushed against his chest. Hard.

He wanted to ignore her wordless refusal, wanted to go on touching, tasting. The strength of his need, more than any promptings of conscience, startled him into lifting his head.

She was breathing hard. And scowling.

He let her create a small distance between their bodies.

"Is that why you've been after me? Because you thought . . ." She stopped and swallowed. Tears glittered in her angry eyes. "I'm not innocent, Damon."

What was she talking about? She was the most innocent woman he'd ever known. "It's nothing to be ashamed of."

"I wouldn't be, if that's what I was. But I'm not a virgin." She surprised him then, shoving against him with unexpected strength. He let go.

She tilted her chin up, somehow keeping those tears from falling. "You wanted to seduce a virgin, didn't you? It was a thrill, a turn-on." She shook her head. "That's disgusting, you know."

When she turned to leave, he let her go.

She was right. It was disgusting.

Damon stood in the cramped, colorless room and ached. He felt the strangest flutter of panic, deep inside. He even recognized it. It was the same sensation he'd had four months ago when that mutt ran in front of his car in the middle of a high-speed-chase scene.

Like a fool, he'd jerked the wheel to avoid hitting the stupid animal.

The Camaro had flipped five times. Damon had been conscious through it all, waiting for the terror to hit. Waiting for the pain. And there had been pain, an ocean of it, arriving in a belated tide that had swept over him like the hellfire his grandmother used to tell him he was bound for. But he never had felt the terror he'd expected, only that odd little flutter of panic—as if, instead of experiencing the horror of someone who has just made a deadly mistake, he'd stopped himself right on the brink of one.

Damon shook his head, irritated. Sexual frustration wasn't likely to prove fatal. He wasn't hurting in any other way, of course. It had been years since any woman possessed the power to hurt him in any way that counted.

That's twice, he thought, *I've put tears in her eyes.*

He stood there and tried not to think about the hurt he'd seen in Felicity's blue eyes. But that just left his mind open to thoughts of her soft skin, her small breasts and hard nipples, and lush bottom.

At this rate it would take him all day to get his body back under control.

It occurred to Damon that Felicity was wrong, both about his motives and about herself. He had no idea how many men she had been with, but it didn't matter. Knowing she wasn't a virgin didn't affect the way he ached to have her. She was still an innocent. And he still wanted her.

He found himself hoping that whatever quality had helped her preserve that innocence would protect her later. After he left.

The pantry off the kitchen was perfect—deep and cluttered and downright dirty in the hard-to-reach places, filled with the accumulated odds and ends of years. Felicity hadn't been certain she could find anything sufficiently messy to satisfy her. Oh, things were a little dusty here and there, but the lawyer had hired a cleaning crew shortly after Mrs. Reed died, and a house sitter after that. Most of the house was discouragingly neat.

Felicity turned the radio up. Music was as necessary to cleaning as soap and water, in her opinion. While she assembled her tangible cleaning supplies, a woman sang about the heart being a lonely hunter.

It was slightly past noon—the country music part of the day. Damon would probably show up sooner or later to put together a sandwich, but he wouldn't hang around. She felt confident that not even he would try to seduce a woman wrist-deep in bleach water.

She brought in the pail she'd stood on last night. While she waited for it to fill, she thought about what Melinda Abbott had told her. Melinda was the mother of one of her third-graders and the sister of one of the Merry Maids who'd cleaned the house after Gertrude Reed died.

The old woman had become eccentric, turning into a recluse in the last year or two of her life, seeing no one but her lawyer and the woman who cleaned and cooked for her. Maybe she'd deserved her isolation, but Felicity couldn't help pitying such a lonely existence.

Did Damon know how alone his grandmother had been when she died? Felicity wondered if he felt any guilt for not having tried to reconcile with the old woman. He was her only kin, after all.

Mrs. Reed's maid hadn't worked very hard in that last year. Felicity's fingers itched when she thought of the disorder Melinda's sister had reported: clothing in piles on the dining room table; stacks of newspapers and old magazines; jewelry in the refrigerator. Restoring order must have been quite a challenge, she thought with a wistful sigh.

And maybe, she thought as she dragged the step stool into the pantry, if she'd been part of the cleaning crew she would have found her mother's mysterious document.

Not that the Merry Maids had turned up anything like that, or the will that Damon was convinced existed. They'd been under strict instructions to put all the papers they found in a large box for the lawyer to sort through. Felicity didn't waste her energy suspecting Mr. Stimmons of anything underhanded. He was a careful, capable, dried-up stick of a man, devoted to the orderliness of the law.

Just the sort of person she sometimes feared she could turn into.

Felicity carried her bucket and sponge into the pantry as the woman on the radio wailed about being driven by a desperate hunger. She stuck her tongue out at the radio, stepped up on the step stool, and started emptying the top shelf. Everything had to be checked as she took it down, from the huge roasting pan to the mysterious bits and pieces that sprout like mushrooms in closets and basements. Someone who had hidden costume jewelry in a Tupperware container in the refrigerator might have hidden blackmail documents almost anywhere.

Or a will. She thought of Damon's determination to have nothing to do with the spiteful old woman who had bullied him and his mother, and felt a tug deep inside her, a tug she couldn't—didn't—name. It wasn't pity, though. What she felt for Damon had nothing to do with pity.

This morning, she'd seen the Damon she remembered . . . or maybe the man she'd once thought he would become. A man who could make her relax. A man who had himself relaxed with her, as if he liked her as much as he wanted her.

She shivered.

The singer on the radio lamented over the way a woman's hunger for love could drive her to risk the dangers of a one-night stand. Felicity grimaced, plunged her sponge into the soapy water, and started scrubbing.

Damon stood in the kitchen doorway. Felicity was too busy to notice him. She stood on a stool in the pantry, scrubbing something and singing along with the radio. Both activities commanded her enthusiastic attention.

She carried a tune about as well as she lied.

He smiled and thought about walking up behind her, sliding his arms around her, cupping her breasts. She'd probably fall off the stool. But he'd catch her, turn her around, hold her tight in his arms . . .

His thoughts bogged down in confusion. *Hold her?*

Damon considered himself a thoughtful lover, one who took the time to make sure his partner enjoyed herself. Because he'd paid attention over the years, he knew women often wanted to be held as much as they wanted the pleasure of passion. But he'd learned these things for purely selfish reasons. He pleased women in order to please himself, and his goal was always the same—a simple, basic act.

He'd certainly never fantasized about *holding* a woman.

He frowned. His priorities were getting confused. He was here to look for that damned will, not to get tangled up with a woman, however appealing. Felicity's seduction could wait a little while, he decided as he turned away. Let her think she was safe. He was going to do what he'd put off too long already, and begin the search of his grandmother's bedroom.

Felicity bobbed in time with the music as she sang along with Trace Adkins. She was on the floor now, wiping down the next-to-last shelf.

It was late afternoon. The rain had stopped, but water dripped from trees and from the roof. The road was undoubtedly still flooded. Felicity had been cleaning for hours. Her muscles ached, her hands were chapped, and even her feet were sore, but her head was clear.

Now that she'd put things in perspective, it was hard to believe she'd really worried about succumbing to Damon. Good grief, she was no risk-taker, and a man like Damon was a dreadful risk for a woman like her.

Felicity's priorities were clear, and always had been. She took life seriously—at least the parts of it that mattered:

the people. While still very small, she'd absorbed the sobering lesson that life is fragile. She'd grown up knowing that the people in her life were what gave it value. She wasn't capable of having a sexual fling without her feelings becoming involved.

Good grief, look what had happened when she lost her virginity in college! She'd gone into that relationship so carefully she couldn't call it an adventure, and she'd still messed up. Charlie had been two years older than her, a big, gentle teddy bear of a man. And she'd loved him. Maybe she hadn't been head-over-heels, but she'd cared, and their breakup had hurt. But even though they'd been friends, they hadn't been right for each other romantically.

It wasn't that Felicity disliked sex. It was pleasant enough, if somewhat overrated. She simply wasn't a very passionate woman. No surprise there. She'd spent far too long repressing anything as untidy and improper as passion to suddenly turn wanton.

And yet . . . now she knew how Damon's hand felt on her breast. She knew the taste of him. He had been able to call up a wild heat in her body, conjuring passion like a magician. He'd given her a glimpse of a very earthly sort of paradise.

But paradise didn't come without a price, did it? If she'd managed to be mildly in love with sweet, pudgy Charlie, how much harder could she fall for Damon?

Fortunately, she reminded herself as she scrubbed hard at a stubborn spot, she didn't have to worry about that. She wasn't a risk-taker. Her cowardice would protect her even if her common sense took a detour. How could she have forgotten that?

The spot finally came off, along with some of the paint. She straightened, rubbed the small of her back, then started putting things back on the shelf. The radio went from a commercial for a local used car lot to some man singing about a woman who only wanted to be wanted.

All those country-western songs were beginning to irritate her. No one, she thought as she shoved boxes of cereal, instant rice, and stuffing mix on the shelf, should have to listen to people moaning about love for hours on end. It wasn't healthy.

When Felicity tried impatiently to make room for a box of bran cereal with the others, she somehow knocked the whole shelf down. Everything she'd just replaced fell onto the shelf below, knocking things helter-skelter to the floor—including an old shoebox that had been on the bottom shelf.

Papers spilled from the shoebox—old utility bills, grocery lists, photographs—along with a small, leather-bound journal. Curiosity fought with propriety in Felicity's heart. She had no right, no right at all, to read what looked like someone's private journal. She reached for the papers to straighten them.

Curiosity won. Felicity picked up the journal.

SIX

Damon sat on the floor, leaning against the bed where his grandmother had died. Her cleaning lady had found her, according to Stimmons. She'd died in her sleep.

Damon still hadn't decided how he felt about that. Part of him wanted to drag her back from the grave so he could tell her how little he missed her, and how little she'd deserved such a peaceful passing. He supposed he would have to let go of the anger sooner or later. Raging against the dead was a futile business.

Yet . . . now he was alone. There were no Reed cousins, no brothers or uncles. There was just him. The bastard.

He held a paper in his hands, a paper he'd found folded and tucked inside the backing of a framed photograph of a grandfather he'd never known. It was an official-looking document complete with seal, scrawled signature, and ornate border.

Damon wasn't looking at what he held, though. He was looking into the past.

He'd been five years old when he got in trouble for bloodying Timmy Wiggins's nose in Sunday school. Grandmother had sent him to get a willow switch as soon as they got home from church, and he'd made the mistake of trying to defend himself. He'd told her the name Timmy had called him.

It was a word he'd heard before, but didn't know the meaning of.

"You're old enough to know the truth," Grandmother had said, her hands folded piously, her features as pinched and narrow as her soul. "And the truth is that you *are* a bastard, born out of wedlock, a disgrace to this family."

Damon's mother had protested. Grandmother had overridden her—and, though she'd spoken to Damon, he'd sensed that her words had been weapons aimed more at his mother than at him. "You have no father, or none who will claim you, because your mother fornicated with some stranger she refuses to name. Perhaps she doesn't recall who it was. Don't glare at me that way, boy. Your mother is to blame for your shameful state, not I. Now bring me that switch."

Damon hadn't brought the switch. That terrible old woman had made his mother cry. He hadn't liked his grandmother much before then, but from that day on he'd known her for his enemy. His mother had cried so quietly, her grief almost soundless as it crumpled her face and broke her heart.

He looked down at the paper he held in his hand now. It was a birth certificate. The place for the father's name was blank. The place for the infant's name was filled in, though.

It read "Felicity Jane Sheffield."

Not Armstrong. Sheffield, her mother's maiden name. He remembered vaguely that Felicity's mother was supposed to have married the Armstrong boy when he went into the Army. She'd gone away with him, then returned home a year later as a young widow with a new baby.

Apparently the part about getting married had been slightly exaggerated.

How in the world had his grandmother gotten her hands on this?

Damon shook his head. That wasn't important now. What mattered was that Felicity was a bastard, too, just like him . . . except she didn't know it. Her mother had protected her from the knowledge all these years.

His mother would have protected him, if she could have.

Damon stood slowly. He supposed that someone with a better-developed conscience than his might say he had no right to conceal what he'd found. But when had he ever worried overmuch about right and wrong? He did what he wanted.

And, for whatever reason, he wanted to protect Felicity.

It remained only to decide whether he would hide the evidence, or destroy it.

It was raining again.

Felicity wiped her cheeks, which were as wet as the dripping world outside. She closed the little leather-bound journal and took a deep breath.

Poor lady. Poor, sad lady.

Felicity had only read the first ten pages or so. Tears had kept her from intruding further. She could scarcely believe any woman could hate her own daughter, yet what else could explain the way Gertrude Reed had treated poor Elissa? She'd known exactly how to hurt Elissa the most, too. Through her son.

Felicity understood a little better now why Gertrude Reed had died alone.

Damon had to see this. Much as she hated to show it to him—how could he help but be hurt?—she had to find him and give it to him. Felicity took a moment to wash away the traces of her tears before going in search of him.

She hadn't seen Damon all afternoon. He might be anywhere in the big house. But the servants' quarters were just off the kitchen.

It had seemed very odd, when he mentioned it earlier, that he would stay in a servant's bedroom rather than his own. Yet she thought she knew why. He meant it when he said he wanted nothing from his grandmother—not this house, and not the implied kinship of sleeping upstairs in one of the rooms meant for the family.

When she opened the narrow door near the pantry and saw the short, drab hallway, she knew she'd guessed right. She could hear Damon's muffled voice.

Frowning, she went forward. The door at the end of the hall probably opened onto the back porch, which would explain how Damon had reached his temporary room without her seeing him pass through the kitchen. There were three other doors—two on her left, one on her right. Damon's muffled voice came from the last door on her left.

Who in the world could he be talking to? There was no one here but him and her.

She stopped in front of his door, her hand lifted to knock. It would be quite horridly improper to just open his door without permission—but who was he talking to?

Proper be damned, she decided as she reached for the doorknob and swung the door open.

The room was small, windowless, bare. It held only a chest of drawers, an unmade double bed, and a suitcase. Damon stood by the far wall of the tiny room, talking on a pocket-sized cellular phone.

He stopped speaking immediately. His eyes met hers. "I've got to go, Phil," he said, and disconnected.

Until Felicity saw Damon in that barren room, she would never have thought such a monastic setting would suit him. He was a hedonist, wasn't he? All too familiar with the pleasures the world offered. Yet when she met his eyes now, she thought she saw an affinity for this room, a place just as bleak and windowless deep inside him.

For a long moment neither of them spoke. She stared at the phone in his hand, disappointed past all reason. "It never occurred to me you might have a cellular phone. I'm more gullible than I thought. After the way you jeered at me for lying, I thought you were being honest, at least."

"I didn't lie," he said, "but I never intended to play fair, either."

"And I'm not playing at all," she said unsteadily. "I don't know how to play at . . . intimacy."

The intensity in his eyes didn't diminish, but she could have sworn something slid between them, as real as a closing door. "No," he said softly, "you don't, do you? That's a problem."

Her heart pounded. Because she suspected she'd already said too much, she held out the journal. "I found this in the kitchen."

He crossed to her, but didn't take the little leather book. "It looks like one of my mother's diaries."

He'd startled her. "You've seen others, then?"

"Did you read it?"

She flushed. "A few pages."

He nodded as if they'd just come to some agreement. "I blamed her at one time."

Felicity had seen Damon angry. She'd seen him seductive, relaxed, aroused, drunk. She'd seen him as a youth and as a man, but she'd never seen him like this. She didn't even know how to name this mood he was in. "What do you mean?"

"I didn't understand. I wanted Mother to leave, to take me with her and escape. At the very least, I wanted her to fight back. But she couldn't," he said sadly, "though it took me years to understand that. She was like a wife who stays with an abusive husband because she believes she *can't* leave. The one time she did escape, after all—she moved away from Cross Creek for two years—she got knocked up and deserted by whatever son-of-a-bitch fathered me.''

The lump in Felicity's throat threatened to choke her. ''What did she die of? I was trying to remember, and couldn't.''

''Cancer. It was quick, at least.'' He glanced at the journal she held. ''I found a couple of her diaries after the funeral. Grandmother had a big box of her things. She was planning on burning them.''

Felicity shuddered. ''She was a dreadful old woman.''

''Yes,'' he said, ''but the bizarre thing is that she truly grieved for Mother. It made me furious at the time. I didn't think she had any right.''

''What do you think now?''

''I think that all those damned poets who sing about love being 'the answer' haven't a clue what a vicious, bloody beast it can be. For some people. Anyone remotely like my grandmother.'' Catching her expression, he shook his head. His mouth crooked up wryly. ''You look more nervous now than you did when I was seducing you. Here.''

He tossed the cellular phone at her. She managed to catch it one-handed, but then she just stood there blinking stupidly at him.

''Go ahead and call your friend to meet you,'' he said impatiently. ''I'd suggest you get out of here right away. It's still overcast, and we could have another storm move in.''

This was it? He'd changed his mind, and now he was all but shooing her out the door? Emotion built behind Felicity's temples, getting stronger with every pulse.

''Don't just stand there staring at me like a confused kitten. It won't help. If you're worried about your car, I imagine I can fix whatever idiotic thing you did to fake having car trouble.''

''That's right,'' she said, speaking slowly and clearly

through the flood of feeling threatening her control. "You do know a thing or two about cars, don't you?" The emotion broke free. *"How dare you!"* She tossed the phone and journal on the bed so she could have both hands free to shove against his chest. Hard.

He staggered back a step, looking as surprised as a cat attacked by a mouse.

Her hands went to her hips. Fury was a fine, heady torrent. "I will *not* have you feeling sorry for me. You think I don't know what you're doing? You decided I was too fragile, didn't you? Too vulnerable. Well, I have had it up to *here* with people I care about making decisions for me because they think I'll crumple in a strong wind!" She leaned forward so she could put her face near his. *"I'll* decide whether I can handle being seduced by the likes of you, Damon Reed, and don't you forget it!"

For a long, breathless moment neither of them spoke, or looked away.

Damon's smile was like daybreak in the mountains— gradual and brilliant, a seduction more shattering than any of his earlier touches. "Well, then. What's your decision, Felicity?" He reached out and slipped his hand beneath her hair. His long fingers caressed the nape of her neck.

She shivered.

"Come here," he said softly, "and tell me what you want."

Felicity hesitated, but only for a second. His smile said that she mattered, her answer mattered. It was enough, for now. Her heart pounded madly as she stepped forward into his arms, but fear was only a small part of the rush. There was desire, too, and the excitement of a challenge made— and accepted.

"You," she said simply, reaching up to circle his neck. "I want you."

His fingers tightened on her neck, and he bent his head.

This time, his kiss wasn't soft. This time, he wasn't courting or seducing. This was the kiss of a man who'd spent years pursuing the thrill of speed. His mouth was hot and avid and everywhere. Her lips. Her cheek. Down the line of her jaw to the sensitive place beneath—oh, there, *yes*. Felicity thought she whispered that word, but couldn't be sure. She was already beyond anything she knew.

Then he pulled her against him, body to body. His hands went to her bottom and he ground her against him.

Need. It slammed into her, quick and hard. She clutched his shoulders, his neck. He grabbed her hair and used it to pull her head back so he could bury his greedy mouth at the base of her throat.

Felicity's mind didn't shut off. It turned loose, letting go of reasons and possible tomorrows. She swam in sensation, a rich current, thick with hunger. She was falling, drowning, flying freer than she had ever dreamed possible. If there was fear, it was only another flavor floating on that mad current.

His hands pulled at her shirt. He made a frustrated noise. "Where does this blasted shirt fasten?"

"In back," she said, tugging in turn at his shirt.

He slid his hand beneath her shirt and up her back. She shivered. Instead of unbuttoning her shirt, though, his long, clever fingers undid her bra, then snuck around front to close over her bare breast.

She moaned, but she managed to tend to most of the buttons on his shirt before losing patience. He shouldn't knead her breast that way if he wanted her sane, now, should he? She ripped his shirt open, sending the last button flying. He made an approving noise and took her nipple between his thumb and forefinger. He squeezed. She shuddered and sent her hands racing over him.

Fascination slowed her slightly. His contrasts captivated her. Hard, rounded muscles jumped at her touch. Sharp collarbone. Small, hard nipples. Smooth skin over his belly. And heat—oh, Lord, everywhere she touched he seemed to be burning up.

"Now," he said, and his hands went to the waistband of her pants. He unbuttoned them. "I want you now, Felicity."

When he pulled her pants and panties down, her mind fell suddenly, jarringly, back into place. She grabbed his shoulders as if he'd unbalanced her physically. She was bare from her waist to her knees. Exposed.

His eyes met hers, glittering like the strong waves of the ocean as they catch the sunlight and toss it back. His face was tight with hunger, and his lips were damp from hers.

"Damon?" She didn't know what she asked, only that she teetered on some uncertain cusp.

All at once, he grinned. She had only a split second to marvel at the transformation before he bent and scooped her up in his arms. She yelped. He took two quick steps and tossed her into the air.

She landed on the bed, bounced, and started laughing. He followed her down. One of his hands went to her face, his fingers curving along it from temple to jaw. His thumb stroked slowly beneath her jaw. Their eyes met.

He stopped moving.

She stopped laughing.

Time itself seemed to snag on the moment, to catch and hang, suspended. Then his head lowered. His mouth took hers once more, and her lips parted for him just as his other hand went to her belly, and below. "Open," he whispered into her mouth as he threaded his fingers through the curly hair covering her pubis. "Open for me."

Felicity shivered, flooded with a vulnerability as terrible as the sensations his clever fingers wrought as they toyed with her. And as irresistible. She opened her legs.

He teased her. Invaded her. Retreated to tease again, and then, when she was helpless, delirious, hanging on the brink of climax, he drew his mouth back while his fingers played.

She tried to draw him down to her again.

"Let go," he said, his face tense, shiny with sweat. "I want to see you."

"I can't!" As desperate for the privacy of his kiss as she was for release, Felicity tried again to pull his face back to hers.

He stabbed inside her with two fingers while his thumb circled the sensitive nub he'd been playing with. "Let go!" He pressed firmly on her clitoris.

She did. Or her body did it for her—bucking in convulsive delight as Damon sent her spinning, spinning, out on a dark spiral. Her body went lax, her mind blank, stunned with pleasure. She lay in an untidy sprawl on the hard bed and blinked at him while he stood and tore the rest of his clothes off.

She came back to herself when she saw him standing, naked, beside the bed, rolling a thin latex sheath on a very interesting part of his body. She frowned. She wanted to do that. She wanted to touch him, and she wanted to be as naked as he was.

When she scrambled to pull her things off, he helped. They got rid of her shoes, pants, and panties, but then he got impatient. She still wore her shirt when he moved between her legs, spreading them wide. She pulsed, helplessly hot and ready, as if her climax had been foreplay rather than release.

Then he cupped her bottom in both hands, lifted, and pushed inside.

He was *big*. Her eyes widened at the sensations shimmering through her. He paused. "I wanted to go slow," he said. "but I had to get inside you. I don't understand—"

His body moved, drawing partway out and slamming home again. He groaned. "I'm sorry." His body moved again. He shuddered. "I can't stop."

Felicity had no idea what he was talking about. She certainly didn't want him to stop. She pressed her hips up and gasped with delight. Moving felt *good*. Very, very good.

He responded immediately, moving faster. She met him stroke for greedy stroke, so lost in what they built together that she slapped up against the second peak before she knew it was there. She cried out.

So did he.

The bare little room was quiet except for the thudding of Damon's heart. Felicity could hear that clearly because her head rested on his chest. One of his hands rested on her hair. The other arm curved around her waist. The musk of their lovemaking filled her nostrils.

Not lovemaking, she told herself. Sex. The most grand and glorious sex of her life, maybe, but she mustn't make it into something it wasn't.

Besides, no one fell in love in the space of one night and a day. Especially not someone like her, a woman who hardly knew the meaning of risk. It didn't matter that this was Damon, the grown-up version of the boy she'd been obsessed with so many years ago. It didn't matter that she felt connected to him in a way she'd never imagined could come true, that her body curved into his as if made for this.

Sex, she repeated silently. That's all this was.

His hand moved. He started stroking her hair, from the top of her head to her shoulders. Over and over.

No, she wanted to tell him. Don't be tender. Don't do this to me. How could she remember all the reasons that she wasn't feeling what she was feeling when, with every stroke, he bound her more firmly to him?

His long fingers brushed the hair back from her face, lingering as if he liked the gentle intimacy.

"I think I'm falling in love with you," she whispered.

He froze. For a long moment he did nothing. "You know," he broke his silence to say lightly, "I still haven't made the acquaintance of your pretty breasts." His hands went to her back. She felt her shirt—the shirt she'd forgotten about—come loose button by button.

He rolled her off of him, onto her back. Somehow he managed to slip her shirt and bra off in the process. What a clever man he was, oh, yes, ever so good at getting a woman out of her clothes. Feelings welled up inside her, nameless and harsh like the rising swell of a dark sea.

Damon leaned over her, his mouth turned up in his usual smile. He looked at her breasts, not her face.

"Damon—"

His eyes met hers—winter-bleak eyes the terrible color of the North Sea when the sunlight is gone. "Don't," he said gently.

He bent and fastened his lips on her nipple. He tugged, and within seconds, he'd carried her off to the mad, temporary place they'd built—a place of great pleasure, where no one spoke of love, or tomorrow.

SEVEN

At odd moments over the next three days, Felicity was able to believe she didn't love him. But she couldn't make herself think of the times when they came together as anything other than making love. That was his fault. She might have convinced herself it was only sex if he didn't insist on holding her so tenderly afterward. Or if he hadn't continued to seduce her—with his hands, with his words . . . with the idea that he needed her.

He never said so, of course, and he wouldn't let her speak of her feelings, but she was sure it was need she saw in his eyes when he reached for her, when he pushed inside her.

Almost sure.

On that afternoon three days after making love with Damon the first time, Felicity headed down the second-floor hallway to his grandmother's bedroom. She'd had to scrounge for things to wear, and today she had on a robin's-egg-blue polo shirt of Damon's and a pair of his silk boxers—pale blue with thin white stripes. He claimed he found the sight of her in his boxers incredibly sexy. Her own clothes hung in the closet of the bedroom she didn't sleep in anymore, since she was sleeping with him.

"I can think of any number of better things to do this

afternoon," Damon said now from behind her.

She smiled. "You can still take your hike." Damon had too much energy to stay cooped up. Every day he took off hiking, heading up and down and all over. She'd gone with him until today. Today she had another goal.

"Come with me."

"Maybe later. I know you've already looked here, but I'm running out of places to search. You don't have to come with me, though." She stopped in front of the door to a room that she suspected might be even more haunted for him than the rest of the house.

"Ah, well, you know how devious I am. While I'm pretending to search, I can try to change your mind about the proper way to spend the afternoon."

She looked over her shoulder, trying to frown. He was right behind her, smiling down at her, ruining her attempt at a serious expression. Damon wanted her. Whatever else he felt or didn't feel, the wanting was real, and it made her as fizzy as a freshly opened bottle of pop. "This is important to me, Damon. I want to find that paper, whatever it is."

He nodded. "I know. But I can't help wondering . . . how long will you look before you decide it isn't here?"

Her mind went blank. This had happened several times in the past three days, pretty much every time she tried to think beyond the present. Her mind refused to peer around the corner to the time when he would be gone. "I don't know," she said carefully, and turned and opened the door.

Gertrude Reed's bedroom was large, and as crammed with Victorian furniture and bric-a-brac as the parlor downstairs. It was just as ugly, too, and very nearly as red. Felicity looked around the room, feeling oppressed at the sheer number of hiding places to be checked.

A painting on the far wall caught her attention. She walked over to stand in front of it. It was a large, framed oil executed with a professional eye, a portrait of a tall young man in an Army uniform with his arm around a striking young woman. She wore the sort of gauzy summer dress that Felicity associated with old black-and-white movies.

"Grandmother was married in 1939," Damon said quietly. "The year the Germans rolled into Poland. He was career Army, one of the first to be sent to Europe. He died shortly before the war ended."

"She looks like you," Felicity said, amazed. She'd never seen the resemblance before, but it was obvious now. Damon's features were a masculine translation of the ones she saw in the portrait—lazy, hooded eyes, ax-handle cheekbones, a strong nose. Even the mouth was similar, and very different from the way Felicity remembered old Mrs. Reed looking. This young woman's lips were full and smiling. "I didn't realize how much you resembled your grandmother, Damon. She was lovely."

"Didn't you?"

Something odd about his voice made her turn to look at him.

"Has it truly never occurred to you how much Grandmother and I are alike?" His tone was casual, even mocking. He was looking over her head—at the portrait.

"No," she said slowly. "No, I never saw any resemblance at all, and even now, the only similarities I see are physical."

His lip curled. "Seeing only what you want to see, dear Felicity? It's a gift, I guess. Like your ability to live in the moment."

His scorn stung. "I don't know what you're talking about." She turned away. "We'd better get started, if we're going to get anything done. I'll take the dressing table." It was closest. She moved over to it. "Good grief. The frame on that mirror alone must weight twenty pounds, don't you think?"

"I'm talking about the way you sidestep discussing the

temporary nature of our relationship. What happens if you do find what you're looking for? If you open that jewelry box and find a whole stack of love letters your mother once wrote to the mailman, will you stick them in your pocket, shake hands, and tell me it's been fun before you head back down the mountain?''

Her hand froze in midair, inches from the ornate jewelry box. The road was clear now. It had been for the last two days. They both knew she could go . . . and they both knew why she hadn't. "I've always been a coward," she said quietly, and opened the gilded lid. "I'm no good at facing things, I suppose."

"You?" He sounded incredulous. "I remember you as being a bit timid when you were a kid, but now—"

"A bit?" She laughed as she looked inside the box and found an assortment of bobby pins, combs and, surprisingly, a couple of old lipsticks. She didn't remember ever seeing Gertrude Reed with a painted mouth. "I didn't climb trees or play softball. I might have fallen, after all. The ball might have hit me. What if I got a concussion? What if I needed stitches and ended up scarred for life?"

His voice softened. "Those were your mother's fears. It was only natural they would affect you."

"Were they? Sometimes the line between our parents' fears and our own gets blurry. Even when I got older, and wanted to rebel . . . Look," she said, "are you going to help me search this room or grill me?"

"I imagine I can do both," he said. He came to stand next to her, and began sorting through the clutter on top of the dresser. His shoulder brushed hers.

"If you're going to look here, I'll pick another spot," she said, annoyed at the way her heartbeat speeded up at the most casual of touches. She moved away and jerked open the drawer of the nightstand.

"Did you ever climb a tree?"

"Maybe you didn't notice back when you lived here, but Mom enlisted the whole town in her campaign to protect me. Everyone watched out for me," she said glumly as she sorted through the debris in the drawer. "The one time I tried climbing a tree, Mrs. Fieldman came out and lectured me about straining my heart and worrying my poor mother."

"Does the entire town still worry about you climbing trees?"

"Oh, Mother shifted the focus of her anxiety as I got older. By the time I was a teen, she mostly worried about boys. She started talking a lot about my father and how he would have wanted me to be 'a little lady.' I was normal enough," she added, "to resent that. She made him sound so . . . perfect. I didn't like feeling I had to live up to the expectations of a man who'd died before I was born."

He didn't respond at first. She glanced over her shoulder to see him standing very still, his back half turned, as if she'd said something truly surprising. "I always rather envied you the father you didn't have," he murmured after a moment. "He seemed a much better sort than the one I lacked. Not that I ever knew much about mine, except that he was married. My mother did tell me that much one day." He looked up and met her eyes in the mirror over the dresser. "Did you ever manage to rebel?"

"A little, here and there. But I was afraid of the consequences."

Softly, he quoted, " 'Now am I cabin'd, cribb'd, confin'd, bound in to saucy doubts and fears.' "

"Is that Shakespeare?" she asked, surprised.

"I've no idea. It comes of hanging around actors," he said apologetically. "They give wonderful parties, but they do have a bad habit of dropping lines from their performances into their speech. Did you never want to get away from here?"

"Oh, I thought about it. I did get away for college, but
... it's ironic, I suppose. While I was in college Mom was
diagnosed with a mild form of heart disease. She really
wanted me to live close after I graduated." Felicity
shrugged away the vague dreams she'd had. Didn't all teenagers fantasize about faraway places? "I might have come
back to Cross Creek eventually, even if she hadn't devel-
oped the heart trouble. There are a lot of things I like about
it here."

"You spoke of consequences," he said. "Were you
afraid for yourself, or for her?"

"I don't know. It gets confusing when we try to sort
out where our ideas about ourselves come from, doesn't it?
Like you thinking that you're like your grandmother. Who
told you that?"

She didn't think he would answer. When he did, he
sounded surprised—though whether at himself for responding, or at what he said, she wasn't sure. "My mother. But
she thought it was a good thing, because it made me a
fighter instead of a victim, like her."

"What do you think?"

His expression changed, closing her out even as he
closed the drawer to the dressing table. "I think," he said,
"that it's pointless to spend this afternoon going over ter-
ritory I've already searched. You never did answer my question, you know. If you find what you're looking for, are you
going to hurry on your way?"

He looked so damned polite and curious. As if her answer might be interesting, but was not particularly important. Her hands clenched into fists. "Why are you making
me say it?"

"There are a number of things I can make you do,
particularly when I have you naked. But I don't think I can
make you tell me the truth."

Maybe, just maybe, he needed to hear it. She held her

head high. "I won't go until you send me away." She didn't ask him when that might be. She didn't want to know.

His face tensed, so she knew her words had affected him. She just couldn't tell what that effect was. He turned away. "I'm going downstairs," he said, heading for the door. "Join me when you get tired of wasting your time here. There are a few things we haven't tried yet." He paused, his hand on the doorknob. "The kitchen, for example. Have you thought about the erotic possibilities there? No? I have. I want to strip you and lay you naked on the table, flat on your back so I could nibble on you a bit." His smile was pure, sinful invitation. "Sound like fun?"

"Do you think I don't know why you're trying to distract me?"

"It really doesn't matter if you know what I'm doing. It works anyway, doesn't it? I'll see you downstairs later." His eyes glittered as he made a mocking little bow. "In the kitchen."

When the door closed behind him Felicity didn't know whether to rage or weep. She'd pushed Damon. She knew that. He wasn't ready to trust, to open up, and she should know better than to push so hard. It had come as no surprise that he'd retreated behind the sexuality he could wield like a weapon.

Yet she had so little time. How could she get him to open up if she didn't try? How could she stop herself from hoping, however foolish her hope was?

Felicity spent three hours making herself go through as much of the old woman's bedroom as she could, and finding nothing significant. Of course, she didn't do a very good job. All too often she'd find herself motionless, staring off into space while she thought about the kitchen, the wooden table there and how it would feel against her bare back.

Among other things.

*   *   *

He wasn't in the kitchen.

A little after four, Felicity poured herself a glass of the tea she'd made for lunch and told herself she wasn't disappointed. She certainly hadn't expected Damon to be waiting here for her . . . *naked*, she thought, her mouth quirking up, *and sitting cross-legged on the table.*

The image warmed her cheeks, among other places. She shook her head, amused at her newly prurient imagination, and set her glass in the sink.

The radio was on. She drifted over to the window, listening to Garth Brooks sing about wild horses and wondering if Damon was outside, or if he'd finished his hike. She stared outside, a little dreamy, distracted by the ache of desire.

The song finished and the deejay reminded everyone that the National Weather Service had issued a severe thunderstorm warning. Felicity found herself hoping the road would flood again so Damon couldn't send her away for another day or two. She bit her lip.

She was pathetic, wasn't she?

"Looking for me?"

She turned around.

He stood near the door. She knew he'd been outside because, while he wore the same dark blue T-shirt, he'd changed to the ragged cutoffs he wore for hiking. He wasn't smiling. "Phil called."

In the past three days Felicity had learned who Damon's agent was, and what sort of things he was likely to call about. Her heart stumbled in sudden fear. "Oh?"

"The studio wants me to come in and sign the contract. I'll have a couple weeks to put things together before shooting starts."

She wasn't ready. No, dammit, she wasn't ready, not this fast. It couldn't be over. Not yet. She dug her fingernails into her palm and concentrated on that sting instead of what was happening inside her. "It's a good deal for you, moving to Stunt Coordinator. A real coup."

"Yes." He came towards her, moving like an animal so at home in his body that the limp became natural, a part of his grace.

"Of course you're going to take it. You'll be leaving. Soon."

"Tonight."

"Oh, but you can't. The will—you never did find the will—"

"It doesn't look like I'm going to, either. But I won't let that keep me from going after what I want." He stopped in front of her. "Come with me."

Her heart did stop. She was sure of it, though when her hand went to her chest she could feel something pounding there: *ka-thump, ka-thump*. "W-what?"

"Come with me." He put his hands on her shoulders. "They want me in L.A. to sign the contract tomorrow. Phil's got me booked on a red-eye flight out of the Stanhope airport. I told him to have a second ticket waiting at the counter. We'll drive into Cross Creek so you can pack a few things, then drive on into Stanhope and fly out of here together."

Her mind and heart whirled. *Together?* The word was magic, opening up possibilities, chances she'd never dreamed of having. But even as the magic spun out dizzy threads of hope, a fist of panic pulsed in her middle, growing larger with every heartbeat, grabbing at each thread and reeling it back in. "I can't just *leave*."

"You can." His hands slid from her shoulder up her neck to cup her face. He stared down into her eyes. "I want you to come with me."

The surge of longing that his words brought was as strong as the fear. She clutched his arms as if she could restore her balance physically. "For how long? A week? Two weeks? Until filming starts?"

He hesitated. "We could—try living together."

If he'd asked her to go to the moon with him, she couldn't have been more astonished. "You want me to live with you."

"I know it's a risk, and you've got this crazy idea that you aren't brave, but you're wrong. You've got the courage to do anything you want—if you want it badly enough." His voice took on the husky, coaxing note she'd heard any number of times since she showed up at his front door in the rain. He bent and skimmed his lips across hers. "I know you want me."

"My job," she said, making a grab for the fading shreds of her reason. "School starts next month."

"That gives them time to find someone else. You don't have to work," he added, that wonderful mouth of his taking a leisurely trip around her face. "Unless you want to. That would be up to you. I have plenty of money. This is going to play hell with my carefree image," he said, lifting his face to smile into her eyes from very close, "but I've got a house outside L.A., in one of the canyons. It's nothing fancy, but I think you'd like it."

"You have a house." That was, somehow, as hard to assimilate as the idea that he wanted her to come live in that house. With him.

His lips smiled, but his eyes . . . his eyes were anxious. Intent. "This is your chance to get away. You always wanted to get away, didn't you? You were afraid to go, but you wanted it. Just like you want me." Now his lips came down on hers, seductively soft. "Let me set you free."

Her lips clung to his. Her hands tightened on his arms. She wanted him, oh, yes, she wanted to throw everything aside—her job, her duty to her mother, a lifetime spent in caution—she *wanted* to take the risk—but what if Damon didn't love her? What if he never loved her?

What if she fell out of the tree and broke her bones . . . ?

What if, once he got her there, he saw how dull, how ordinary she was next to the glamorous women he was used to?

What if a ball hit her in the face and she was scarred for life . . . ?

"No!" Panic swallowed her whole. She felt herself falling down its black inner walls, sliding down an endless, suffocating gullet. She shoved out of his arms, panting. "No, how could you ask me to do that? You haven't promised me anything. I need time—"

His face turned fierce. "When I leave, I'm not coming back. Come with me." He gave her a little shake. "Don't let your mother's fears shape your life."

Her mother—"I have to find the paper," she babbled. "I can't leave yet. In a day or two, after I find the paper, then I—maybe then I could go. You have to give me a little time to think it over."

"How many things have you talked yourself out of doing over the years by 'thinking things over'?"

"I'm not an impulsive person—"

"It took you less than twenty-four hours to decide to go to bed with me," he said flatly. "That seems pretty damned impulsive to me. But maybe that wasn't such a risk. You don't know what I'd be like to live with, but you were pretty sure I'd be a good fuck, weren't you?"

She recoiled, tears springing to her eyes.

He stepped back, his eyes cold. "I'm going to pack. If you want to come with me, fine. If not, be sure to lock up behind you when you go."

She couldn't move. For the longest time she stood frozen, staring at the open door and the short hallway that led to Damon's room. She could hear him moving around in his room.

Something was nagging at her, something . . . she

closed her eyes and put her hands to her head and rubbed, as if she could force the thought out physically.

What was she so afraid of, anyway?

Her eyes opened. She was afraid of being hurt, of course. That was obvious. She was in love with Damon—there, she'd admitted it. And finding out he didn't—couldn't—love her back would be devastating.

But would it be any worse than spending the next thirty or forty years wondering if he might have come to love her if only she'd taken the chance?

Don't be ridiculous, she told herself. *Not only has he never said he loves me, he's made it clear he doesn't want to hear about my feelings for him, either.* Damon had gone out of his way to be sure Felicity didn't think in terms of love and happily-ever-after . . . but then, why had he asked her to go with him?

She remembered the anxiety in his eyes. As if her answer mattered. As if he needed her.

It was enough to give her hope, and hope, she discovered, was as strong and stubborn as fear. She bit her lip. Maybe she was a fool—but wouldn't she be a bigger fool to let the man she loved walk out the door without finding out if he could learn to love her back?

She was crazy. She was stark, staring nuts, but she didn't care. Felicity took a step forward, glanced down and realized she was wearing a man's *underwear*, for heaven's sake. She couldn't go on a plane dressed like this.

She took off running for the stairs.

Five minutes later she stood in what had been her room for only one night, zipping the green pants she'd worn for her first-ever adventure. The room was at the front of the house. When the front door slammed, she heard it clearly, and froze. He wouldn't have just left, would he? Without her?

She ran to the window, thinking she could lean out and call to him—but the damned thing was stuck. Paint and weather had welded the wooden frame in place. After a fierce but futile struggle she gave up and raced out of the room.

Felicity took the stairs so fast it would undoubtedly have given her mother a heart attack. She skidded on the floor in the hallway, actually sliding into the big front door. Wrenching it open, she ran outside—just in time to see his rented Porsche disappear around the first curve.

He must have taken off like the proverbial bat out of hell. She stood there trying to blink away the sudden fuzziness in her vision as thunder rumbled overhead. She'd never be able to catch him. Her car was hidden half a mile past the end of the driveway, and she'd have to put the solenoid back before she could start it.

No, she'd never catch him. Not as fast as he was driving.

Lightning tore a hole in the sky, followed by thunder and the hushed sound of rain sweeping toward her in a thin, gray curtain. Felicity watched the storm arrive. This one seemed mostly noise and lightning with a bit of rain thrown in, but with the river already swollen, it wouldn't take much to make it flood the road again.

This time, she'd be stranded here alone.

It was just as well he was gone, she told herself as she turned and went back inside. Obviously he'd regretted asking her to go with him. Look how fast he'd gotten himself out of here. He must have been afraid she would be crazy enough to take him up on his offer. She should be glad he'd kept her from doing something so incredibly stupid.

When thunder boomed so hard the pictures on the wall shook, she didn't flinch. She hardly noticed. She did notice, vaguely, that there was something wrong with her vision as she walked down the hall toward the kitchen. Everything kept getting blurry, no matter how much she blinked. Damp and blurry.

She stopped and used both hands to wipe the tears away, but it didn't help. They kept coming. So she just kept walking in spite of them.

She didn't know where she was going until she stood in the doorway to the tiny bedroom she'd shared with Damon. He had left in a hurry, hadn't he? His suitcase was gone, but the bed wasn't made, and she saw a sock on the floor by the chest of drawers . . . and something on top of the chest.

Slowly she stepped into the room. At the chest of drawers she stopped and looked down at the little leather journal she'd found. His mother's journal.

Pain stabbed through her, sharp as a knife. She picked up the journal and held it to her and wished he'd wanted to take this with him, wished he'd wanted any of the things she'd been so ready to give him enough to wait a few more minutes for her. If he'd only waited a few minutes longer . . .

A folded paper fluttered out of the journal. Mechanically she bent to pick it up. She started to tuck it back inside, thinking it was a loose page, but something about the thickness and size of the paper penetrated her daze.

She unfolded the paper and looked at it.

A minute later Felicity still stared blankly at a room she no longer saw, her world uprooted and her heart shaken by what she'd learned. This time, the lightning was so close it was truly blinding, like a dozen flashbulbs going off right in her face. This time, she felt the thunder as well as heard it, felt it in the soles of her feet as the old house shook from the blow.

She stood there, dazed and frightened, clutching the journal and blinking away the last, dazzling afterimages. Then she heard the crackling of the flames.

EIGHT

The Porsche handled beautifully, even on wet roads. When Damon took the last turn before the intersection at a speed he had no business hitting, though, the car fishtailed.

He corrected automatically. Driving fast, like living fast, came all too easily to him.

Ahead of him lay three miles of a straight, downhill stretch veiled in the deepening dusk of storm. He pressed on the accelerator, knowing it wouldn't help. No matter how fast he drove, the woman he was trying his damnedest to leave stayed with him, lodged solidly somewhere near his heart. He saw her eyes again, angel-pure eyes the color of hope and redemption—eyes filled with hurt and fear.

Because of him.

Didn't that prove how right he was to leave? If he'd stayed another day, another damned hour, he'd have told her the truth—and truth, like love, wasn't always a good thing. He knew that. His childhood had proved it. His grandmother had loved her daughter, but it hadn't been healthy for either of them. No, the old woman's obsessive love, her inability to let go, had been both the cause and the means of destroying what she cared most about.

And he was like her. Felicity didn't want to see that,

but it was true. He'd grown up strong in that house, but not straight. From the moment when, at five, he decided his grandmother was his enemy, he'd been unable to compromise. He'd fought her at every turn, in every way—and his mother had suffered the consequences. Like his grandmother, he'd never been able to give in—like her, he was selfish in his strength.

He couldn't take the chance of what the love of a man like him might do to a woman like Felicity in the long run. But he hadn't been able to just walk away. So he'd asked her to come with him. He'd pushed her, pressed her, refused to give her what he knew damned well she needed—some kind of assurance that he cared. This way, they could both tell themselves it was her choice when he walked out.

He'd committed any number of sins in his life, but he hadn't numbered hypocrisy among them. Until now.

The intersection was coming up on him fast now. Too fast. He realized he'd waited almost too late to start slowing, considering the condition of the road and the river that lay just the other side of the intersection—bloated and brown now from runoff. It flashed through his mind that he didn't have to slow down. He could just keep going—and if he wiped himself right off this earth, who would care?

Felicity would.

Fear touched him, clammy and as livid as the lightning that chained across the sky behind him, lighting up his rearview mirror for one blinding moment. If anything happened to him, Felicity would mourn. No matter whether he deserved it or not. Felicity would grieve for him.

What the hell was he doing?

Self-disgust and determination flooded him in equal parts. He didn't want to die—and he didn't want to be on this damned road, racing away from the best reason he'd ever found for staying alive. Since when, he demanded of himself, had he turned his back on what he wanted?

He took his foot off the accelerator and pressed on the brakes. The car skidded and barely slowed. He tapped the brakes again and again, but it wasn't enough—he was nearly in the intersection already.

He downshifted.

The engine whined. The car slewed into a spin. Somehow, he promised himself as the world spun around him dizzily—somehow he'd make it right for her. Make himself right for her.

If he lived through the next few seconds.

Damon ended up with the rear of his car five feet from the edge of the swollen river. He'd spun completely around twice and was half off the road now, pointed back the way he'd come.

Good enough. He pressed down the accelerator. The car leaped forward.

The rain had lessened to a mere drizzle already, though clouds still hung heavy overhead. He kept his speed down out of respect for the wet road that wound up towards the house he refused to think of as his.

Then he saw the orange glow through a thinning in the trees.

Fire.

Damon took the last curve at a speed a little short of deadly. His fingers were white-knuckled on the steering wheel, his mind white with fear. His first glance at the old house calmed him slightly—it wasn't completely engulfed in flames. The fire must have started at the back, because the front was still untouched, except for the sullen orange glow in the windows. But even as he raced down the long drive he saw flames lick up above the roof in the back.

There wasn't much time. And he didn't see Felicity.

Damon had learned a few things about fire in Hollywood. He'd driven through small, planned fires and he'd worked with experts in explosives who arranged the careful conflagrations needed for special effects. But there wasn't time to use any of his knowledge, which involved special clothing, timed charges, and men standing by with firefighting equipment. The one thing he figured he had going for him was that an old house crammed with old things should burn clean, without the toxins in the smoke that make modern house fires so deadly.

But it would burn fast, too.

He slammed the car to a shuddering stop and jumped out. First he looked around frantically, telling himself that surely she was somewhere outside. Safe. Surely the lingering drizzle, the overcast and his own haste had made him miss seeing her.

Only he still didn't see her.

His gaze went to the second floor of the burning house. The window he knew to be hers was as vacant as the rest, but it was dark. The fire hadn't reached it yet. He had time to get her out. There *had* to be time. He ran for the front door. The doorknob wasn't hot to the touch—good. He jerked it open and saw smoke and darkness, took a deep breath, and stepped forward.

A hasty figure stumbled into him and sent him staggering backward through the doorway.

His arms went around her. He dragged her back, back away from the smoke and danger—down the stairs, off the porch. By the time they reached his rented car, she was bent over, coughing. He held her and cursed himself. "Are you all right, sweetheart? Damn my eyes, I left my cellular behind so you'd have a phone. I can't call for help. We'd better get you in the car—"

"No!" She straightened and tried to pull away.

"I know you don't want to go anywhere with me. I don't blame you, but smoke inhalation is nothing to fool around with."

"I'm all right," she said, but her voice was hoarse.

Still, she managed to push away enough that he saw her face clearly for the first time.

She was a mess. Her face, her hair, her clothes—all were blackened from the smoke, and rapidly growing more filthy as the continuing drizzle dampened the soot without washing any of it off. The whites of her eyes were the only part of her that looked clean. "You came back," she whispered.

"I shouldn't have left. I should never have left, but—" Then he saw what she clutched—a Dr. Seuss book and his mother's journal.

The one he'd stuck Felicity's birth certificate in.

He gave himself away. He knew. The despair and guilt he felt must have been stamped on his face plainly as he stared at the journal that would put an end to the hopes he'd barely begun to claim. But maybe—maybe she hadn't seen it, hadn't read it . . . "You saved this for me?" He reached for the little leather book.

She stepped back, clutching both books closer to her. "I saw what you put in the journal. You hid it from me, didn't you?"

He didn't answer. He couldn't make himself lie. That was his only hope—to lie in order to persuade her he hadn't lied, hadn't been lying to her for days. But somehow he couldn't make his mouth form the false words. "I'm sorry," he said, because that was the one true thing he could think of—sorry for her, because he'd wanted to spare her this painful discovery. And sorry for himself.

She looked up at him. The drizzling rain drew furrows of paler skin along her sooty face. Lightning flashed, but it was more distant now. Behind her, the house continued to burn. "How could your grandmother have gotten hold of my birth certificate?"

"Actually, I think it was my mother's doing." She looked incredulous. He explained mechanically. "She de-

scribes the events in her journal. Apparently she and your
mother were closer friends than I'd realized . . . at least, they
were for a time. Until my grandmother put an end to it.
Your mother—I'm sorry, Felicity, but apparently she falsi-
fied your birth certificate when she enrolled you in school,
and she was showing my mother how to do the same thing
for me when my grandmother discovered them plotting like
schoolgirls. Grandmother, of course, was enraged because
your mother was trying to help mine get away. That's when
she found out your mother's secret, and that's when—and
why—the blackmail began.''

She bit her lip and looked down.

"You must know I won't tell anyone," he said gently.
"I would have destroyed the copy I found—" He wished
to heaven now that he had "—But I was going to return it
to your mother. I thought . . . I wanted her to know her secret was safe.''

"You weren't going to tell me, were you? Not at all.''
She didn't look up.

"No.''

"I'm not an Armstrong. At least, not by name. Maybe
by blood, but . . .'' Now she raised her head and shocked
him. She was smiling—a wobbly smile, true, but the hope
in her eyes that went with that shaky smile made no sense
at all.

"Felicity?'' That was all he could think of to say, just
her name. Hope left him more wary and uncertain than fear
had ever done.

"Do you know what this means?'' she demanded.
"Mom's fears never were about me, not really. The one big
adventure of her life, running off with my father without
getting married, ended in such pain she never dared take
another. But that was her. That's not *me*.'' Her smile had
widened as she spoke until she was beaming at him.

"You mean—you don't mind? About your parents—?"

"About them not being married? Oh, no! It shook me up at first, until I realized—don't you see? This means I'm not who I thought I was, not the person everyone else thought I was, either. Maybe I *am* a risk-taker. Maybe," she said, her dirty face glowing as she hugged the little journal to her, "I can decide for myself what kind of person I am. And maybe . . ." Here she faltered, but her chin went up stubbornly. "I think you do care about me. You hid this because you didn't want me hurt, didn't you? You were protecting me."

Dumbly, he nodded.

She took a deep breath. "In that case, I *will* go to L.A. with you. And don't tell me it's too late," she said, scowling at him. "You care about me, so you're just going to have to give me another chance. And you're going to have to get used to me telling you how I feel, too, because—"

His paralysis burst. He grabbed her and spun her around. "You can have all the chances you want," he said, pressing his mouth to hers in a quick, hard kiss. "You can *take* all the chances you want. As long as you take them all with me. And," he said, pulling her up against his rapidly responding body, "I expect I will have to let you tell me what you feel, from time to time. Because I want—I feel—" Courage failed him.

"You what?" she said, her face radiant. She gave a wicked little wiggle, rubbing herself against him. "You feel pretty wonderful to me."

Off in the distance, but drawing steadily closer, a siren sounded the approach of the town's one fire truck. But it would arrive too late. The big old house was burning well in spite of the misty rain . . . and, along with the smoke and the ashes of the past, Damon tasted a new flavor.

Freedom.

It seemed that, when the fire was hot enough, even the stubbornest sort of past could lose its hold on the present. "I love you," he told the woman in his arms, grinning like a fool.

She glowed brighter than the fire behind them. "Good," she said, looping her arms tighter around his neck, "because you're going to have one heck of a time getting rid of me. Now," she said, her voice suddenly husky, "let's see if we can shock old Joe McGinney and the other volunteers when they get here in their big, shiny fire truck, shall we?"

EPILOGUE

Cross Creek's volunteer firefighters were indeed shocked when they pulled up in front of the blazing ruin of the old Reed house and discovered sweet little Felicity Armstrong locked in a passionate embrace with Damon Reed. The very next day, the entire town was stunned when poor, misguided Felicity ran off with the scoundrel.

Still, the real surprise came seven weeks later, when the notice of their marriage appeared in the *Cross Creek Journal*, along with the suggestion that those who had been "unable to attend" could catch part of the ceremony on an upcoming PBS special about daredevils. The producer had gotten permission to film the happy couple as they exchanged their vows while holding hands . . . in midair . . . before pulling the cords on their parachutes.

ONCE BURNED

Dee Holmes

·ONE

"This is a helluva bad idea."

Mariah Thornton froze. The dress she was holding slid to the floor. She'd been packing for the trip north to celebrate her father's birthday. She pressed her hand to her heart, and took a deep breath. She didn't need to turn around to know it was Deke Laslo.

She knew his voice. Dark, husky, low, and controlled.

She knew his body. Lean and strong, with a snakebite scar high on his right thigh.

But most of all, she knew he didn't want her.

He'd walked out of their relationship, refusing to explain his reasons; she knew better than to expose herself to that kind of rejection again. Now a year later, and determined to prove to herself that she no longer loved him, she'd made arrangements, through a mutual friend, to travel to Rhode Island with Deke.

"How did you get in here?" she asked, glancing at him and feeling the too-familiar catch in her throat. The man was just too damn sexy. And, here, leaning against the doorjamb of her bedroom on a hot June evening, brought back memories of a year ago. He'd returned from South America unexpectedly, and they'd made love before he ever got into the room.

"I used a key."

She scowled. He'd returned her key when their relationship collapsed. "What key?" But the moment the words were out of her mouth she knew. It was the key she kept under her pot of gardenias. "Don't you say one word."

"Didn't I warn you a long time ago that one of these days you'd turn around and be looking at some stranger with more on his mind than unlocking your door?"

"Like you?"

"I'm not a stranger, foxy." His deliberate use of an endearment from happier times made her mouth go dry. "Lucky for you I'm in the mood to behave myself."

He straightened, moving toward her with that loose-limbed walk that was so familiar it sent a shiver down her spine and through her legs. Black jeans and soft black shirt, bourbon-brown hair that swept back from a narrow face, and eyes as deep a blue as a stormy Miami night.

"You could have knocked," she said, irritated that he could unnerve her so easily.

"And miss all those second thoughts you're trying desperately not to let me see?"

"I am not having second thoughts," she said flatly. "I've made the decision to go north with you, and I'm perfectly happy with it. I haven't changed my mind."

"As I already said, it's a helluva bad idea."

"On the contrary," she argued. "We're both adults. Just because we were once lovers is no reason for us to avoid one another. When Buzz told me you were driving, and intended to stop and visit my dad for his birthday, it seemed silly for me to go separately."

He stared at her for too many beating moments. "Safer, foxy."

He'd said it so softly, she was sure she'd misunderstood, but the boring of those dark-blue eyes told her she hadn't.

"Surely you can handle a couple of days."

"Can you?"

She laughed. "Really, Deke," she said, deliberately dismissing any erotic directions his question intended for her mind to take. "My life is quite happy without you in it." The majority of the time, she corrected silently. "From what Buzz told me, you've bought that property in New Hampshire that you always talked about. Dare I ask if you plan to drop out of life and spend your retirement years as bitter as he said you were?"

"Buzz has a big mouth."

"He also worries about you."

"He worries about whether the sun will come up tomorrow."

She grinned. Deke was right. It was their very opposite personalities—Buzz, the worrier, and Deke, the risk-taker—that had cemented their friendship for so many years.

Mariah folded the dress and placed it in an open suitcase. "So what time do you want to leave?"

"The sooner the better." He glanced at his leather-strap wristwatch. "Like in an hour or so."

She blinked. "An hour? Deke, it's almost dark, and I haven't finished packing. I thought we'd be going in the morning."

"Why wait?" He crossed to the bed, picking up a black bra that she had decided not to take. He brought the garment to his cheek, brushing the lace cup along his jaw. Mariah held her breath, her ears ringing, his words and gesture taking on intoxicating intimacy. He laid the bra beside her suitcase. Then in a husky voice, he added, "Less traffic at night. You can buy extra clothes in Rhode Island. The sooner we get out of Florida, the sooner it will be over."

Mariah shuddered. Perhaps this *wasn't* a good idea. "Please tell me we're not going in your Corvette."

"What did you think? I was going to buy a new car?"

"No, but . . ."

"Don't worry, I won't remind you about the time you—"

She clamped her hand over his mouth, touching him for the first time in a year. His hand gripped her wrist, and she prayed he didn't feel the sudden jump in her pulse.

They stood close, while his gaze shattered any ideas she might have entertained about liking him as a friend.

"Please let me go."

"I did it once a year ago. I did it for your own good. Nothing has changed. What I was then can't come close to what I've become. Be warned. I don't want to play games with you, Mariah. I don't want to touch you, and I don't want you touching me."

She swallowed, her eyes wide, alert, and sympathetic. His hard words were typical of Deke when he wanted to close down, and push everyone and everything out of his life. In the past, she'd seen him bitter and cold, but this attitude had a savageness that didn't frighten her as much as catch at her heart. She wanted to defend him, protect him, and lash out at anyone who had hurt him. It was ridiculous. He was an ex-mercenary, and more than capable of taking care of himself. He'd made that clear when he walked out on her. He neither wanted nor needed her, and she seriously doubted anything she did or said would change his mind.

Mariah forced herself to ignore her softening feelings. She would not let herself be hurt by him again. In an even voice, she said, "You're wrong about one thing. Something *has* changed. You."

"And you don't want a goddamned thing to do with who I am now."

They stood rigid, tension firing back and forth between them. Mariah mentally repeated her resolve, and reminded herself that Deke, true as his word, wouldn't touch her unless he had good reason. For sure, he wouldn't touch her in a sexual way. She glanced up at him, her eyes wide and determined. He stared back at her, and it took all her courage not to lower her lashes.

"Are you trying to intimidate me?"

"I'm trying to get you to rethink this asinine idea. You could find another way north. Like take a plane."

She took a deep breath. "You know I don't like to fly, and doing what I hate at last-minute prices is ridiculous."

"I'll buy your ticket. First class."

She planted her hands on her hips. "Oh, I get it. You don't care that I hate to fly. You don't care that it might be nice that my father sees that we are still friends, even though the relationship didn't work out." Her father had once speculated that Mariah was the one woman who could convince Deke to settle down. That, of course, was wishful thinking; she couldn't even keep him interested in a relationship. "You don't care that I got over you, Deke. And I have. Since you never wanted anything more than sex, I would think this would please you enormously that I'm not hanging on you, and begging you to take me back."

"You beg me to take you back?" His laugh was deep and brought a basketful of good memories. "Mariah, I might have spent too much time in the hot sun of South America, but when it comes to you, my mind isn't half-baked. You aren't the begging type."

She grinned. "Thank you."

He scowled, glancing at her partially-packed suitcase. "No room for all that stuff. Just take the necessities, the tighter the better."

"We could take my car."

"And then am I going to take your car to New Hampshire?"

"Oh. That's right. I was thinking we'd be coming back here together." At his dark look, she walked to a closet, and took out a rawhide-trimmed leather duffel bag. Deke had bought it for her when they'd once vacationed at a resort in Texas.

He glanced at the bag, the black bra he'd handled, and then, turning his gaze on her, he shoved a hand through his hair. In a low, raw voice, she heard, "Christ, I don't need this."

"Deke?"

"I'll be back in an hour," he snapped, stalking to the door. "Be ready to go."

The door closed behind him, and Mariah sat down hard on the bed. Her heart was racing, and those second thoughts Deke had mentioned rushed forward. Don't get rattled, she reminded herself. All she had to do was endure this tension for a few days.

Surely she could do that. Couldn't she?

Two

Ninety minutes later, they were caught in an endless stream of northbound traffic out of Miami. Deke downshifted, cursing Buzz for his stupid idea of taking Mariah with him, but more than that, he cursed himself for not saying no, and then backing up that decision with determined action. Leaving Miami. Alone.

He didn't want her near him.

He didn't want to spend the next couple of days with her practically in his lap.

But most of all he didn't want her to touch him.

Christ. How could he have forgotten how easy she was to touch and feel and taste. Her very eagerness for him had been part of her charm.

At the moment, however, he might as well have been infested with poison ivy given the distance she'd put between them.

Better this way, he thought, even while he wondered how long he could hold out.

She was sexy and sophisticated and elegant, and taking her to bed had been riding his thoughts ever since he'd unlocked the door of her condo.

But he had his reasons for not wanting her near him. He feared he'd hurt her, feared that even in a consensual sexual context that he'd lost his ability to be gentle, to be patient, to give her the satisfaction she deserved. He had nothing warm inside of him anymore. His soul had died that night in El Salvador when he'd screwed up royally.

Flashbacks of that gruesome scene shimmered through his mind. The gunfire, the screams, the aborted rescue, the dictator he killed too late to save the village of women and children. And the blood. Deke couldn't forget the blood. His nostrils flared at the acrid smell. He could still feel the layers of stickiness on his hands.

Now he glanced at his hands on the steering wheel, fully expecting to see his flesh stained crimson. *Good God*, he thought, *get it together*. Nevertheless, he gave an involuntary shudder.

Mariah continued to hug the door, her silence deafening. He'd been harsh and direct with her, and still she was here with him. Gutsy. Yeah. She'd always been gutsy, with a mind of her own.

Miles sped by as they headed north on Interstate 95. It was close to midnight when they passed the West Palm Beach exits, and Deke pulled off at the last one, looking for the fast food joint Josh had mentioned.

He parked in the area with the fewest cars; a habit born from living on the streets. Never put yourself in an ambush situation. And a tight parking lot bred all kinds of trouble. Not that he expected any, but Deke had learned a long time ago that one careless chance taken could mean never getting a second one.

He shut down the engine.

"Mariah?"

She didn't turn to look at him. She didn't answer him at all.

"Are you pouting?"

"I'm being quiet, and letting you pretend I'm not here."

"You smell too good for that."

She turned enough to peer at him. "You say those things so easily. Do you mean them, or are you just trying to keep me unbalanced?"

"Both." He opened his door and climbed out. "Come on, let's get some coffee."

He waited while she got out of the car, watching her with as detached an interest as he could. Her blond hair was held back by combs and she wore a pink summer skirt and jacket with the elegance of a fashion consultant, which was what she was. They weren't exactly clothes to travel in, but he guessed she didn't want to appear too relaxed.

Buttoned-up and uptight were not terms he would have applied to Mariah in the past, but this was now and he knew she was being overly wary of him.

"Hungry?" he asked.

"Thirsty, mostly."

They were walking in silence, when Deke touched her arm to draw her closer to him.

Three guys in gangsta pants and muscle shirts swaggered toward them. One carried a boombox, one pointed, and one whistled. Deke reacted instinctively, and dropped an arm around Mariah.

"Don't make eye contact," he murmured.

"They wouldn't dare do anything," she said, but without conviction. She pressed against him.

The three slowed, looking Mariah over. Deke counted the seconds he'd need to pull the blade from his boot.

"Pretty pussycat, man," said the leader.

"Meow, meow," said another.

"Bet she's good even in the dark."

Deke tightened his grip, his hand coming over her shoulder to cup her breast. She caught her breath, but he kept his hand in place.

"She only purrs for me, man," Deke said, his tone filled with sexual innuendo.

"Could make it worth your while to give her up."

Deke whispered, "Show them you're mine."

"How?"

"Touch me."

To her credit, she didn't ask questions. He expected her hand on his chest, or the snap of his jeans, he didn't expect her to slide it down his zipper to tuck on the inside of his thigh.

Deke thought the top of his head would go off. His eyes ached and his mouth felt desert dry. In a casual, meaningful voice, he managed a husky snarl. "Ain't nothing worth givin' this up, man."

They made a few more comments, but all the time they talked, Deke was easing Mariah in a wide arc that was putting distance between the three guys and the two of them.

"You're a cool dude. Better find some place you can bang her. She's lookin' as juicy as a ripe peach."

They all guffawed at that, and then apparently deciding not to push anything, they moved on into the dark lot.

Mariah sagged against Deke, and he continued to hold her, walking her over to a white bench splattered with graffiti.

"Sit down."

"Oh God, Deke."

"It's okay. They're gone."

"If you hadn't been with me."

He stood above her, and drew her against him, his hands tangling in her hair, her cheek against his belly. His own heart was none too steady.

They stayed that way a few moments, her clinging to him and Deke allowing it.

He chuckled, pressing her to him, moving his hands down across her shoulders. He could feel her relax, her total trust in him rewarded by his total protectiveness of her. That instinctive compliance was why he'd been drawn to her so long ago. She knew when to fight and when to cling. Those three would have eaten her alive if they'd sensed she was anything but his devoted woman.

"You were a cool cookie, foxy."

"I was terrified."

"So was I."

"You? I don't believe it."

"Hey, I'm no fool. Three against one when the prize is a gorgeous blonde not wearing a bra, and who probably would have opened my zipper if I'd asked her to . . . They probably figured they couldn't handle you."

"I would have gone down on you to get us out of that," she said flatly.

He grinned. "And speaking from experience, you do it like a pro."

"Oh, Deke, don't joke. It wasn't funny."

She pulled away and stood, straightening her clothes.

Deke watched her, amused, and more intrigued than he wanted to be.

She pushed her hands through her hair. "For someone who didn't want us to touch each other, we sure blew it."

"Necessary, babe. But you can relax. It was all for show. Didn't mean a damn thing."

The fast-food place was nearly empty. A couple of truckers getting coffee, and three teenagers giggling in one of the booths.

"What do you want?" he asked, his hand touching the small of her back, indicating she should go ahead of him. He was amazed he could feel the heat of her skin through her clothes, but he could.

"A shot of bourbon," she muttered, "But since they don't serve that, then a large Coke with lots of ice."

He glanced toward the side entrance where a man leaned against the wall next to a newspaper vending machine. It was Josh.

He pulled some bills from his pocket and pressed them into her hand. "Get me coffee and a cheeseburger and fries. I'll be right back." He turned to walk away, then stopped. "You remember I like—"

". . . Your coffee black with three sugars," she said as if she'd never forget such an important detail. "Where are you going?"

"Just to take care of some business."

"Here?"

"I'll be back in a few minutes."

He moved away, walking across the dining area to where Josh waited. His old friend straightened, his expression breaking into a grin.

Josh Otis was a comrade, friend, and preacher of peace even to Deke. Unfortunately, Deke had long ago stopped believing such a state would ever exist for him.

Nearing fifty, and as lean as a fast moving panther, Josh offered his hand. "Didn't expect to catch up with you until I came north."

Deke had invited Josh up to New Hampshire for a week of fishing, drinking, and poker. "You been waiting long?"

"'Bout an hour."

"Sorry. Got jammed up in traffic coming out of Miami. I really appreciate this. Last-minute favors can be a bitch."

"Are you kidding? What fascinates me is that you're going to so much trouble."

"Don't give me grief." He glared at Josh, who merely smiled.

"Don't have to, buddy. You do that all by yourself." He nodded toward Mariah. "She's lookin' good. Classy, sexy, but still a little too skinny for my taste."

"Good thing your taste isn't an issue."

Josh grinned. "Do I detect a bit of territorial marking?"

"Just driving her north."

"Uh-huh."

Deke pulled an extra set of keys to the 'Vette from his pocket. "Come on, let's get this done."

"Gonna cost you, you know."

"I don't want to know how much."

"Oh, I don't mean money. I mean an invitation to the wedding."

"What the hell are you talking about?"

"You and your lady."

"Mariah? And me? About as much chance of that as a cobra and a mongoose becoming long-lost friends."

Josh straightened, his expression more patient than exasperated. "You know, Deke, you and I go back a long way. Knew you when you were the idealistic kid who wanted to right the world, when you were dying in the jungles of Peru, when you killed that bastard who raped the kid in Hong Kong. Lots of skirmishes with you, Deke. Not many of them made you happy, even when you were the winner. But then there was that period when you were with Mariah. You were relaxed and reasonably content—"

"And looking at a commitment that was an occupational hazard. End of story. Back off, Josh. I mean it. You're a good friend, one of the best I've ever had, but nosing around in this part of my life is off limits."

Josh peered at him, and Deke was beginning to think this brilliant idea he'd had a few hours ago had become one of his dumber ones.

"Okay," Josh said, resigned. "New topic. What happened in El Salvador? I heard you got the wrong info on the dictator. That the so-called good guy ended up being the rat. True?"

It was hard to imagine that this was easier to answer than anything concerning Mariah, but it was. "Yeah. Solugia was on our side, or so I thought. Then me and my men walked into the village that Solugia was supposed to be protecting, and found him on a murdering rampage. For a few weeks, I'd been suspicious of him, but his old lady had died, his kid got killed in that raid. I figured the double losses had just rattled his bones. Made him testy and depressed—God knows losing his family should have. Obviously, I misread the bastard, and got jerked around big time.''

"No way you could've known, Deke.''

"I was being paid to know, for crissake,'' he snapped, irritated by his own ineptness. "We wouldn't have caught him at all if we'd arrived twenty minutes later. That had been his plan. Take control of the village for some up-and-coming drug cartel, then clear out, and reappear after we did, so he could commiserate about all the deaths and destruction. A real two-faced spook.''

"You weren't the only one who trusted him,'' Josh said softly.

"Then we were all a bunch of damn fools. I should have known better. Old saying about keep your friends close and your enemies closer. He'd practically been in my back pocket. Should have seen that. Solugia always had been a loner like me. For him to be so cozy was a clue I missed.''

"It happens, Deke. Can't do it perfect every time.''

"Innocent women and kids died. I can't forget that or forgive myself for letting it happen.'' He sighed. "It won't happen again. I'm out. Mordike will find another body to fight the lizards and do his bidding.'' Then he gave Josh a fierce look. "No more questions. Let's get this done. My cheeseburger is getting cold.''

"One more. Heard Solugia is dead. True?''

Deke shrugged, but their eyes met in silent unity and understanding.

Josh waited a moment, then nodded. "I'll meet you by the 'Vette."

Deke crossed to where Mariah was waiting.

"Was that Josh?" she asked, just as Josh disappeared out the side door. "What in the world is he doing here?"

But Deke was directing her back outside to the parking lot. Josh was just pulling his dark red Ford Expedition up beside the 'Vette.

Deke took the bag of food from Mariah, while she made her way over to where Josh was climbing out of the vehicle.

"Josh, I can't believe it's you." She flung herself into his arms and he lifted her up, swinging her around.

Deke unwrapped his cheeseburger, took a bite, and washed it down with the coffee. He ate while he watched and listened. Mariah laughed, and Josh talked with his trademark drawl that had been drawing women since Deke met him fifteen years ago on the streets of L.A.

Now, in those few seconds of greeting, Josh had managed to get from Mariah the easy companionship that some deep part of Deke's soul had wanted since he walked into her condo. Sure it was a helluva bad idea to want even that, but seeing her, listening to her, had shown him how much he'd missed her laughter and affection.

Stupid. You don't want anything with her. You're just feeling lonely and empty, and remember too well how good it was. How sweet she tasted, how fiercely she held him when he was about to leave her, how eagerly she'd always welcomed him back.

Until a year ago. He'd come back for two weeks, and then before leaving, he'd told her it was over between them. She'd been stunned and disbelieving, but he'd been adamant. If she asked him why once, she must have asked ten times. He still hadn't answered her.

"Hey, you two," Deke said, finishing his fries, and stuffing the papers into a nearby trash receptacle. "Getting reacquainted time is over."

THREE

"I can't believe you did this," Mariah said, stretching out in the soft leather bucket seat. The Expedition, although a sport-utility vehicle, rode like a dream. Cushy, roomy seats, plenty of leg room and distance between her and Deke.

They'd said good-bye to Josh, watching him roar off in Deke's Corvette. Now, back on the interstate, Mariah felt a little thrill deep within her that Deke would have gone to all this trouble for her.

"I aim to please," Deke said.

"So when did you work this all out?"

"Right after I left your condo. You were right. The 'Vette is too small for two people on this long a trip. I called Josh and asked him if we could switch vehicles. He was going north to see his sister, and then drive to my place in New Hampshire. He's been hasslin' me about sellin' him the 'Vette. Once he rides in it for more than a thousand miles, he might change his mind."

"Josh is a sweetheart. And so are you."

Deke didn't respond.

Mariah shook her head in exasperation. "Am I allowed to say thank you?"

"You're welcome."

She yawned and curled up in the seat. "Do you object to me going to sleep?"

"Go ahead."

"We could stop, you know. I mean driving straight through is a little rough."

"I'm fine. I'm used to going days without sleep."

"Well, I'm not." She leaned sideways to take Deke's denim jacket from the backseat. "Do you mind?"

"Of course not."

"Sometimes you're touchy about anyone handling your things."

"For you, I always make an exception."

"Always?"

"Have I ever lied to you?"

Mariah took a deep breath. "As a matter of fact, I think you have."

His body stiffened as if he were gearing up for battle. But his reaction made her realize it had been this same leery body language that had dominated all of their conversations since they'd left Miami.

Deke definitely wanted total control of this tense reunion in a way that intrigued Mariah. If she didn't know better, she might even believe he was frightened of her.

Suddenly Mariah felt emboldened with new resolve. Deke scared? And of her? The idea was so ludicrous she wanted to laugh, but at the same time she knew this man. His wariness of anything as straightforward as a woman asking him some questions had never been a problem for him. Something was going on inside of him. Something she very much doubted he wanted her to know about.

"I thought you were going to sleep."

"You're trying to change the subject."

"Change it? I don't even know what the hell the subject is."

"What it always is when we're together. You and me."

"There is no you and me."

"For the sake of argument, I disagree."

"Christ."

She settled down in the seat, bundling his jacket on the console for a pillow. "Hear me out."

"Do I have a choice short of jumping out of the car or gagging you?"

She grinned, feeling very sure of herself. "When you broke off with me, you said you didn't want permanent commitment and that you knew I did."

"Mariah, we've been over this."

"No, you've been over it. I was just told the relationship is finished as if it was a done deal. You made it sound no more important than a casual good-bye."

"Believe me, not once since I've known you have I ever applied casual to anything about you. Intense, emotional, stubborn, and angry, but not casual." He pulled into the left lane to pass an eighteen-wheeler.

"Well, that's some progress," she said, pleased that at least he was responding. "This is the way I see it. In addition to wanting to stay free of any ties, you made it pretty clear that our relationship had run its course. It was time for me to move on, and for you to do the same."

"You win the memory game."

"And it was all a lie, wasn't it?"

"It wasn't a lie," he snapped. "It was for the best. Proven by the fact that you have moved on. Buzz told me you were seeing some investment banker and might marry him. Randy something-or-other."

"It's Andy."

"Whatever."

But Mariah wasn't interested in talking about Andy Ridgeway. Not now. "What do you mean breaking off with me was for the best? Whose best? Obviously yours since you never made any attempt to call me."

"No point. It was over," he said, but she was sure she heard the tiniest pause of regret.

Mariah reached across and slid her hand around his forearm. The heat and muscle filled her hand with pleasant sensations. He wouldn't look at her, and in the very dim light, she couldn't read his expression. "Why did you agree to take me with you?"

"Good question."

"Deke, please tell me. I really need to know why."

"You want the truth?"

She nodded.

He slowed the car, easing into the breakdown lane, and came to a stop. He put it into park, turned around, and slid his hands into her hair. "Here's the truth, foxy. I was nuts. Should have said no, and then driven out of Miami, and away from temptation before I changed my mind. Instead I rationalized that I could resist this."

Then he lowered his head and kissed her. Mariah gasped from the possessiveness, and the hunger that poured into her from his mouth. Not gentle, not tentative, not even experimental. It was as if no time had passed, no anger, no regrets, just the clawing yearning between the last time he'd kissed her and this time.

She slid her arms around him, awkward and uncomfortable in the car. His mouth opened wider, his tongue plunging deeper, and for just a few moments Mariah forgot she was supposed to be in control, she was supposed to be cool, and not allow him to touch her heart again.

"I should be pushing you away," she murmured, when he lifted his mouth to kiss her throat and nuzzle above the edge of her raspberry shell.

"Yeah. You should."

"You didn't want me to touch you."

"Starting right now." Then he released her and set her back in her own seat. She sat for a moment, her head reel-

ing, her pulse thumping, her questions many. He eased the
vehicle back onto the highway.

She grinned, feeling a bit like the cat who'd pounced
on the proverbial canary. She began to rethink her thoughts
of staying cool and reserved to prove he meant nothing to
her anymore.

She knew different. In fact she'd known within five
minutes of seeing him in her condo. But telling him? Not
anytime soon. Deke would be furious. He believed there was
nothing between them, and he wanted to believe that when
they reached Rhode Island, he could walk away without a
glance back or a single regret.

Maybe. But if there was a chance for them she had very
little time to find that tiny part of Deke that she desperately
hoped still cared. Changing vehicles proved he wasn't totally unfeeling about her.

And that kiss. She licked her lips, still tasting him.

"Deke?"

"What?"

Once again she snuggled her cheek into his denim
jacket. "It's nice to know you still find me a little bit desirable."

"Go to sleep, Mariah."

She closed her eyes, her mind still edged with anxiety.
Her feelings for Deke notwithstanding, it was very likely
she could be in the throes of making the biggest mistake of
her life.

He'd found a radio station of soft country music. The
raw, bluesy ballads of love and heartbreak relaxed her, and
made her eyes heavy. Deke brushed his hand across her hair
and then palmed her cheek. She thought she heard him say
something about her being too patient and too willing, but
when she tried to rouse herself, he gently pressed her cheek
back down, and she slowly drifted off to sleep.

She had no idea how long, but she was jarred awake

by the car turning suddenly, then braking, then coming to a skidding stop.

She jackknifed awake, blinking and looking at Deke, who had slumped over the wheel.

"Oh my God!" She got out of the seatbelt and scrambled across the console. "Deke?" She touched his face, and he groaned, then slowly raised his head and let it fall onto the headrest. She smoothed his hair, her fingers brushing his cheek and his temples.

He turned and stared at her, his eyes somewhat glazed. He asked, "You okay? Not hurt?"

"What happened?"

"I don't know. One minute I was on the road and the next I was on the shoulder."

"You fell asleep."

He rubbed his eyes. "Yeah, well I'm sure as hell awake now."

"Let me drive."

"Not necessary."

"Stop being so stubborn." She glanced at the clock. "It's nearly three. I've been asleep for a few hours. You could use some."

"I said I'm okay."

But Mariah was determined. She reached over and pulled the keys from the ignition. "Then we sit here."

His look was fierce. Added to his bristly cheeks, his rumpled hair, and husky voice, good sense told her she should return the keys, and not press the point. Wisdom however prevailed.

"I want to drive."

He put his head back on the rest and closed his eyes, his thumb and forefinger rubbing the bridge of his nose.

"Come on, Deke. Just this one time let me have the last word."

Finally, he nodded.

They switched sides, and she noted he had slumped down in the seat, mouth set in a grim line. He folded his arms, looking straight ahead, and then mumbled something.

"I didn't hear you."

"I said, I could have killed you."

"And yourself."

"That, babe, would be no great loss." He waved away any follow-up comment, but Mariah couldn't get his words from her mind.

They settled within her as the miles sped by, and took her heart in a whole new direction. Losing Deke, this second time, would be a loss she couldn't have survived.

FOUR

Deke awakened with a start, muscles aching, eyes gritty, and his mouth tasting like the inside of a moldy cave.

Sun poured through the windshield, making him squint. For a few seconds he was disoriented, but then it all came back.

Mariah, the trip, dozing off, and almost sliding Josh's Expedition down that grassy embankment.

He rubbed his eyes, then came fully awake when she walked in front of the vehicle. Still wearing her pink suit, although the skirt was wrinkled, and the jacket had a dirty streak on the sleeve, she moved with a willowy elegance that would have passed muster on a New York fashion runway.

With Mariah, nothing was forced or affected—just a natural grace that made him even more aware that his decision a year ago, although painful and difficult, was best for her. God, the woman deserved silk suits and hand-painted ties on the man she married, not jeans and boots and a disease of the spirit.

Yeah, and Randy—or Andy or whoever the hell he was—probably fit the silk-suited description, which in turn caused Deke to instantly dislike him.

She continued walking as Deke tracked her steps down

an asphalt walkway, his scowl deepening when realization hit him. They were at a motel, for crissake. What in hell did she think she was doing?

"Mariah!" His shout was husky, and obviously unheard or ignored. She'd already inserted a key into a door, pushed it open, disappeared inside and a few moments later, she reappeared. She walked toward the car, and Deke opened the door. The blast of sunshine nearly blinded him.

"No," he said succinctly, putting on his dark glasses.

"Too late," she said cheerfully. "It's already paid for, it's clean, and I for one want a shower and a change of clothes."

She was all bouncy and smiley, and Deke glared at her. "You tricked me."

"Actually, I only thought of it when I saw the sign a few miles back."

"Where are we anyway?"

"North of Savannah."

"We should be in Charleston," he grumbled.

"Sorry, but I don't have your penchant for driving at ninety miles per hour."

He glanced around, the morning heat already sinking into the black pavement. The air felt like a steam bath. A line of perspiration grazed her upper lip. As if suddenly realizing she'd be cooler without the jacket, she took it off, leaned into the car, using his shoulder for balance, and tossed the garment into the backseat. Her raspberry-colored top was soft and lacy, and covered her breasts as if the material had been placed there by skilled hands. His attention was riveted on the outline of her nipples, and he was grateful he'd put on his dark glasses. Deke clenched his hands recalling the way her breast had felt in his hand when those three goons had threatened them.

". . . Seemed like a good idea. You were asleep, and watching you try to get comfortable made me ache. So I decided we should stop for a while, get some sleep, and then we'll both feel better."

"I feel fine."

"You're cranky."

"I am not cranky. I don't get cranky. I get angry and right now I'm furious."

She patted his cheek, brushing her knuckles across his overnight stubble. "Right now you're acting like a little boy. You might have endless marathon energy, but I don't. The room has A/C, two double beds, a hot shower, and there's a nice restaurant right around the corner. It's run by Jocelyn, and she cooks all the food herself."

Deke stared at her. "You know the cook by name? How the hell long have we been here?"

"Only about fifteen minutes. She was very nice and welcoming. She wore one of those waitress dresses with a name tag, which is how I knew her name."

Deke rolled his eyes and wished he hadn't asked.

Mariah continued nevertheless. "Jocelyn offered me coffee, and we started talking about clothes. She asked where I'd bought my suit because she loved the color."

"Good God." Deke lowered his head, shaking it slowly.

"I told her I was a fashion consultant currently living in Miami, but I'm considering a move to Tampa where a man I've been seeing wants me to live. She has a cousin in Tampa and told—"

"Enough. You're giving me a worse headache than I already have." Deke could feel the summer heat take up full residence inside his gut. "I don't believe I'm being jerked around like this. This is my trip, and you're the un- invited guest—"

"That you've so gallantly endured, poor baby." She gave him a commiserating look, her eyes filled with mock devotion. "And you saved me from those jerks, gave up your beloved Corvette, and the absolute best gift in the world. You let me drive.''

''Obviously a goddamned mistake.''

''Oh, absolutely. The alternative could have been an intimate encounter with soft, gentle things like trees, rocks, and the bottom of that embankment.''

''Very funny.''

''Can I get just a hint of a smile out of you?''

''No.'' He waved her away, when she tried to take his arm. ''I'm going along with this motel gig so I don't have to listen to you bitch all the way north.''

''Good reason. Bitching is my most favorite thing when I'm not trying to figure out a way to keep my hands off of you.'' She grinned with such guile that his annoyance collapsed. She was charming as hell, and sparring with her— damn, he'd forgotten how much he enjoyed it.

She opened the back door to get her bag. Then she pulled his canvas duffel out at the same time he reached for it.

''I can carry these. My gallantry can endure one last act.''

''It's room twenty-seven. The door is open. You go ahead. I'll lock the car, and I'm going to get us some orange juice.''

''I want coffee.''

''I thought you wanted to sleep.''

''No, I want to be in Charleston.''

''You know,'' she said tipping her head so that the sun created gold streaks. ''I'd forgotten how ornery you could be. All right. Coffee it is.''

''Thank you,'' he snapped, wondering why he felt as if he'd lost every comeback attempt in this asinine conversation.

Deke's back ached, a cramp jammed his left thigh, and he had a headache from hell. He felt about ninety and probably looked it, too. But he'd be damned if he'd let her see any of it. He straightened, hefting the two bags and concentrated on walking like a man with boundless energy.

He got to the room and out of sight, dropped the bags and practically staggered into the bathroom.

He turned on the shower, shed all his clothes, and was under the hot spray in a minute flat. The water was blistering, and he let it sluice over him to ease his tight, sore muscles. He soaped his hair and his body, rinsing and finally turning off the water. When he pulled the curtain back, his toiletry case was on the counter along with clean underwear. The dirty clothes he'd shed were gone.

Grimly resolute, he thought, *Why am I not surprised?* In the past when they'd been together, he always forgot to haul his stuff to the bathroom, and she always had it there waiting for him when he got out of the shower. Damn, but it was tough to stay mad when she was being so considerate.

He grabbed up a towel and dried, while the scowl on his face, reflected in the steamy mirror, threatened to become permanent. He knew he should be, at least, reasonably tolerant and cooperative because she'd been anything but a bitch. That was the problem; she was sweet, considerate, and a good sport, and it irritated the hell out of him. Next thing he expected was to find her wearing nothing but panties, that black bra, and a come-do-me smile.

No way. He intended to resist going down that road if it took every bit of control and stamina he possessed.

Reluctantly, he admitted the hot shower had felt good, and the thought of stretching out on that bed beckoned more than a shot of forty-dollar bourbon. Suddenly, he wondered why he'd been so ornery and adamant about driving straight through.

"Idiot," he muttered as he shaved and brushed his teeth. It wasn't stopping to sleep that he'd wanted to avoid. It was stopping to sleep *with* her.

Feeling refreshed, awake, and back in control, he gathered up the clean underwear and toiletries and opened the bathroom door. He dropped the entire pile on a chair, standing naked in front of her and taking some pleasure in that she swallowed once, blinked twice, and to his satisfaction, a flush spread across her cheeks.

She sat in an armchair, legs crossed, shoes off. So much for his theory that she'd be undressed.

"I don't sleep in anything," he said. "You should know that better than anyone else."

"But I thought that since you, uh . . ." She swallowed again, her gaze so obviously riveted above his hips that he had to work to hide his smile.

He folded his arms. "Go on."

"Uh, since you didn't want anything to happen between us, well, I wouldn't have thought you'd want to sleep naked."

"You're joking. You thought if I put on underwear that would stop my two million salacious thoughts from rushing into sheet action with you? Not even if I was dead. Besides, I wasn't aware you planned to sleep with me."

"I didn't."

"Then I'm safe."

She licked her lips, then asked, "Two million? Really?"

"And that's before I started counting."

His coffee and her carton of orange juice sat on the nightstand between the two beds. She hadn't moved, and looked as if she preferred not to chance it until he was safely out of the way.

The room was dim, only a shaft of light coming through the tiny crack where the edges of the drapes met. The air, with its lingering trace of pine-scented room freshner, blew cool from an A/C that rumbled like a rusted-out muffler.

Instead of going to the bed, he walked closer to her, taking note of her widening eyes.

He halted. "Scared?"

"Of course not."

"Want me?"

"No."

"Liar."

He braced his hands on either side of the armchair and leaned down. "Tell you what. If I'm still awake after you take your shower, and if you ask me nice, I'll make you come before I'm even inside of you."

She shoved him back. "You are crude and disgusting."

"Hey, what can I say?"

"Start with an apology."

"And ruin my horny style that you used to love?"

"Oh, shut up."

He grinned, liking things much better now that he was back in charge. Amazing what a shower, a naked entrance, and a few prurient words could do to change the dynamics.

He stretched out on the bed, hands stacked behind his head, ankles crossed and took great pleasure in watching her. She moved to her open bag, pulling out items, and deliberately not looking at him.

"Need some help?"

"No."

"I could come in and wash your front."

She whirled around, hands full of tubes and jars and bottles. Then, as if she decided the offensive was much better than allowing him the last word, she said, "Tell you what, when I come out, if you can wait that long, I might just let you rub lotion on me. Front and back."

The words hung in the air between them for a few seconds before Deke rose from the bed, crossed to her, and backed her up against the wall. He took all the things she held, and dropped them on the same chair where he'd put his own stuff. Then he gripped her wrists and pulled them above her head where he pinned them with his left hand. His body caught at hers, and he heard her breathing become a quick pant. He moved, hiking up her skirt and insinuating his leg between hers so that he could feel the heat and dampness. He rocked a bit and when her body responded, she closed her eyes.

"You're making me rethink my resolve, foxy," he whispered, kissing her once, and then again, urging her mouth open and tangling their tongues.

"I've missed having sex with you," she said so softly, he was sure he misunderstood her. Hell, he had to have misunderstood. It wasn't the kind of thing Mariah would say, but it made him wonder why he was resisting this.

But when her lashes lifted, he saw something else in her eyes. Not just the need for sex with him, but the need for commitment and a future and all the promises that came with both. This might start with sex, but as sure as midnight ended one day and began another, he was dealing with a lot more than a hot romp in the sack when it came to Mariah.

Promises and commitment—he couldn't handle it. A year ago, he'd concluded that she deserved better. Right this minute, he knew it again, but he also knew something else.

He needed her in a way he'd never needed anyone. And that scared him. With that new revelation opening up inside of him, he let go of her and turned around so she couldn't see the terror in his eyes.

By the time she'd taken her shower and returned to the room, Deke was sprawled on his belly across one of the beds. He watched her, saying nothing when she crawled into the other bed.

One thing was no longer in question about Mariah. She was in his heart because sometime in the past few hours, his soul had invited her in.

FIVE

L ater that afternoon, after about seven hours of sleep, Deke and Mariah ate country-fried steak and fresh tomatoes and drank iced tea with mint in Jocelyn's Roadside Restaurant. They listened politely to her tales of her son, who was in the Marines, and her daughter, a fledgling country singer trying to break into the Grand Ole Opry in Nashville.

Deke wanted to get on the road, but Mariah did more than listen; she got involved. She took Jocelyn's address, promising to send her the names of nearby department stores where she might find clothes by the same manufacturer as Mariah's pink suit.

They packed up the car, having said nothing about the tension and desire and mutual silence that both had unwittingly embraced since he'd kissed her.

Deke, not one to dwell on something he didn't want to change—that being his restraint with Mariah—went out of his way to act cool and reserved. His hope was that she had concluded that this trek north was just that. Nothing more involving than traveling with a female companion. Mariah, on the other hand, wasn't feeling quite so calm and disinterested.

She'd had trouble sleeping, quite frankly, because crude

suggestions or not, she'd wanted to sleep with him. She'd been very tempted to crawl in with him, but had resisted. If they'd made love, she would have been left empty and unfulfilled because sex was all he would offer. Then there was always the possibility that he would have said no. To have him turn away, and ignore her like she was some sexually obsessed female . . . that would have been too humiliating.

Begging a man offended her, but begging a man she once loved? That would be the ultimate degradation if he refused.

She had few illusions about Deke. He did what he wanted when he wanted, and while he might change his mind about sleeping with her, he wouldn't change his mind about loving her. Selfish, perhaps, but it wasn't as if she didn't know what she was getting. If anything, Deke was brutally forthcoming.

Not once in their relationship, even at the best of times, had he ever said he loved her. Oddly she had respected him for his honesty, but honesty was a lousy salve for her heart.

Now, settled back in the passenger seat of the Expedition, Deke drove from Savannah to Charleston and into North Carolina. Mariah was surprised at how easily the conversations and their mutual camaraderie settled around them with a warm familiarity.

The following morning, after sharing the driving during the night, they bought a bag of peaches from a roadside stand and made a mess eating them at a picnic area, then washed up in a nearby brook. They listened to Josh's gospel CDs, and to Mariah's delight, Deke knew the words to a favorite hymn of hers. They sang along together, and she rediscovered his rich bass voice.

As they crossed the border into Virginia, she told him that her mother, who had been divorced from her father for years, was now on husband number three and living in Paris.

Deke laughed, commenting that Eliza would probably

turn Paris into one long social event. Mariah had laughed, too.

"She always liked you, you know," Mariah said.

"I liked her, too. However, I didn't like the things I heard about the way she treated you. Always running off on the next whirlwind trip when she should have been home with her daughter."

Mariah's face tightened at the old buried resentment. For the most part she'd put her childhood neglect behind her, but with Deke she'd never hidden her feelings. Perhaps because of his own parents, who had never married, and had preferred cheap booze to paying attention to their son. And while her mother had provided the physical necessities, Mariah and Deke had both grown up feeling like unwanted distractions to disinterested parents. In the past few years, her father had become more interested in her, and while it had come late, she relished it.

But for her and Deke, their wants in a relationship had little in common. She wanted the stability of a home and family, and Deke balked at commitment and love and all their ultimate results such as marriage and children.

"I hated her at one time," Mariah said, realizing it was the first time she'd verbalized that particular word when it came to her mother.

"But not now?"

"Not anymore. I'm not sure if I got past it, or if I just came to the place of realizing she was never going to be June Cleaver, even though she has the world's largest collection of pearl necklaces."

Deke reached over and squeezed her hand. "You're a remarkable woman, you know that? A mother who was born with a passport instead of a birth certificate, and a father who spent his best years in the jungles of South America. It's a wonder you're not a druggie, or booze-soaked."

"You didn't turn out so bad yourself," she said, thinking that despite his shortcomings, there was no man she trusted more with her life and her property. It was only her heart—and a future with him—that remained in jeopardy.

"Careful," he warned. "Too many of these mutual compliments and we might end up liking each other."

"I do like you. I always have."

"Yeah, I guess even I can admit that when it comes to sassy broads you're my favorite."

"Gee, I don't know when I've had such a flattering comment," she said dryly, but not really taking offense.

Deke would never fit into the politically correct, New Age male roles that society, workplaces, and many women demanded.

Andy Ridgeway wore that role with ease. He adapted because his work and social atmosphere demanded it. Savoir faire to the max, and always a gentleman.

Never would Andy have faced down those jerks the way Deke had; Andy would have been insulted, defensive, and proper. And she probably would have been roughed up or worse, she thought grimly. Nor would he have come out of the bathroom naked and backed her to a wall to kiss, fondle, and make remarks that should have outraged her, but only aroused her.

Maybe there was something wrong with her that she would respond in such a primal way to Deke, while at the same time feel much more stable with a man like Andy. Wasn't stability what she'd always wanted? Wasn't balance, mutual wants and needs the glue of a good relationship? Wasn't knowing what to expect, and not being in constant upheaval, the best way to develop that relationship?

The answers were all a resounding yes, and yet there was Deke Laslo. He failed every test for an ideal man in a committed relationship, and what's worse he was the one who made it clear what a bad choice he was.

But. But. But.

Deke was the man she couldn't forget, the man she longed to have love her, the man she loved.

Realization of her true feelings for him weren't a surprise, as much as honest acknowledgment of what she'd always felt, would always feel, no matter how Deke viewed commitment and love.

But she wouldn't tell him. Not yet.

Mariah turned toward the window, watching the scenery whiz past just like her life had since Deke broke off with her—her life passing by without her touching anything of value. Loving Deke had value, but even her honest admittance that she loved him, that she'd wanted to come with him because she might never have another chance, or the guts to tell him, wasn't working very well.

She'd held onto a small hope that he might have changed or mellowed. But to her regret, he was more cynical, more raw, more determined to keep her shut out of his life.

She sighed, chastising herself for placing her expectations too high. Once she'd been burned by him, and had vowed she would never put herself in that position again. And yet here she was, longing for him like some lovesick teenager. Stupid and emotionally painful, she thought, exasperated by her own actions. Andy Ridgeway was so much more reasonable and acceptable and boring.

They rode in silence, with Mariah puzzling over her unsolvable dilemma, when Deke asked, "So what do we do about the sex stuff?"

Instantly, she turned and stared at him. His expression was bland and unreadable; he could have been talking about the darkening sky and thunder in the distance.

Mariah said, "I don't know."

"I expected you to say 'nothing' or 'let's find a motel now.' "

Mariah shifted, wanting to say okay, but instead asked, "Have you changed your mind?"

"No."

"Now you're the one lying. You wouldn't have brought up the subject if you weren't thinking about it."

He chuckled. "Foxy, I'm always thinking about sex with you. It nearly got me killed a few times."

She stared at him, more than stunned that she'd taken up such an enduring place in his thoughts. "You were thinking about sex with me when you should have been focused on your work?"

"Yeah." That was all he said. No explanations, no rough laughter, no cryptic remarks.

Knowing she was leaping to huge conclusions, she pondered only a second and leapt anyway. He had raised the subject, he had told her of his own accord, and some deep piece of herself fastened itself to his words.

Maybe Deke felt more for her than even he realized. Maybe he claimed to think about sex with her all the time because that was simpler and less committed. And most of all, less likely to push against his inner wall of self-protection than anything as immutable as loving her.

Mariah stayed silent as if the moment was too fragile to explore. Raindrops splattered on the windshield. "Tell me about those times you were almost killed. I'm glad I didn't know before, or I would have begged Dad not to let you go back there."

"It was my job to go, and Sabastian's job to send me."

Until her father, Sabastian Thornton, retired earlier this year, he had been in charge of the elite mercenary team funded by the government for secret missions in the South American drug wars. It was through her father, and at a party in Washington, that she'd met Deke.

"Tell me."

He paused as though mentally selecting an event that

wouldn't breach any security. "One time was an encounter with an angry water moccasin."

Mariah winced. "To add another snakebite scar to the one on your thigh."

"That one was from a rattlesnake hunt in Texas when I was a kid. I thought I was a hot shit with my first snake and found out the snake was much smarter. The moccasin was more curious about my neck."

"Your neck?" She shuddered. "My God, Deke."

"Sabastian shot him. Never have met a sharpshooter like your old man. He put a bullet between its eyes. Damn snake was so close to me I could count the scale jags in its dark stripe." Deke turned on the windshield wipers. "Looks like we're gonna get a downpour."

She folded her arms, shivering and shaking her head. "Please, I don't want to hear anymore."

"Snake guts in your face are the pits."

Her stomach heaved with a wave of nausea. "And you're telling me you were thinking about sex with me?"

"Uh, not at that particular moment. But when I was tramping through that swamp, I was, which is why I tripped on that baby."

"It's a good thing Dad was there. What did he say afterward?"

"You don't want to know."

"Yes, I do."

"Trust me, Mariah, you don't."

"Deke. I do."

She reached out to take his arm, and he slowed the vehicle to take an upcoming exit.

"What are we doing?"

"Gotta get gas, plus I'm thirsty and my eyes are turning yellow. Better get it all done now. This rain looks like it's gonna get heavy."

Mariah glanced at the rolling clouds. Dark, restless, and streaking with jagged lightning.

He exited the interstate onto a two-lane highway that looked as if the area was trying to cash in on every traveler who got off for gas or food. There were motels, an amusement park, fast-food joints from the famous to the obscure, service stations with ladders leaning against the price-per-gallon signs to change the numbers and beat their competitors. In the distance was a huge shopping mall.

Deke pulled into one of the service stations. Fifteen minutes later he'd paid for the gas and climbed back into the Expedition. Mariah had used the bathroom and bought two cold soft drinks. She had no sooner closed the door than the rain began in earnest.

Back in the car, she handed a can to Deke, and popped the top on her own. "Let's go over to the mall."

"For what?" He drank, draining half the can.

"To shop for some clothes for the party. I didn't bring anything fancy because you didn't have room in the Corvette. Now we do. And I bet you don't have anything but those jeans."

"I like jeans. Your dad is used to seeing me in them. He isn't going to care."

"But I will. It's his sixtieth birthday, and it would be so nice if you looked like a sexy, handsome man instead of a mercenary who just came out of the jungle."

Deke scowled. "Tell me something, Mariah. Why is it that every conversation I have with you, I end up doing what you want instead of what I want?"

You don't want to make love, and nothing, including me, has changed that. But she kept the thought to herself. Instead, she said, "Well, on one thing you skidded by. You haven't told me what Dad said after he killed the snake."

He started the vehicle and drove to the mall parking lot. In minutes, the rain was blowing and sweeping across the windshield. He found a space, and pulled in before he spoke again. "Unless you want to get drenched, we're going to have to wait out this squall."

"We can wait. Tell me what he said."

"Trust me, you won't like it. It's the kind of thing that sends women into hysterics."

"I want to know," she said stubbornly.

Deke drummed his hands on the wheel. Thunder cracked and rain poured down. Clearly, he didn't want to tell her.

"I won't be shocked. I won't even act shocked if I am."

He turned, settling his back against the driver's door, finished his soda and set the can aside. He brought his right leg up so that it lay nudging the console, then hung his dark glasses on the visor. The longer he remained silent, the more intrigued she became.

Lounging there, watching her, she was pinned by the midnight blue of his eyes. His mouth was set, his arms relaxed, his chest moving with each breath. Mariah was so tense that when a bolt of thunder cracked, she jumped. Deke never moved.

"Bring your foot up here in my lap," he murmured, his voice slipping over her like warm syrup.

She moved so that her shoulders were braced by the passenger door, and did as he asked. She wore sandals and a skirt and no hose. Deke cupped her ankle, his thumbs moving over the bones so that she felt his touch all the way to the tips of her ears. The rain poured, their breathing fogging the windows and creating a humid cocoon. Deke didn't speak, and her own mouth was so dry, she kept sipping from her soda even though she didn't really want it.

He removed her sandal, smoothed his hand from her toes down the sole, and caught her heel. She jerked.

"Ticklish?"

"What are you doing?"

"This." He then placed the bottom of her foot against the zipper of his jeans. He felt hard and warm and pulsing with life. Mariah swallowed when he slid his hand up her calf.

Massaging his fingers around her leg, he said simply, "It's raw guy stuff, and it makes me look like an idiot."

Mariah's head buzzed. "What?"

He grinned. "For someone who wanted to know so bad, it sure didn't take much to make you forget."

"You're distracting me," she grumbled.

He leaned forward, pushing her skirt so that her thighs were exposed. Then he kissed her knee, lingering a moment, then kissing again, his tongue touching. Mariah caught her breath, aroused and tantalized.

"If I wanted to distract you, I'd make you wet."

She licked her lips. "Too late," she whispered. "I already am. Now tell me what he said."

Deke stared at her, again bringing his hand down to her ankle and holding her foot in place against him. Then he looked away, watching the water pour down the windshield. "He told me if I was going to refuse to hump any of the handpicked and paid-for women he'd provided for the guys, then I'd better do some private hand jobs to get rid of the stress before I got killed."

Mariah was stunned. But not by the rawness, or the use of women for sex, or even that her father—prim as an old maid when it came to his own daughter—showed his cruder side. She was stunned that Deke had refused to indulge in the easy sex.

"But why did you refuse? My God, Deke. You could have any woman you wanted. I've been pea-green with jealousy at the way they look at you."

He shrugged, his knuckles brushing back and forth along her arch. "Never noticed any of them. I was always too busy wanting you. Like right now. I swore when I heard you were coming with me, nothing would happen. We were finished. You had your life with Randy—"

"Andy."

"—And I had mine with . . . the decision I made."

"To break off with me."

"Yes."

This time, she made herself not ask why. "But you do want me." She didn't have to say the words, she could feel him. "How long has it been since you . . . ?" She let the question trail off, ducking her head, astonished she would even ask him about other women. Quickly, she added, "I'm sorry. That was inappropriate."

Deke tipped his head back and laughed. "From the lady who just told me she was wet? Come on, foxy, there's no such word as inappropriate between you and me. Anyway, you wouldn't believe me."

"Is it so many?"

"Two."

Mariah stared, mouth slightly open. "Two as in twice? You've only had sex twice? You broke off with me a year ago."

"Eleven months and ten days."

Mariah's heart swelled. "Oh, Deke."

"Hey, your old man was right. Hand-jobs do ease the stress." He took a deep breath. "Despite the prevailing wisdom that men want sex more than food or sleep, I'm here to tell you sex can be boring as hell with the wrong woman. Then again, you weren't around. You spoiled me, foxy. You spoiled me bad."

She'd spoiled him? My God. She embraced his admission as if it were sealed in gold. He hadn't expressed it in so many words, but this small step convinced her that Deke felt more for her than just sex and desire. It had to be more, or he would have happily gone to the women her father had provided. And after their breakup, he would have found someone new, or many someones.

But he hadn't; he'd been almost celibate. And he'd been that way by choice; he'd never wanted anyone else. The profoundness of that left her speechless.

"Rain's stopped. If we're going inside, we better make a run for it." He put her sandal on and lowered her leg. She touched his hair, her fingers tunneling into the thick strands.

She took a breath. Heart overflowing and fear clutching her as well, she rallied her determination despite the risk. "I want us to make love," she whispered.

"I know." His tone indicated all his earlier resistance was melting away.

"Please don't say no."

"Let's do the shopping first." He opened his door, got out and came around and opened hers. "I need to give *you* time to change your mind."

SIX

The mall was three-tiered, diamond-shaped, boasting over three hundred stores, a roller-blade rink that became an ice rink in winter, and a central fountain that reached clear to an intricate glass dome.

Deke looked around, and wondered how anyone knew where to start. And if he and Mariah got separated, he'd never find her.

He took her hand.

She glanced at him and grinned. "You look like you're about to attend your own execution."

"Let's just get it done. I hate shopping."

"I offered an alternative," she said with a sideways glance to catch his reaction.

He dropped an arm over her shoulder, and brought her against him, lowering his head and whispering, "I offered anticipation. Unless, of course, you change your mind."

She groaned. "You know I won't. And you're making my knees wobbly."

He nipped her ear. "Good." He released her, saying, "Lead the way, foxy."

And for the next hour they wandered into one store after another, but didn't find exactly what Mariah wanted. To Deke, one pair of pants looked the same as the next, but the fashion consultant side of Mariah was in full gear. Outside of what seemed like the zillionth window display, she pointed across the mall to thirty more stores. Deke groaned. They all looked crowded and cluttered.

"There's a casual men's store. Come on."

"On one condition, when we come out, we've bought the stuff."

"Agreed."

For the next hour he tried on clothes, finally emerging with lightweight slacks and a jacket. The shirt was cotton knit with an open collar. By the time they were back in the mall proper, he'd vowed that he wouldn't go into another men's store in this lifetime.

"You're going to look so handsome."

"Can we leave now?"

"I have to get a dress." She squinted, then took his arm, drawing closer to a store window with sexily clad mannequins. It was called Delilah's.

"I don't believe it," Mariah said, as if she'd found her dream store.

"Neither do I. Victoria's sister opened her own place," Deke muttered, his imagination racing in a hundred erotic directions.

"Delilah's is different."

"Yeah, I just bet it is. Good thing I'm allergic to haircuts," he said sagely, shifting the box from one arm to the other.

"Never mind. Didn't you see it?"

"See what?"

"The red dress."

"What the hell are you talking about?"

She gave him an exasperated look. "Don't you remember that time we had dinner in Miami, and that woman came out of the bar wearing a red dress, and you said it was the kind of dress that men fantasize about?"

"No."

She gave him an amused look. "You do so remember. It had all those buttons."

"A nightmare, not a fantasy," he muttered.

She turned and gave him a curious look. "Okay, what is your idea of a fantasy dress?"

"One I don't have to work to get you out of."

"Okay. Then all the more reason why you need to help me pick it out."

"Hold it." He halted her forward motion and turned her around. "I'm gonna help you pick it out, then you're gonna put it on, and I'm gonna see how easy it is to get it off?"

"Yes."

"I'm not staying at your father's party long enough to test it out."

"Who said anything about the party?"

He raised an eyebrow. "I don't need inspiration, foxy. You're it. All I need is some place where we won't get arrested."

"Delilah's is very indulgent about men coming into the dressing rooms. In fact they encourage it, and provide lots of private rooms with comfy chairs for you to, uh, wait. It beats leaving you out here in the mall where you might get picked up by some woman who wants her way with you."

Deke started to balk, but she took his arm, tugging him inside. The air undulated with some exotic scent, the lights placed at strategic points so as not to interrupt the intimacy of the boudoir displays.

Deke muttered, "Christ, this place looks like a high-priced whorehouse."

"Shhh." She pulled him along while he gaped at the erotic trappings, and wondered if he'd get out of here without embarrassing himself.

Mariah sorted through a rack of dresses, and removed

the red one. She spoke to the salesperson, got a key, and tugged Deke along with her. Thick carpet muted their steps as she turned into a circular area with about a dozen gold-embossed doors. Each had a number and a lock.

Inside number six, the alabaster and orchid rose walls were backlit with soft low lights. The air wafted that same intoxicating perfume. A satin tufted couch and a matching chair were arranged opposite an oval free-standing mirror.

Deke stood in the center of the room feeling trapped, turned-on, and hot.

"All you have to do is sit over there and watch." And before he could respond, she disappeared behind a folding black-and-gold screen.

Deke sat down in the tufted chair, stretched his legs out, tented his fingers and hooded his eyes. Her skirt and her top were flipped over the top of the screen.

"Oh, damn," he heard her say.

"What?"

"I should have brought in some high heels."

He took a breath, his libido instantly disappointed. She looked sexy as hell in spikes.

"Ready?" she called.

He grinned. He was ready all right. "Let's see it, babe."

But when she emerged from behind the screen, any earlier sexy thoughts became primers for the scene before him.

She stood with her head tipped so that her hair fell forward, her eyes sultry, her body like poured cream in the red silk. Buttons marched from hem to a deep neckline that showed the tops of her breasts. Straps just dipped off her shoulders, and when she placed one hand on her hip and lifted one leg, the dress fell open, exposing the knee he'd kissed in the car. She moved again and her thigh came into view. She reached down to open more buttons, and Deke quit breathing.

"Sweet Christ."

He stared and she stared back. Then she started toward him. Deke closed his eyes. If she touched him, it would be all over.

Deke got to his feet, although he wasn't confident his own legs would hold him. He held up his hand to halt her.

Mariah licked her lips, and took a step closer. Her scent enveloped him. Heat poured into his groin, bringing him pain like he'd never known.

"No closer. Buy the dress. It works." He took another desperate breath. "I'll wait out by the entrance."

"Deke, the door's locked. No one will come in."

But he backed away when she reached to touch him. He fiddled with the lock, lifted the handle, and glanced back.

"Hurry the hell up."

She grinned. "Yes, sir."

He stalked out, closing the door firmly, and leaned against the wall, hauling oxygen into his lungs. He reached down to ease the tight throb, but it had expanded to his thighs, and worse, had taken up blazing residence in his brain. This was crazy. It was raw, primal sex.

Yeah, but this was Mariah. This was more. This would likely kill him.

SEVEN

Seventeen minutes passed between exiting Delilah's, driving to the first motel Deke came to, then paying for the room, and getting the key into the lock.

Mariah clung to him, unable to stand still. Her clothes weighed her down, her mouth ached for his, and her body hummed with the need to mate.

Deke's face was fierce, not with anger or frustration, but with a raw, pulsing desire that had no name.

He opened the door to a room that smelled musty and was artificially chilly from a cranked-up air conditioner. A double bed, covered with a gray-and-purple bedspread, sat between two end tables, with lamps screwed to walls the color of bean sprouts.

Deke kicked the door closed, backed up against it and hauled her tight to him. His hands plowed into her hair, his mouth crushing hers, his tongue sweeping deep. Mariah was no less eager; she fitted her mouth to his, basking, absorbing, straining, and whimpering for more. Desperate to get rid of their cumbersome clothes, her fingers fumbled with the snap on his jeans.

He drew back, brushing her hand aside, breath hissing between his teeth. "Don't, don't . . . I'll come."

"I want to touch you. Please, please . . ." she murmured before once again devouring his mouth. He hiked her skirt high, tore the panties from her, and cupped her.

A ring of tiny bubbles popped inside of her, a prelude to the power coming. "Oh God . . . Deke . . . the bed."

"Can't . . . No time . . . Here, now, I want you."

He took one shuddering breath, then slid his fingers inside of her. She gasped.

Deke swayed, straining, his memory of the smudge of wet curls acute and hot. "Jesus, you're burning for me . . ."

She hugged herself to him, felt it begin a long way off, rising and swelling and then hurtling toward her in a rush of energy. She arched away, trying to contain the force of it, desperate to slow it down, to control it.

She panted, sweat breaking out across her neck. Despite his earlier objection, she got his jeans opened, but struggled with a stubborn zipper until he pushed her hands away and released his sex.

"You have to h-hurry, Deke, hurry . . ." White and black dizzying pinpoints danced in front of her eyes. She squeezed them closed, nearly terrified of the power that pounded and roared closer now, mere moments from completion.

"Hang on, baby . . ."

He bent his knees slightly, then cupped her bottom, lifting her, turning to give her legs room to wrap around him. She came up and then sank down on him.

Deke devoured her mouth, his hands steadying her while she moved, her breathy pants matched by his husky groans.

He felt swallowed and possessed and scorched.

She welcomed his sweet, hot invasion. He sealed within her the wonder of hope and happiness and all their tomorrows. For so long, she'd wanted and waited and yearned for him. She wanted to wrap him in her body, and show him that she'd already wrapped him in her heart.

"I love you," she whispered, barely aware of the coveted words spilling from her mouth into his, her own raging passion screaming at a perilous pitch.

Deke stilled, drawing back, trying to cool the beats of craving, trying to tilt toward a level of sanity. His mind scrambled, flailed, but her words had already buried themselves deeply and permanently.

Then his own rush began, no longer trapped, no longer ignored, no longer eating at his gut. His release burst forth in a clamoring, tearing spree of raw heat that erupted into a dazzling blaze. "Christ, sweet Christ . . ."

"I can't," she whispered desperately. "It's too much, it's been too long . . ." But even as she spoke, her aroused body began to move.

"Come on, baby, ride me." He held her, feeling her lift and lift and lift, her climax rolling closer with each plunge downward. Her breathing came in a ragged pant, her body squeezing his with the power of life itself. He kissed her to take the sound, milking her mouth, easing her down, holding her until she was quiet, until her body softened against him.

She clung, her mouth buried in his neck; he anchored her, his body whipped and exhausted, his mind empty, his heart reclaimed, renewed and full with wonder. Neither spoke but for a few reedy gasps, both sagged under the weight of their own spent frenzy.

Moments later, Deke tumbled her onto the bed, and then collapsed beside her. His body felt used, abused, and more satisfied than he thought possible. Flat on his belly, he reached out and wrapped an arm around her waist.

Mariah twisted. She was naked under her wrinkled skirt, her knit top still on, but stretched beyond repair.

Deke had dispensed with his jeans, but his shirt had been torn open, his back sporting red streaks.

"Did I do that?" she asked touching the marks with her mouth.

"Everything you did was sensational," he mumbled, his face buried in the pillow he'd pulled to him.

She kissed the center of his back. "That's what I love about you, Deke. A little good sex and you're putty in my hands."

"A little! God help me if you gave me a lot."

"So when are we going to do it again?" she asked, amusement bridging her words.

"In about a year."

"A year!"

"Too long, huh?"

"You're teasing me." She gave him a playful slap on the butt, then leaned down and kissed the spot.

Deke groaned. "Careful, foxy, or you'll be getting me sooner than you thought."

"I want you forever," she murmured, feeling complete and satisfied, and totally in love. She barely noted the slight stiffening in his body. She curled next to him, inhaling the smell of their lovemaking, savoring the taste of his warm skin, drowsy under the rhythm of his breathing.

"Deke?"

"Hmmm."

"Why did you break us up?"

He lay still, then slowly rolled away. She grabbed his arm to make him stay and answer. If he wouldn't answer her now, when they were at their happiest, she had no hope of ever finding out why.

He swore. "You sure know how to get us back to reality, don't you?"

"I need to know. I don't believe you could be nearly celibate for a year, then make love with me so thoroughly if you didn't care for me."

"I like you, I care for you. Can't you just leave it there?"

She needed to stop, to shut up, to kiss him and make him forget she'd ever asked. She knew that was smart, that was what he wanted, that would save her pride. She knew it all and yet . . .

"No, I can't leave it there. What just happened was too powerful for just liking and caring. You feel more; you have to. Is that why you broke off with me? Is that why you were so angry about taking me with you? Is that why you're being so cold now?"

He sat stone still, his back to her. She'd run out of questions, and he'd answered none of them. Silence, but for their breathing, beat between them.

Finally he asked, "Is the quiz finished?"

His distance and calm reaction infuriated her. "How can you be so closed down? So cold and cruel?"

Again he didn't answer, again the unending silence.

"Damn you, Deke Laslo. Damn you to hell." She shuddered, folding her arms about her, dragging in the tangled rags of her own humiliation.

He carefully removed her hand from where she was gripping his arm. He rose, and turned on one of the lamps. They both blinked and squinted at the explosion of light. He found his jeans, pulled them on, not bothering with underwear. He dragged his hands through his hair, taking a deep breath and expelling it.

Mariah watched him, hearing the sound of her own heart permanently breaking. He opened the door.

"Where are you going?"

"To get our stuff. As long as we're here, and I paid for the room, we might as well get my money's worth. We can shower and get cleaned up." He glanced at his watch. "I want to be back on the road within the next hour. Already this trip has taken longer than I wanted."

With her mouth agape, she stared at him, his words slicing through her like tiny knives. *Get his money's worth? Trip took longer than he'd wanted? My God.* If the place between her legs hadn't still been tingling, if the smell of him wasn't still on her hands, she would have believed she'd fantasized it all.

How could she have been so gullible, so blind to the truth, so misdirected in her own assessment of his feelings? Her heartbreak turned to anger, and by the time he returned with their things, she was seething.

He glanced at her. "You want to go first?"

"I want you to go to hell."

He shrugged, opened his duffel, and took out toiletries and clean clothes before going into the bathroom and closing the door.

Mariah sat, tears glistening, anger seeping away and leaving emptiness. He'd done it to her again. Burned her again, and this time it didn't just hurt, it scalded. Maybe because she'd honestly believed she'd had another chance with him. Before, she'd simply been shocked and hurt. This time, she'd not only asked for his rejection by her insane idea of coming with him, but had made herself even more vulnerable when she falsely assumed she could convince him he loved her.

Fool. She was a damn, stupid fool, and she had no intention of allowing him to humiliate her any further.

She got up, dressed, gathered her things, slung her purse over her shoulder, and then spotted her torn panties. She tossed them on the bed and walked out.

EIGHT

Deke, showered and dressed and finding her gone, flung his duffel across the room. Furious, he stalked over to the motel's office.

"Did a woman come in here? About thirty, pretty, blond hair, wearing a skirt, top, and sandals."

The gray-haired man, chunky and unshaven with a Marine buzz cut peered at Deke. "Lot of women come in here."

"Couldn't have been more than fifteen minutes ago."

"Maybe. Maybe not." He glanced down at the girlie magazine he was reading.

Deke narrowed his eyes. "How much?"

"Twenty should do it."

"If I'm gonna pay you for information, pal, it better be worth my while. I want to know if she was here, if she made a phone call and to who." Deke envisioned her calling Randy or Andy or whatever the hell his name was, then asking the silk-suited jerk to come and rescue her from Deke's dirty clutches. Except he wasn't clutching or holding or spouting promises he had no ability or courage to keep.

"For thirty, I'll tell you that and where she went," the man offered.

Deke dug the bills from his pocket, and dropped them on the counter.

He snatched them up. "She was here and looked ticked off. She called a cab to take her to the airport."

"The airport! She hates to fly." But something more about Mariah brought him up short. She was so desperate to get away from him that she would do anything, including boarding an airplane.

For reasons that weren't at all logical, since he'd never promised more than he gave her, he was swamped with shame and remorse. In his world those subjective emotions could get a man killed. He'd never allowed himself to embrace them, or any of their cousins like love and commitment. And yet here, with his anger still pumping, he realized that Mariah's ease in handling those same emotions was the reason he'd never forgotten her. She was the reason he had zero interest in recreational sex, and she was the reason he had been more excited about taking her north than anything else he'd done in the past year.

Those final moments of lovemaking had been wondrous, and instead of taking a clue from his own pleasure and building on it, he'd blown her off.

The man looked at the wall clock. "She left about five minutes ago."

"How far is the airport?"

"Forty miles north."

Six minutes later, Deke had dumped his stuff into the Expedition. He tore out of the parking lot, eating up the forty miles to the airport in thirty-five minutes. But despite identifying the Providence flight that she'd boarded, by the time he got to the gate, the 737 was taxiing out to the runway.

Deke leaned his forehead against the glass wall and closed his eyes. "Shit."

*　　*　　*

Her father's house in Newport looked out over the harbor. Even though summer had barely begun, sailboats and yachts dotted the June waters of Narragansett Bay.

The silvery wood-shingled cottage, with a porch and crushed quahog shells in place of the lawn, was compact and pricey. Inside the breezy interior, baskets and vases had been filled with flowers, a buffet table had been set up, and on the porch, the bar was doing a brisk business. Music played, and a few couples were dancing.

For the past hour, friends and relatives greeted Sabastian, bringing best wishes and expressing delight that Mariah had been able to come.

She'd managed a smile, many hugs, and more than a few handshakes, while fielding questions about her business and garnering compliments on the red dress.

Her father, tall and lean with silver-streaked hair, looked more handsome at sixty than she ever remembered. He put his arm around her shoulders and drew her aside.

"You know, honey, I thought you were coming with Deke."

"My plans changed," she said demurely. By her up-swept hair, her flushed cheeks, and the red dress, no one would have guessed that she'd flown into Green Airport, gripping the armrests. She'd deplaned wobbly and exhausted, taking a shuttle for the thirty-minute ride to Newport. Then she'd checked into a room at the Harborside Inn in the downtown area. Her father's house was too small, and she wanted the freedom to shut herself in her room without having to explain her moroseness.

"Hmmm," he said, studying her far too closely. "Those plans sure must have changed for you to fly. But never mind, you're here, and I want you to stay for a visit after the party. I don't see enough of you." He turned her so that he could see her face in the late afternoon light. "Mariah?"

She tried to smile, to look bright and chipper, and she hated Deke all over again for clinging to her thoughts, and stubbornly staying in her heart with such tenacity.

"You've been crying."

"Just some summer pollen."

But her father wasn't buying. "Are those tears connected to Deke?"

She opened her mouth to deny it, then lowered her lashes, taking a shuddering breath. "I don't want to spoil your party."

Sabastian tipped up her chin. "Your happiness and comfort are more important. Tell me what happened."

She promised herself she wouldn't do this. On the flight north, she realized and accepted that whatever misery she felt because of Deke was of her own doing. She didn't want to hash and rehash the obvious—he didn't love her, would never love her. Cold facts.

She was too aware that if she allowed herself the luxury of dwelling on her anger and pain and disappointment, she would fall victim to obsessive and ongoing heartbreak. That happened before, because she took so long to face the truth. This time she intended to face it head on.

"He rejected me," she said bluntly. "And I walked into it like a stupid fool."

Her father nodded. "Ah, stupid like the day Deke stepped on a snake."

She glanced up. "He told me that story."

"Did he now? Did he tell you it happened after he broke off with you? That he'd been drunk for four days, and I had him in the swamp to get him sober, and clear-eyed enough to handle a crucial assignment that would take nearly a year to complete?"

She blinked. "No, he didn't tell me all that."

"Nor, I imagine, did he tell you that he quit the group for a bigger reason than retirement in New Hampshire. He quit because that crucial assignment, the one he'd worked a year to get in place, blew up in his face. The guy he thought was on our side was a rat who killed a lot of innocent people that Deke believed the bastard was protecting."

She shook her head, stunned by this new information.

"And did he tell you he blamed himself for those deaths? It was a situation he couldn't have prevented unless he could have seen the future, but despite commendation from his superiors, because many other lives were saved, Deke wanted out."

She shivered. "So that's why he looked so raw and pained."

"But here's his real problem," her father continued. "It's been his problem for too damn long. Deke has been trying to rid himself of feelings for you. He has the problem, honey, not you. You are neither a fool or stupid, you simply fell in love with a man who is terrified that if he loves you back, he'll lose you."

Mariah stared at him. "Lose me?"

He turned her a bit, and pointed to the porch. "Ask him, and he gives you any garbage about not knowing what you're talking about, you bring him over to me."

Mariah stared. Deke, indeed, was there. He looked tired and irritable, but he was dressed in the slacks and jacket they'd purchased in Virginia. Mariah took a step toward him, hesitating, still unsure. Then he moved forward, shaking some hands, nodding to a few, and finally came to a stop in front of her.

For a few seconds, they simply stared at one another.

"You look like a fantasy in your red dress, foxy."

"You look entirely too handsome for your own good."

"Come and dance with me?"

She hesitated. "You hate dancing."

"I don't know," he said with a shrug. "I think I've

done some pretty fast and tricky steps, especially when it comes to screwing things up with you.''

He slipped his arm around her, and she folded into him.

He drew her closer, his mouth nuzzling her hair. ''What do I have to do to get another chance with you?''

Her eyes filled at the vulnerability in his voice. ''You need to tell me the truth. Are you afraid to love me for fear of losing me?''

He paused, and then murmured. ''Sebastian has been busy.''

She pulled back, and narrowed her eyes. ''I don't want you blaming Dad. Because of what he told me, I'm dancing with you. Otherwise, I would have—''

''I know. Told me to go to hell.''

''I already did that.''

''And I've been there. More times, in the past year, than I want to think about.''

She had been, too. ''Tell me why you're afraid of losing me.''

He remained silent, while Mariah held her breath. Finally, he murmured, ''I knew, after our last time together, that I was in love with you. It wasn't a revelation as much as a realization that I didn't want to leave you. And that had never happened before. But thinking about myself in a marriage—no way. I knew that was what you deserved from the man who loved you. I couldn't visualize it ever working with me. I was afraid that one day you'd wake up, take one look at me, and decide you'd made a mistake.''

''Oh, Deke,'' she murmured.

''Pushing you away, walking out, and ending things between us was self-preservation. It was a way of saying I'd never let you hurt me, never let you leave me, if I did those things first.''

Mariah swallowed, his words filling her heart to overflowing. "Didn't you believe me when I told you I loved you?"

"Sexual chemistry has people saying all kinds of things. And most of the time when you said it, it was during or after we made love."

She touched his mouth, her fingers lingering. "Maybe because it felt the safest to say it then. You were more pliable and warm."

"Until yesterday."

"Yes."

They were silent, staying close, moving with the music.

Finally, Deke said, "I want another chance." He ventured the words out, testing them on his tongue. Mariah smiled inwardly, but didn't offer any prompts. It was important for him to get it all said. He continued, "I want a chance to make you believe I love you. Coming out of that bathroom, and finding you gone, with nothing left behind but torn panties . . . God."

"I'm sorry. I was just so furious with you. I, well, I wanted to leave something to show you how hurt I was."

"It worked. I felt like a bastard. Then racing to the airport to stop you from doing what you feared terrified me worse than any jungle encounter of the past fifteen years. It's a wonder I got here in one piece."

She looked up at him, taking in the hard lines, the midnight-blue eyes, the new vulnerability that made her want to weep with joy. She made her own confession. "I'm still afraid, but I love you too much not to try again."

"You're afraid?" He drew in a deep breath, and then expelled it. "Christ, I'm terrified."

At his poignant admission, her once-burned heart healed completely. She hugged him even harder, whispering, "Guess we can test our fear-conquering abilities together."

"Only if you promise to marry me."

"Marry you?" She was truly stunned. "Are you serious? I'm still amazed that you love me."

"Hell, I figure if I'm going into this relationship, then I ought to be willing to give more than great sex."

"Just so that's included."

He dipped his head and kissed her. "Count on it."

As they danced through the evening, and later excused themselves to explore their newly discovered love in Deke's hotel room, Mariah knew these changes and promises were real and forever. Because he'd said them, yes, but making those words magic and enduring for her, was Deke's admission that he was terrified. Not of snakes and death, but of loving and losing her.

"You know," she said as she straddled his hips, "you're stuck with me forever."

"Not long enough," he murmured, while exploring her breasts with his hands.

She leaned down and kissed him, lingering. "Do you remember what you said to me when you came into my condo in Florida?"

"Yeah, taking you north was a helluva bad idea."

"Care to make any changes?"

"Yeah, it was one helluva *great* idea."

And with her in agreement, those were the last words either spoke for a very long time.

MELTING ICE

Stephanie Laurens

·One

"If you believe the family will continue to countenance such profligate hedonism now that you've stepped into your poor brother's shoes, you are fair and far out, sir! *You—will—marry!* Soon. And well!"

With his great-aunt Augusta's words ringing in his ears, to the tune of emphatic raps from her cane, Dyan St. Laurent Dare, most reluctant fourth Duke of Darke, sent his gray hunter pounding along the woodland track. Outlier of the New Forest, the wood was thick enough to hide him. The pace he set was reckless, a measure of his mood; the demon within him wanted out.

The gray's hooves thundered on the beaten track; Dyan tried to lose himself in the driving rhythm. After an entire afternoon listening to his relatives' complaints, he felt wild, his underlying restlessness setting a dangerous edge to his temper.

Damn Robert! Why did he have to die? Of a mere inflammation of the lungs, of all things. Dyan suppressed a disgusted snort, feeling slightly guilty. He'd been truly fond of his older brother; although only two years had separated them, Robert had seemed like forty from the time he was twenty. Robert's staid, conservative personality had shielded his own more robust and vigorous—not to say profligate—

character from their exceedingly straitlaced family.

Now Robert was dead—and he was in the firing line.

Which was why he was fleeing Darke Abbey, his ancestral home, leaving his long-suffering relatives behind. He had to get out—get some air—before he committed a felony. Like strangling his great-aunt.

Tolerance was not one of his virtues; he'd always been described as impatient and hot-at-hand. Even more critical, he had never, ever tolerated interference in his life, a point he was going to have to find some polite way to make plain to his aunts, uncles—and his great-aunt Augusta. Naturally, they still saw him as his younger self. They had descended on the Abbey, intent on impressing on him the error of his rakehell ways. They all believed marriage would be his salvation; presumably they thought securing the succession would be a goal in keeping with his talents. They had made it plain they thought marriage to some sweet, biddable gentlewoman would cure him of his recklessness.

They didn't know him. Few did.

Jaw setting, Dyan swung the gray into a long glade and loosened the reins; the heavy horse plunged down the long slope.

He'd only just arrived back at the Abbey—for the past ten years, India had been his home. A decade ago he'd left London, intent on carving out a new life—that, or dying in the attempt; even now, he wasn't sure which of those two goals had, at the time, been his primary aim. His family had been relieved to see him go; the subcontinent was reassuringly distant, half the globe a comforting buffer against his scandalous propensities. Under India's unrelenting sun, his recklessness had found ample scope for danger, intrigue, and more danger. He'd survived, and succeeded; he was now a wealthy man.

On being informed of Robert's death and his ascension to the title, his initial reaction had been to decline to be found. Instead, a nagging, deeply buried sense of responsibility had goaded him into liquidating his assests, realizing his investments—and disengaging from the clinging embrace of the Rani of Barrashnapur.

By the time he'd reached London, Robert had been dead for well nigh a year; there'd seemed no need to rush into the country. He'd dallied in town, expecting to slide into the indolent life he'd enjoyed a decade before. Instead, he'd discovered himself a misfit. The predictable round of balls, select parties, and the pursuits of *ton*nish gentlemen engendered nothing more than acute boredom, something he was constitutionally incapable of tolerating.

Worse, the perfumed bodies of discreetly willing ladies, as ever at his beck and call, completely failed to stir his jaded senses. For one who, for the past ten years, had had his every sexual whim instantly and expertly gratified, abstinence for any measurable time was the definition of pure torture.

And self-imposed abstinence was the definition of hell.

Reluctantly, knowing his family was lying in wait for him, he'd returned to the Abbey, his childhood home. Only to be met by the family's demands that he marry and ensure the succession without delay.

It was enough to send him straight back to India.

And the Rani of Barrashnapur.

Memories of golden limbs, all silk and satin, wrapped around his senses; gritting his teeth, Dyan shook them aside. The end of the glade was rapidly approaching, the gray all but flying over the thick grass; Dyan hauled on the reins. Slowing the huge hunter to a canter, he turned into the bridle path that led from the glade.

He was searching, still searching, as he had been for years. Searching for something—an elusive entity—that would fill the void in his soul and anchor his restless passions. His failure to discover that entity, to fulfill his inner need, left him not just restless, but with his wildness—that demon that had always been a part of him—champing at the bit.

His predator's instinct was to focus on his target—then seize it. To be unable to define what his target was left him directionless. Like a rudderless ship in a storm.

Drawing rein in the clearing that marked the next bend, he sat still, breathing deeply, letting the gray do the same.

Through the trees, lights twinkled. Shifting to get a better view, Dyan saw that the entire ground floor of Brooke Hall was ablaze. His childhood friend Henry, now Lord Brooke, and his wife, Harriet, were obviously entertaining. From the extent of the lights, a house party was in progress.

Hands relaxed on the pommel, Dyan stared across the fields. Wisps of conversations caught during his stay in London wafted through his brain. Allusions to the Brookes, and the house parties they gave. A vision of his relatives' faces, particularly his great-aunt Augusta's, if he failed to show for dinner—failed, indeed, to return at all that night—rose in his mind. His long lips lifted, then curved.

He hadn't seen Henry and Harriet in ten years; it was time to renew old friendships. Twitching the reins, Dyan swung his hunter toward Brooke Hall.

"I realize it's inconvenient, but I would like to speak to Lady Brooke, please, Sherwood." Her bag at her feet, Lady Fiona Winton-Ryder tugged off her gloves, and ignored Sherwood's scandalized expression.

"Ah . . . indeed, Lady Fiona." His calling coming to the fore, Sherwood relocated his butlerishly impassive mask and turned.

The drawing room door opened; Henry, Lord Brooke, looked out. "What is it, Sher—" Henry broke off, his gaze sweeping Fiona, taking in her travelling bag and her pelisse. He stepped into the hall, firmly closing the drawing room door. "Fiona!" Plastering a smile over his transparent surprise, he advanced. "Is there some problem at Coldstream House?"

"Indeed." Lips firming, Fiona lifted her head. "Edmund and I have had a falling out—the most *acrimonious* disagreement! I have *sworn* I will not stay at Coldstream another hour—not until he apologizes. So I've come to beg houseroom until he does."

Henry's jaw slackened.

Fiona swept on: "I realize the timing's inconvenient." A regal wave referred to the drawing room and the sounds of the gathering therein—in reality, she had planned her arrival to the minute, for just before dinner, so Henry, with guests waiting, would be hard pressed to argue. "But I know you've plenty of room." She smiled confidently; Henry couldn't contradict her—she'd known this house from her earliest years—she knew very well how many beds it held. More than enough.

"Ah, yes." Henry lifted a finger, easing the folds of his cravat.

Squirming—as well he might; Fiona fought not to narrow her eyes. If she had her way, Henry would squirm even more before the evening ended. The doorbell pealed; assuming it was a late-arriving guest, Fiona did not turn as Sherwood bowed and moved past to the door. Her gaze firmly fixed on Henry's face, she waited, brows raised in polite question.

"I suppose—" Henry began, then he blinked and stared past her.

"Good evening, Sherwood."

The deep, rumbling voice sent Fiona's eyes flying wide.

"Good evening, my lord—er, Your Grace."

Fiona's heart stopped, stuttered, then started to race. She stiffened; shock skittered down her nerves and locked her lungs. She spared one instant in pity for old Sherwood, stumbling in his surprise. She'd known Dyan would eventually return to take up his brother's mantle—but *why* did he have to turn up *now*?

She resisted the urge to whip about; slowly, regally, with all the cool haughtiness at her command, she turned, her composure that expected of an earl's daughter—only to discover Dyan almost upon her.

His eyes met hers instantly, the dark, midnight-blue gaze more piercing than she recalled. Her heart in her throat, she lifted her chin—a necessity if she was to continue to meet his eyes.

She'd forgotten how tall he was, how intimidating his nonchalant grace. Large, lean, and distinctly menacing, he prowled—there was no other word to describe the languid arrogance of his stride—to her side. His name rhymed with lion; she'd always thought of him as a dark jungle cat, black king of the predators. Dark brown hair, black except in bright sunlight, one thick lock falling rakishly over his forehead, contributed to the image, as did the hard, austere, planes of his face, set in an arrogantly autocratic cast.

The years in India had changed him. She was struck by that fact as he drew closer and her gaze took in the alterations, some obvious, others less so. Gone was all vestige of youth, of innocence, of any lingering softness; his features, now heavily tanned, had been stripped to harsh angularity, leaving them more dramatically forceful, more compelling than she recalled. His gaze, always sharp, was more penetrating, his intelligence more obvious in his eyes. His expression was world-weary, more deeply cynical; his movements were slower, more languid, more assured.

Gone was the youth, the young man she had known. In his place was a black leopard, mature, experienced in the hunt, in the full flush of his masculine strength. India had honed his dangerous edge to lethal sharpness.

He was dressed with negligent grace in buckskin

breeches and a dark blue coat, his Hessians gleaming black, his linen faultless white. His expression was studiously impassive.

He halted by her shoulder; his presence engulfed her. Her gaze locked with his, Fiona discovered it took real effort to breathe. "Good evening, Dyan." She raised her brows haughtily. "Or should I say, Your Grace?"

A frown flashed in his eyes. "Dyan will do." His accents when irritated were as clipped as she recalled. For one instant longer, he stood looking down at her, at her face, then he switched his gaze to Henry. And smiled, effortlessly charming. "Evening, Brooke."

The devil-may-care grace worked its magic, as it always had. Henry relaxed. "Dyan." Smiling, he held out his hand. "We hadn't heard when you'd be back. What brings you this way?"

"My relatives." Dyan grasped Henry's hand. "Or," he drawled, as he released Henry and turned to gaze, rather speculatively, at Fiona, "should I say my great-aunt Augusta?"

Henry frowned. "Your aunt?"

"Great-aunt," Dyan corrected him, his gaze still on Fiona's face. "Believe me, there's a difference."

"Don't have any, myself, but I'll take your word for it." Henry tried unsuccessfully to catch Dyan's eye. "But what's this great-aunt done?"

"Driven me from my home." Deserting Fiona's stubbornly uninformative countenance, Dyan looked back at Henry. "And my bed. I wondered if I might prevail on you to put me up for the night?"

"Certainly," Henry gushed—then glanced at Fiona.

Who smiled winningly. "Perhaps," she suggested, "if you summon Harriet—"

Harriet didn't need to be summoned—she slipped out of the drawing room at that moment, carefully closing the door before turning to see who was keeping her husband from his guests. When she saw who it was, she paled—then flushed—then paled again.

Dyan viewed the reaction with acute suspicion. It wasn't, he knew, due to him. Finding Fiona Winton-Ryder here, a bag at her feet, had shaken even him—more deeply than he could credit. Despite not having done so for fifteen years, despite his firm conviction Fiona was no longer any business of his, his immediate, almost overpowering impulse was to grab her by her honey-gold hair, haul her out of the house, give her a thorough shake, then throw her up to his horse's back and cart her straight home to Coldstream House.

Given what he'd heard of the Brookes' house parties, and having a more than academic understanding of the subject, he was not just surprised to find Fiona here, he was— the realization was a shock in itself—shocked. For one unholy instant, his mind had reeled with all manner of visions—visions of Fiona. But, as he'd looked deep into her eyes, all hazel-greens and golds, he'd seen, clear and true, the same girl he'd known years before. Relief had hit him like a blow, right in the center of his chest.

She hadn't changed. Not in the least.

Which meant she was up to something.

That conclusion was borne out by her next speech.

"Harriet, dear." Smiling serenely, Fiona opened her arms to Harriet and they exchanged their usual kiss. "I fear I am come to throw myself on your hospitality—as I explained to Henry, Edmund and I have had a falling out and I've refused to stay at Coldstream until he apologizes."

Dyan frowned. He knew Fiona's explanation was a lie, but why the devil was she staying with her brother at Coldstream House? Where was Tony, Marquess of Rusden—her husband? He looked at Fiona, but she avoided his eye. Harriet's reaction to Fiona's tale was more revealing. She blushed fierily—and glanced helplessly at Henry. Who, muffin-faced, looked helplessly back.

"Ah . . ." Wide-eyed, Harriet stared at Fiona, who smiled encouragingly; Dyan knew the precise instant Harriet inwardly shrugged and bowed to fate. "Yes, of course." Her words sounded like the capitulation they were; a fleeting frown tangled Fiona's brows, then was banished. Wringing her hands, Harriet continued, "I'll get Sherwood to show you to your rooms." She smiled weakly, but with a hint of hope, at Dyan.

He smiled reassuringly and held out his hands. "It's been a long time, dear Harriet, but I, too, am claiming refuge from my relatives. I hope you can find a pallet somewhere."

"Oh, I'm sure we can." Harriet's smile turned to one of relief. She took his hands; under cover of planting a kiss on his cheek, she squeezed them warningly. "We'll have to reorganize a trifle but . . ." Shrugging lightly, she turned aside. "Sherwood—"

Harriet's hope—her relief—had communicated itself to Henry. Leaving Harriet to issue her orders, he faced his unexpected guests and fixed Dyan with a significant look. "Well! Just like old times—isn't it?"

Dyan studied Henry's face; so, he noticed, did Fiona. "Old times" referred to their joint childhoods, when, as a small army, he, Fiona, Henry, Harriet, and an assortment of others—all children of the local gentry—had roamed far and wide through the New Forest. He had been their leader; Fiona, two years his junior, had been his second-in-command, the only one of them all who would, without a blink, argue, remonstrate—simply dig in her heels—if some escapade he suggested was too wild, too reckless, too altogether dangerous. She had jerked his reins any number of times, usually by invoking his conscience, a sometimes inconvenient but surprisingly forceful entity.

Conversely, he, as far as he knew, was the only person

presently alive who had ever succeeded in managing Fiona, mettlesome, argumentative female that she was. Dyan surmised it was that aspect of their "old times" of which Henry was attempting to remind him. Which confirmed his guess that the entertainment Henry and Harriet had planned for this evening would not meet with Fiona's approval. But that still didn't tell him what had happened to Fiona's husband.

"Indeed," he drawled, politely noncommittal.

Fiona flicked him a quick, suspicious glance, but said nothing.

"If you'll follow Sherwood," Harriet said, gesturing towards the stairs, "he'll show you to your rooms."

Smoothly, Dyan offered Fiona his arm; she shot him another suspicious glance but consented to rest her fingers on his sleeve. In silence, they followed the stately Sherwood up the wide stairs; a footman followed with Fiona's bag.

Dyan held his tongue as they ascended—for the simple reason that he couldn't formulate a single coherent thought. His predator's senses were well-honed, acutely sensitive. They were presently screaming, far too adamantly to be ignored. Their message left him reeling.

Fiona, strolling haughtily beside him, was, indeed, the same girl he'd known before. Unchanged. Untouched.

Unmarried.

He knew it—felt it—deep in his bones. One glance at the fingers of her left hand, presently residing on his sleeve, confirmed it—no band, not even any lingering trace.

As they reached the top of the stairs, Dyan hauled in a not-entirely-steady breath. The foundations of his life had just shifted.

He couldn't interrogate Fiona in front of the servants. Forced to hold his tongue, he slanted her a glance as she glided regally on his arm. She was of above average height—her head just topped his shoulder. Her hair, lustrously thick, was pulled back in a chignon; her face was a perfect oval rendered in ivory satin. Her glance, delivered from large hazel eyes set under finely arched brown brows, still held the same directness, the same uncompromising honesty—the same uncompromising stubbornness—that had always been hers. That last was obvious in the set of her full lips, in the elevation of her chin.

He squinted slightly—and saw the band of freckles across the bridge of her nose. She was exactly as he remembered.

So what had happened to Tony? And why was she here?

He frowned. "How's your brother?" In Sherwood's wake, they turned down a long corridor.

Fiona kept her eyes forward, her chin up. "Edmund's in perfectly good health, thank you."

The urge to shake her returned; Dyan set his jaw and held it back. They'd reached the end of the wing. Servants were scurrying everywhere.

The rooms Harriet had assigned them were next to each other—Dyan suspected for a very good reason. A maid appeared and Fiona, with a haughty nod, disappeared into her room.

"I've brought some fresh cravats, Your Grace." Henry's valet hovered at Dyan's elbow. "If you'll let me take your jacket, I'll have it brushed."

His gaze on Fiona's closed door, Dyan nodded. "You'll need to be quick."

He was waiting for her when she came out.

Lounging in the shadows, his shoulders against the wall, Dyan watched as, unaware of his presence, Fiona exited her room. Looking down the corridor, she closed the door. Hand still on the knob, she cocked her head, listening. Light from a nearby sconce bathed her in golden light.

Dyan's chest locked. For a long minute, he couldn't breathe, couldn't drag his eyes from the figure robed in turquoise silk poised before the door. This was a Fiona he'd glimpsed only briefly, in the ballrooms of London ten years ago. Guinea-gold curls fell from a knot on the top of her head, a few shining locks artistically escaping to frame brow and nape. The smooth sweep of her jaw and the graceful curve of her throat were highlighted by delicate aquamarine drops depending from her earlobes; the expanse of ivory skin above her scooped neckline played host to the matching pendant. Dyan fought to draw breath, fought to ease the vise locked about his chest; her perfume reached him, violet and honeysuckle—the scent went straight to his head.

His blood rushed straight to his loins.

Before, in London, seeing her only through breaks in the crowds surrounding her, he'd never been able to let his gaze dwell on her, as it was dwelling now. Dwelling on the ripe curves of hips and derriere clearly outlined as she leaned slightly forward; when she relaxed, letting go of the doorknob and straightening, another set of curves came into view—her breasts, full, Rubenesquely abundant, positively mouthwatering.

Desire ripped through him—hot, strong, violent.

Abruptly, Dyan straightened and pushed away from the wall. Fiona heard him and swung around. And frowned.

Dyan strolled forward. "Now we're alone, perhaps you'd like to explain what you're doing here?"

Up went her pert nose; down came her lids. "You heard." Turning, she started down the corridor. "I had an argument with Edmund."

"And pigs flew over the forest this morning."

"I *did*." Fiona heard the tartness in her tone. Trust Dyan to thrust in his oar. "You've been away for years— things have changed." They hadn't spoken in fifteen years, but here he was, as usual, trying to take her reins.

"Try again," he advised, falling into step beside her. "It takes generations, not mere years, to change a man like Edmund. I'd believe he's got a mistress stashed away in the north wing of Coldstream House faster than I'd believe he'd waste his time arguing—*attempting* to argue—with you."

"*Be* that as it may, I assure you—"

"Fiona."

She only just managed not to shiver. The three syllables of her name were infused with steely warning—a warning she recognized only too well. The stairs were in sight, but she knew she'd never make their head—not unless she told Dyan the truth. She knew his propensities; minor considerations like her dignity—or the possibility of her screaming—wouldn't stop him. She drew in a deep, much-needed breath. "If you *must* know, Harriet spoke to me last week, when she came to tea."

She kept walking; the less time she spent alone with Dyan, the more certain her goal would be. "She told me about these house parties Henry organizes." She paused, conscious of the blush rising in her cheeks. But it was, after all, Dyan she was talking to. She lifted her head. "About the activities the guests Henry invites delight in. Expect. Engage in."

Beside her, Dyan blinked. "*Henry's* guests."

Fiona nodded and started down the stairs. "Precisely." Sherwood was waiting by the dining-room door; leaning closer to Dyan, she lowered her voice. "You know what Harriet's like—she's got no gumption at all. I decided the least I could do was come and support her. At least that way she won't have to spend the entire time in fear for her virtue."

"Fear for her . . . ?" Dyan was stunned. He stepped off the stairs in Fiona's wake. "Fiona—" Blinking, he refocused—and discovered her forging ahead. "Here—wait a minute." Striding after her, he caught her arm and halted her, swinging about so his body screened her from Sherwood. "Listen—"

Fiona looked down, at his fingers wrapped about her elbow.

"I don't know what Harriet claimed, but that's not—"

"Dyan—let go. *Right now*."

Dyan did. Instantly. The quaver in her voice momentarily threw him.

Fiona didn't look up; she stepped back but didn't meet his eyes. "I didn't expect you to agree with my views—I don't expect you to help." Her chin firmed. "Just don't try to stop me."

With that, she whirled from him. Lifting her head, she swept into the dining room.

Dyan cursed, and strode after her.

He crossed the threshold just as Sherwood opened his mouth to announce Fiona. Dyan planted his boot on Sherwood's foot.

Sherwood cast him an anguished, somewhat reproachful glance. "Miss Winton," Dyan hissed, and removed his boot.

With commendable aplomb, Sherwood announced Miss Winton and His Grace of Darke.

Dark was precisely how Dyan felt as he stalked up the table. Harriet had left two seats vacant, next to each other in the middle along one side. Equidistant, Dyan noted, from Henry at the head and Harriet at the foot. Chairs scraped as the gentlemen hurriedly stood; all heads turned to assess the late arrivals. With the single exception of Henry, every male reacted similarly as their gazes connected with the vision that was Fiona—their eyes widened, taking in her abundant charms; their lips lifted in anticipatory smiles. More than one reached blindly for their quizzing glass before recalling where they were.

Following on Fiona's heels, Dyan fought back a scowl.

He was peripherally aware of the response his own appearance was provoking—the flaring interest that lit many feminine eyes, the sudden increase in attentiveness, the subtle preening—the slithering tendrils of sexual excitement that reached for him. He ignored them.

He waved the footman back and held Fiona's chair. His logical mind patiently reminded him that she had rejected him—very thoroughly—fifteen years ago; she was no responsibility of his. The lecture fell on deaf ears. Seeing one so-called gentleman reach for his monocle under cover of the general re-sitting, Dyan caught his eye—a second later, the gentleman flushed; letting his monocle fall, he turned to the lady beside him.

As he waited for Fiona to settle her skirts, Dyan looked down the table; Harriet met his saber-edged glance with an imploringly helpless look. Dyan swallowed a furious oath, and sat.

"Such a *pleasure*, Your Grace, to see you here." The lady on Dyan's left, a handsome woman with almost as much bosom on show as Fiona, leaned closer and smiled warmly. "I hadn't realized you were acquainted with the Brookes."

"Childhood acquaintances," Dyan informed her tersely, and turned to Fiona.

Only to discover a soup tureen in the way. She was helping herself, apparently concentrating. Finished, she held the ladle out to him, still refusing to meet his eyes. He reached for it—and caught it in midair; she'd let go before his fingers touched it. Frowning, Dyan helped himself to the thick oyster soup, then waved the footman away.

"Did you hear about the party old Rawlsley held at that manor of his in Sussex?"

The other guests, well ahead of the two of them, were spooning up the last of their helpings and starting on the next phase—tossing conversational balls about the table.

"Gillings said he'd pop up tomorrow—he had to stay in town until his wife retired to Gillings Hall."

By keeping his eyes on his plate, Dyan avoided the many waiting to capture his attention. Fiona, too, kept her eyes down. He shot her a sidelong glance; lashes decorously lowered, she sipped her soup. Looking back at his, Dyan frowned. What had happened in the hall?

Deaf to the conversations about them, Fiona breathed deeply, steadily, and ate her soup. And struggled to settle her nerves. Dyan's touch had jerked her back fifteen years— to that moment when he'd kissed her in the forest, and her world had stopped turning. Just a simple touch—and her knees had gone weak; she'd felt like crying for all her lost dreams, dreams that had come to nothing, that had turned to dust. Forcing the old memories into the deepest mental drawer she could find, she slammed it shut—there was no point letting their past torment her.

Gradually, a measure of calm returned; she could actually taste the soup.

Beside her, Dyan had been frowning at his, absent-mindedly stirring it; apparently reaching some decision, he lifted the spoon and sipped. "You're obviously as stubborn as ever." Glancing sideways, he caught her eye. "You're on some damned righteous crusade, aren't you?"

Fiona raised a haughty brow. "Better than a licentious one."

The riposte stopped him in his tracks—for all of half a minute. "Fiona, can I at least suggest—just introduce the idea to your mind—that Harriet might not be *quite* as innocent as you're supposing?"

Fiona's lips compressed; she fought to hold back her words, but they tumbled out, acid and tart. "You may suggest what you like, but I would hardly accept your word on the matter. I know you find it difficult to distinguish between a virtuous lady and a lightskirt."

Dyan's brows snapped together. "What the hell's that supposed to mean?"

Fiona shrugged. "You confused me with some wanton scullery maid years ago."

"What?!"

It was just as well the rest of the table were loudly enthusing over the dishes comprising the next course, which Sherwood and his helpers had just set forth. Fiona merely raised her brows and took another sip of her soup.

The turbulence to her left didn't abate, although Dyan lowered his voice. "I *never* confused you with anyone."

His words were harsh—and bitter. Dyan frowned ferociously and viciously stirred his soup. He'd never confused any other woman with Fiona. "What the *devil* are you talking about?"

He glanced up in time to see Fiona color delicately. She shot a brief glance his way, then looked down and carefully laid her spoon precisely in the center of her plate. "When you kissed me in the forest. You've probably forgotten."

Forgotten? Dyan stared at her. One didn't forget major turning points in life. He bit the words back; jaw clenching, he looked away. He had an exceptional memory, particularly when it came to Fiona. In the blink of an eye, he was reliving that scene in the forest—something he'd not allowed himself to do for over ten years. Nevertheless, it was easy to go back—to the clearing where they'd stopped to rest the horses after he'd deliberately lost Henry. Too easy to hear the hot words Fiona had heaped on his head the instant he'd released her and she'd been able to draw breath. *"Don't you dare confuse me with some wanton scullery maid!"* She'd paused, and looked briefly, expectantly, at him—stunned and stung, he'd simply stared back. Then she'd drawn a second breath, and a tirade had tumbled out—a scornful, scathing, hurtful denunciation. She had dismissed the incident, tarnishing it, rejecting what should have been—hell, *had been* to him—a glorious moment.

Dyan frowned; he glanced at Fiona. "I didn't think you were—or confuse you with—a maid. Or any other woman."

"Oh?"

Her haughty disbelief hit any number of nerves.

"*No.*" The single syllable vibrated with suppressed fury. "I didn't."

A footman reached between them to clear their plates— Dyan looked away, ostensibly scanning the guests, in truth seeing nothing more than a blackly swirling haze. The old hurt was still there—unhealed, throbbing, and raw. He could still feel his shock, feel the totally unexpected pain. Taste the bitterness that had flooded him.

"Excuse me, Your Grace."

Fresh plates were laid before them; stiffly, her expression a polite mask, Fiona served herself from the already plundered dishes. With an effort, Dyan forced himself to do the same—he supposed he had to eat, or at least preserve the appearance.

"Here, my dear Miss Winton. Allow me." The gentleman on Fiona's right held a large platter for her inspection; Fiona rewarded him with a brief smile. As she made her selection, the gentleman's eyes strayed downward—an instant later he looked up, blinking dazedly. Dyan gritted his teeth—and jabbed his fork into a slice of roast beef.

Other gentlemen and ladies, too, were exceedingly helpful; Dyan blankly refused all invitations to interaction. Beside him, he felt the cool wall of Fiona's hauteur slide into place, deployed between her and any too-overt advances.

Sherwood hovered between them. "Wine, Your Grace?"

Dyan nodded curtly. Sherwood filled his glass, then Fiona's. She was still making her selections; as she finished with each dish, she slid it toward him. Grimly, Dyan piled food on his plate. From the corner of his eye, he saw Fiona lift her head and scan the table, then imperiously wave up one last dish. Eagerly, gentlemen reached to pass it to her; she smiled benignly and accepted it—then handed it wordlessly to him.

Frowning, Dyan received it; he looked in—pork in wine sauce. Fiona hated pork, but the dish was one of his favorites. With a grunt, he helped himself, glancing at her from under lowered brows. She was calmly eating—she didn't look his way; he wasn't sure she even realized what she'd done.

The simple act helped him get his temper back on its leash. Picking up his knife and fork, he growled through still-clenched teeth: "I didn't kiss you all those years ago because I thought you were some sort of loose woman."

Fiona slanted him a suspicious, slightly wary glance. "Why did you kiss me then?"

"Because I wanted to." Dyan sliced into the roast beef. "Because I wanted to kiss *you*. Not just any woman, but *you*. Strangely enough, I thought you'd enjoy it—that I'd enjoy it."

"And did you?"

"The kiss, yes. The rest—no."

The rest—the words she'd heaped on his head, had used to flay him—was engraved on her heart. Watching him from beneath her lashes, Fiona shifted in her chair. Dyan never lied. He could bend the truth with the best of them, but he never directly lied. Lips compressed, she chased peas around her plate. "I thought . . . that you were just seizing opportunity." Without looking up, she shrugged. "That it was just because I was there—a willing female."

"*Not* so willing." A pregnant moment passed, then he said, his voice very low: "I *never* thought of you like that."

Her world was tilting on its axis; Fiona couldn't believe

she'd read him so wrongly. Her stomach lurched, then sank; her heart contracted. Her mind rolled back through the years, through all her hopeful, hopeless dreams; gradually, she steadied.

She hadn't been wrong. She'd given him opportunity enough to tell her if he felt anything for her—had, indeed, all but asked him outright for a declaration, a clear statement that she wasn't just a wanton scullery maid to him, that she meant more to him than that. He hadn't made that statement—not then, nor at any subsequent time. She'd waited, telling herself she'd surprised him, asked for too much too soon. But she'd already been so far gone in love she hadn't been able to believe he, always the leader, was not; that he didn't feel for her as she did for him. So she'd waited through the years while he'd been away at Oxford; he hadn't even come home for the vacations. He'd been laying the foundations for his future career while she'd been deluding herself in Hampshire. But she'd learned the truth—*seen* the truth—when she'd gone up to town. Oh, no—she couldn't forget all her wasted years, the rivers of wasted tears. Lifting her head, she reached for her wineglass. "If you found it so enjoyable, I'm surprised you didn't seek to repeat the exercise."

"*After what you said?* I'd have had to don armor."

Fiona humphed and set down her glass. "You could at least have come up to me in London and said hello—not just nodded vaguely over a sea of heads."

"If you'd looked my way just once, I might have."

"*Once*?" Swivelling in her chair, Fiona stared at him. "*Once*? If I'd looked at you any more a blind scandalmonger would have noticed!"

Dyan opened his mouth—Fiona held up a hand. "Wait!" She closed her eyes, like a seer looking into the future, only she was looking into the past. "Lady More-

cambe, Mrs. Hennessy, and the Countess of Cranbourne."
Opening her eyes, she glared at Dyan.

It took him longer to place them—three of his mis-
tresses from that time—the Seasons both he and Fiona had
been in London. Disconcerted, he snorted, and eyed her suspiciously. "How did you find out? Not from watching—I
was never that obvious."

"*You* weren't—*they* were." Her expression mutinous,
Fiona skewered a broiled shrimp. "They made themselves
ridiculous, trying to hold your attention. So if *you'd* actually
looked *my* way just once—"

"Heslethwaite, Phillips, Montgomery, Halifax, and, of
course, Rusden—I can go on if you like."

Her most assiduous suitors. Turning, Fiona stared at
him.

Narrow-eyed, Dyan met her gaze. "Why the hell did
you think those ladies had to work so hard to hold my attention?" He spoke softly, through clenched teeth. "Because it was forever wandering. To *you*! When I think of
the contortions I went through to hide it—"

"It would have been more to the point if you'd thought
to look at me while I was looking at you." Shaken, Fiona
swung back to her plate. "Well,"—she gestured wildly with
her knife—"you could even have made the *huge* effort of
crossing the floor and asking me to dance."

"What? Fight through the hordes to secure a place on
your dance card?" Dyan snorted derisively. A moment later,
he added: "Aside from anything else, I never got to balls
early enough."

"You could have made an exception—made a real effort."

"Oh, undoubtedly—and set every gossipmonger's eyes
alight. Just think—the notorious Lord Dyan Dare actually
turning up to a ball early just to get his name on Lady Fiona

Winton-Ryder's dance card. I can imagine what they'd have made of that.''

Fiona sniffed disparagingly. ''You could have paid a morning call—although I daresay you never even saw the mornings, having to recuperate from the nights before.''

''My recuperative powers are rather stronger than you suppose. I don't, however, believe your parents would have appreciated a morning call from me. One whisper of that, and the gossip mill would have cranked with a vengeance. Besides—*if* you recall—I had every reason to believe my advances were unwelcome.''

The undercurrent of bitterness in his tone was impossible to ignore; Fiona didn't believe him capable of manufacturing it. She bit her lip, and studied her half-empty plate. ''I really didn't think you'd be that easily discouraged—not if you were in earnest.''

Chest expanding as he dragged in a deep breath, Dyan sat back and reached for his wineglass. If they had the scene in the clearing to play again—and she said what she'd said then? He forced himself to consider it, to study her words as dispassionately as he could. Fifteen years on—so many women on—her words held a different ring. No, he was forced to concede, he wouldn't be discouraged—not now—understanding as he now did how women often reacted, their uncertainties and fears, the bees they sometimes got in their bonnets. But then? Slowly, he exhaled. ''Well, I was.''

He made the admission quietly, looking back down the years. He'd been seventeen, just getting into his stride with women. And Fiona had been . . . well, he'd always thought she'd been—would always be—his. He'd thought she'd welcome his advances. When she'd spurned him . . . *That* had been a blow from which he'd never quite recovered.

Frowning slightly, he shifted and set down his glass. A point that had forever puzzled him nagged for clarification. ''Incidentally, what was that nonsense about you not being able to waltz? I taught you to waltz myself.''

Fiona set down her knife and fork. Picking up a dish of sweetmeats, she turned and handed it to the gentleman on her right. Bemused, he took it. Fiona smiled encouragingly—and didn't turn back. Dyan, after all, had answered his own question. She couldn't waltz *because* he'd taught her.

All the other dances she'd managed perfectly well; none required the degree of physical contact—familiar contact—necessitated by the waltz. Luckily, she'd discovered her problem at a small, informal dance party before she'd made her come-out, where they'd been permitted to practice the waltz. When Dyan had taken her in his arms, she hadn't had the slightest problem; when her partner that night—a perfectly innocent young gentlemen, brother of one of her friends—had tried to do the same, every muscle in her body had locked. Not from fright, but from a type of revulsion. She'd tried to fight the reaction and had ended by swooning. After that, she hadn't tried to waltz again. Her veto had driven her mother to distraction, but she'd held to it; she'd never waltzed with anyone but Dyan.

She could feel his gaze on her half-averted face—any second he would press for an answer. She glanced about; but the other diners, having finally accepted their disinterest, were all engrossed in their own conversations; there was no one free to rescue her. Fiona tried to ease the knots in her stomach—tried to breathe deeply enough to calm herself and think.

At the end of the table, Harriet stood; heaving an inward sigh of relief, Fiona grabbed her napkin and placed it by her plate.

Dyan frowned down the table at Harriet—her timing had always been woeful. To his experienced eye, she looked slightly tipsy, her inhibitions nicely softened by the heady wine she'd ordered served. Fiona, thankfully, had barely taken two sips.

Rising with the rest of the gentlemen, he drew out Fiona's chair. As she turned, he blocked her way. "For God's sake," he whispered, "develop a headache." He caught her eye—and poured all the emphasis he could into the instruction: *"Retire early."*

She studied his eyes, his face, clearly considering his words, and his motives.

Dyan opened his mouth to clarify both—

"My dear Miss Winton—I'm Lady Henderson."

Fiona's polite mask, all assured confidence, slid into place. As she smiled and shook hands with Lady Henderson, an older blonde, Dyan inwardly cursed. Forced to stand back, to let Fiona escape, he couldn't help wonder how long it would be before one of the guests realized that Fiona's innately gracious, lady-of-the-manor airs were just a little *too* assured for plain Miss Winton.

With a last, cool, noncommittal glance for him, Fiona fell in beside Lady Henderson; head high, she left the room. Beneath his breath, Dyan swore. Grimly, he resumed his seat.

And prayed that, for once in her life, Fiona would simply do his bidding.

Two

Fiona grasped the few minutes as the ladies milled in the hall to try to bring order to her suddenly chaotic thoughts. Only to conclude that making head or tail of them was presently beyond her—the only point of which she felt certain was that Dyan had interpreted her words in the clearing as rejection. Rejection—the dolt! How could he have been so blind? So deaf? *"Don't you dare confuse me with some wanton scullery maid,"* was what she'd said, having already heard of his exploits with at least two of the species. And then she'd waited—for him to reassure her that she was special to him. That she was his love, as he had been hers.

The stupid man hadn't said a word. He'd stared at her blankly, then let her pour her hurt scorn over him. *Then* he'd gone off to consort with countless beautiful women, as if to illustrate that she was nothing special to him.

And *then* he'd gone off adventuring in India and left her behind.

Well! What was she supposed to think?

The impulse to brood darkly on that point was almost overwhelming, but she hadn't forgotten she was here on a mission.

Realizing from some lady's startled glance that her lips

were grimly set, Fiona forcibly relaxed them into a serene smile. She fell into line as the ladies trailed into the drawing room.

Pausing beyond the threshold, she scanned the room, noting the groups of ladies deploying about its gracious expanse. One group broke apart, laughing immoderately; the raucous note jarred on her ear. The wisest strategy seemed clear—deal with Henry's guests, protect Harriet, then retire gracefully at the appropriate time.

Then she could deal with Dyan.

"Excuse me, Miss Winton."

Fiona turned as Lady Henderson, who had been chatting with some other ladies, came up. Her ladyship—Fiona placed her in her forties—smiled, genuinely friendly. "You seem somewhat lost, my dear—I do hope you don't mind me mentioning it. Is it your first visit here?"

Supremely assured, Fiona smiled back. "Indeed no— I've known Henry and Harriet for . . . quite some time." Sherwood—she presumed at Dyan's behest—had concealed her identity; there seemed no reason to bruit it abroad. "But," she added, looking over the room again, "this is the first time I've attended one of these house parties."

Lady Henderson blinked. After a slight hesitation, she asked, "Pardon my curiosity, my dear, but do you mean the first time at Brooke Hall—or the *first time* altogether?"

The note of concern in her ladyship's voice drew Fiona's gaze back to her face. "I've attended many house parties, of course. But I have to admit this is the first of this . . ." she gestured airily, "ilk."

"Oh, dear." Her ladyship, concern clear in her face, stared at Fiona. Then she glanced across the room to where Harriet was holding forth by the chaise. "What *is* Harriet thinking of?" Looking back at Fiona, Lady Henderson placed a friendly hand on her arm. "My dear, if you truly are not . . ." With her other hand, she mimicked Fiona's earlier gesture. "In the way of things, then I would really not advise this as the place to start. The evening revels here can get quite . . . well, quite *deep*, if you take my meaning."

Despite not being "in the way of things," Fiona suspected she could. She looked across the room. "Perhaps I'd better speak with Harriet."

"Perhaps you had." Lady Henderson removed her hand. "But just so you know how things progress should you decide to join us, once the gentlemen return, we take about half an hour to choose our partner—or partners, if you decide on more than one. Then the games start. Sometimes there's a specific goal to begin with—like who can make a lady reach ecstasy first. But before very long, things just naturally evolve."

Again, her ladyship's hands came into play; Fiona, her expression studiously blank, nodded. "I see." Drawing a deep breath, she turned toward Harriet. "Thank you, Lady Henderson." With a regal nod, she glided away—straight to Harriet.

Whether or not Dyan was right about Harriet, retiring early, as he'd advised, *before* the gentlemen returned, would clearly be prudent. Fiona fetched up by Harriet's side.

"And then his lordship declared I was quite the best—" Harriet, highly animated, glanced up—and jumped. "Oh!" She paled, then smiled weakly at Fiona and gestured about the circle of ladies. "This is my dear friend, Miss Winton. Ah—" Eyes wide, Harriet scanned the room. "Pray excuse me, I must speak with Mrs. Ferguson." She swept the circle with a wavering smile, sent a startled glance at Fiona, and fled across the room.

Fiona watched her go through narrowing eyes.

"Miss Winton, I declare you must tell us all you know about Darke." A lady sporting a profusion of red ringlets laid a familiar hand on Fiona's arm.

Forsaking Harriet's retreating figure, Fiona fixed the

lady with a decidedly cool glance. "Must I?"

"*Indeed* you must!" another of the laughing ladies assured her. "Harriet told us you know him better than she does, and, of course, here we always share." The lady smiled, archly coy. "You really must warn us—is he as *vigorous* as he appears?"

"Or even *half* as inventive as his reputation?"

"Does he prefer a slow waltz—or do his tastes run more to a gallop?"

The smile Fiona trained upon the circle of avid faces was a study in superiority. "I'm afraid," she murmured, her tone drawing on centuries of aristocratic forebears, "that there's been some mistake. *I* do not share." Her smile deepened fractionally; inclining her head, she smoothly moved away.

Leaving a stunned silence behind.

Fiona scanned the crowd—and saw Harriet's startled-rabbit face peeking out from behind an ample matron. Harriet promptly ducked; eyes narrow, lips firming, Fiona set out in pursuit.

She knew the routine of *ton*nish house parties to the minute; she had plenty of time before the gentlemen arrived. Time and more to catch Harriet and give her a piece of her mind, before retreat became imperative.

But Harriet didn't want to be caught. Shorter and slighter than Fiona, she used her status as hostess to flit from group to group. Disgusted with such craven behavior, Fiona gave up the chase. Sweeping around to head for the door, she spied Lady Henderson. On impulse, she stopped by her ladyship's side.

When her ladyship glanced her way and smiled, Fiona smiled, rather tightly, back. "I just had one question, Lady Henderson, if you would be so good as to humor me."

Her ladyship inclined her head and looked her interest.

"Who signed the invitation that brought you here?"

Lady Henderson's eyes opened wide. "Why, Harriet, of course. As usual."

Fiona's smile grew steely. "Thank you."

She turned to the door—

It opened, and the gentlemen streamed in.

Thanks to Henry, garrulously eager for his approval, Dyan was among the last to enter the drawing room. The first thing he did on crossing the threshold was scan the room; the second thing he did was swear, volubly if silently, his gaze fixed on Fiona, trapped at the center of a crowd of eager gentlemen.

Dyan gritted his teeth. Even if she'd come to her senses and swallowed her pride enough to take his advice, she wouldn't have expected them back so soon. Given the number of males present, it shouldn't have been possible to pass a decanter around in less than thirty minutes—so Henry had had three smaller decanters placed along the table. The guests had quaffed the wine—understandable, given its quality.

And so here they all were, back in the drawing room, blocking Fiona's retreat.

Disguising his interest in her, Dyan prowled idly down the long room, his heavy lids at half-mast, concealing the direction of his gaze. If Fiona had managed to slip away, he'd have followed; upstairs, in the seclusion of their rooms at the end of the wing, they could have sorted out what had really happened fifteen years before—and all that had, or hadn't, happened since. Instead, here she was, acting honeypot to a swarm of bees.

He shot her a glance as he drew level; she was looking down her nose at one impulsive gent—a Mr. Ferguson, if he remembered aright. Even from a distance, he could see the chill rising as she acidly requested Mr. Ferguson to remove his foot from her hem.

It was an old trick; Mr. Ferguson, startled, stepped back and looked down. Fiona smoothly turned, giving him her shoulder.

Dyan's lips twitched; his brows quirked as he continued his prowl. Lady Arctic had been Fiona's nickname among the more sporting rakes in town; it had been said no man could melt her ice—he'd die of frostbite first. Right now, Lady Arctic looked to be holding her own. He'd half a mind to retire and let her weather this alone.

Then again. Eyes narrowing, Dyan swung back, studying those gathered about Fiona.

"Your Grace!"

The title was still unfamiliar; it took Dyan a moment to recognize what the two ladies bearing down on him were after. Him.

"I was just speaking to Miss Winton," the possessor of myriad red ringlets informed him. "She quite sang your praises, my lord."

Dyan raised his brows. "Indeed?"

"Your efforts left her utterly prostrated, she said." The redhead leaned closer—any closer and she'd have pressed her breast to his arm.

"So we've come to offer our services in her stead." The second lady, a sultry brunette drifted close; her musky perfume rose like a cloud—Dyan fought not to wrinkle his nose.

"I fear, madam, that I'm already spoken for." With a nod, he stepped aside and turned away.

"But you *can't* be!" the redhead protested. "You've only this minute walked into the room."

Dyan glanced back, cynically dismissive. "I'm here to consort with an old friend."

Leaving the two ladies whispering vituperatively, he strolled languidly on, not stopping until he'd reached a wing chair placed in one corner of the room. He lounged in its comfort, long limbs sprawling; a nearby ottoman caught his eye—he nudged it closer, then propped both booted feet, ankles crossed, upon it.

And fixed Fiona, on the opposite side of the room, with a dark and brooding gaze.

He needed to talk to her—fully intended to talk to her—but he was obviously going to have to wait until she learned the truth of Harriet's innocence the hard way. Turning his head, he searched for Harriet and discovered her chatting blithely—too blithely—with a Lord Pringle. His lordship already had his arm about her waist. Well on the way. Inwardly shaking his head, Dyan looked away. Why on earth had the witless wanton painted herself to Fiona as an injured innocent? The outcome—the present imbroglio—was all too predictable. Fiona had always been a loyal friend, steadfast and true. A friend one could rely on, with a strong, very forthright character. It wouldn't have occurred to her to doubt Harriet's word.

"Might I interest you in a wager, Your Grace?"

Dyan glanced up—a well-developed blonde smiled seductively down at him. Deliberately, she leaned forward, bringing the ripe swells of her breasts to eye level.

"I'm sure," she purred, "that we could think up a most *satisfying* challenge—and an even more *satisfying* reward."

"I've been informed by my great-aunt that, having succeeded to the title, such endeavors are now beneath me." Dyan waved dismissively. "Something to do with my dignity."

His great-aunt Augusta might as well be useful for something; she had, indeed, made such a comment. Taken aback, the blonde blinked and straightened, then, seeing his gaze once more fixed across the room, tartly shrugged and walked off.

A shrill shriek cut through the rising hum; Dyan recognized it—so did Fiona. She stiffened. The glance she threw Harriet—an ice-bolt—should have transfixed her; their hostess, well away, clinging to Lord Pringle, didn't even notice.

Fiona's chin went up another notch; her expression turned a touch colder, a touch haughtier. His gaze fixed on her face, Dyan narrowed his eyes. Perhaps fate wasn't being unkind—with any luck, Fiona would be so incensed, so distracted by Harriet's perfidy, he'd be able to learn what he desperately wanted to know without being too obvious. Perhaps even without showing his hand.

"I declare, my lord, that my legs are quite *exhausted*." Artistically flicking a fan, a gorgeously arrayed brunette paused beside him, her large eyes greedily surveying his long frame. She licked her lips. "Perhaps I could—"

"No." Dyan spoke quietly, coldly. His fingers closed around the woman's elbow before she could swing about, her clear intention to plant her lush derriere in his lap. His eyes, cold and dark, trapped hers. "If your limbs have weakened so soon, dear lady, there are chairs by the wall. I suggest you avail yourself of one."

He withdrew his hand and his gaze, leaving her to retreat with whatever dignity she could muster. She left with a heated glare, but not a single word.

His expression growing grimmer, Dyan looked again at Fiona—at the gentlemen still surrounding her. Some, sensing the state of play, had drifted away; only the most determined remained. Four—four too many for Dyan's liking.

He'd studied the male company over the port; they were not of his circle; none were familiar. More importantly, they were not of the *haut ton*, the rarefied elite to which Fiona was accustomed.

She'd been presented at eighteen, and had instantly attracted the very best of attention. The most eligible gentlemen had flocked about her; she'd never lacked for suitors. Dyan's frown deepened; the single most important question he had for Fiona resonated in his head. Why hadn't she married Anthony, Marquess of Rusden, as he'd fully expected her to?

A quick shake of Fiona's head had him tensing. She turned from one gentleman, imperiously dismissive; the man frowned, hesitated, then strolled off. Three left. Dyan forced himself to relax—at least outwardly. Despite the Seasons she'd spent in London, he doubted Fiona would find her remaining suitors-for-the-evening quite so easy to dismiss. Her very presence would be interpreted as a declaration that she was available. Beneath his breath, Dyan swore. It was just as well he was here to haul her out when she got in over her head. Then she'd have to be grateful.

As well as distracted. Fleetingly, he raised his brows. Perhaps there was hope yet?

He wasn't, however, enjoying the situation. Another lady swanned close—he froze her with a glance. She quickly changed tack and swanned out of his sight. Dyan glowered at Fiona. He felt like a dog watching over a particularly juicy bone—or a wolf over a particularly bountifully endowed sheep.

Fiona saw his glower—and inwardly glowered back. Her face felt stiff, having been held in a distant, impassive expression for too long. She was beginning to wonder how much longer she could maintain it, along with her hold on her temper.

"You really need to relax, my dear Miss Winton." Sir Magnus Herring, on her left, inched closer. "A little flirting's so innocent."

Fiona fixed him with a severe glance. "That, my dear sir, is hardly my style." Earl's daughters didn't flirt, but she couldn't tell him that.

Sir Magnus inched closer; regally, Fiona waved the two would-be cicisbeos on her other side back and started to stroll. "A little fresh air would be more to my liking." The

French windows behind Dyan's chair were open to the terrace and the soft shadows of the evening outside.

Not that she had any intention of setting foot on the terrace. She was heading for Dyan. He might be annoyed enough to look like a human thundercloud, a reincarnation of Thor, the god of war and lightning, his dark hair falling, rakishly dangerous, over his forehead, his eyes dark and stormy—but for her, he represented safety, security; he wouldn't let her down.

Her three encumbrances clung like barnacles as she glided over the parquetry. She was used to dismissing unwanted advances—Mr. Moreton and Mr. Coldthorpe she was sure she could handle. Sir Magnus was a model cut from a different cloth. A bluffly genial, heavily built, and handsome man, he was, she sensed, used to success.

He wasn't going to accept failure easily.

She'd blocked a score of his subtle advances, turned aside a host of glib propositions—and still he persisted.

"Perhaps," he murmured, holding fast by her side, head bent so the others couldn't hear, "we could view the moon together, my dear? Moonlight, they say, can have a quite liberating effect on a lady's passions."

Fiona met his warm gaze with a blank look. "There's no moon tonight." There would be, but much later; she doubted Sir Magnus would know.

The chagrin that showed fleetingly in his pale eyes said he didn't; the flash of something else Fiona glimpsed—an almost grim determination—brought Lady Henderson's timetable forcibly to mind.

She looked ahead—and saw a band of ladies—the redhead, two brunettes, and two blondes—descend, in a froth of silken skirts, on Dyan.

Fiona blinked. Then, plastering a bright smile on her lips, she headed for the melee. She swept up as Dyan, scowling blackly, was fending off two females by main force.

"Enjoying yourself, my lord?"

Her cool query, ringing as it did with the assurance of old friendship, made all five women pause. Dyan grasped the moment to set aside his two tormentors. "As always, my dear." Carefully, he reset his cuffs.

The undercurrents between them ran deep; they always had. Mr. Moreton and Mr. Coldthorpe, the hopelessness of their cause evident, opted for second best. With glib and ready charm, they moved in on the disappointed ladies.

Lady Henderson had been right—all the ladies, some with last, disgruntled glances at Dyan, accompanied by Mr. Moreton and Mr. Coldthorpe, headed off to join the large group of couples gathering at the center of the room.

Sir Magnus did not follow. He studied Dyan, still lounging with no overt show of interest, then turned to Fiona, and smiled. "Well, my dear, shall we?" He lifted a suggestive brow. "Would you rather the terrace or are the bright lights more to your liking?"

Fiona raised her brows. "Neither holds any appeal."

Sir Magnus's smile deepened. "Ah, but you see, you really must choose." With a nod, he indicated Dyan stretched beside her. "I rather think it's me—or Darke." His teeth flashed; smoothly, he slid an arm about Fiona's waist. "Now tell me—which would you rather?"

Fiona froze—literally. Her spine locked; every muscle in her limbs clenched. Her gaze, cold before, turned as chill as hoarfrost. When she spoke, her words froze the very air. "You are mistaken."

Watching, even Dyan fought back a shiver. He had never seen Lady Arctic in action. Knowing Fiona as he did, he could hardly credit the transformation—but he recognized the look in Sir Magnus's eyes instantly.

Braving the ice, Sir Magnus leaned closer. "I don't believe you understand, my dear." Teeth clenched, presumably to stop them chattering, he spoke softly. "You have no choice *but* to make a choice."

Dyan didn't think—he reacted; the next instant, Fiona was safe in his lap. He met Sir Magnus's surprised gaze over Fiona's curls. "Unfortunately, Herring," he drawled, settling his arms comfortably about Fiona's waist, "it's you who have, as Miss Winton said, made a mistake." A languidly bored expression on his face—and a fell warning in his eyes—he smiled urbanely at Sir Magnus. "Miss Winton and I made our choices long before we arrived tonight."

Sir Magnus's face set. He hesitated, looking down on them. Safe in Dyan's lap, Fiona looked coldly ahead and refused to even glance at Sir Magnus, leaving him with no option but to accept defeat. With a curt nod, he turned and strode away, toward the congregation at the room's center.

The instant he moved off, Fiona drew a long breath. *"Well!"* Incensed she glared after him. "Of all the *coxcombs—*"

She'd always had a good line in tirades. Dyan listened with half an ear; she was as incensed as he could have wished.

"It's outrageous! What sort of friends are these for Henry and Harriet? Old Lady Brooke would turn in her grave! That hussy with the red hair and the blonde in the green—do you know what they asked me?"

The question was rhetorical; Fiona didn't pause for an answer but swept straight on.

Leaving Dyan to consider the sight of her, the feel of her, as she sat across his thighs, his arms loosely about her, and railed at the company. She was distracted, certainly; she was also relaxed—with no hint of the frigid rigidity that had attacked her the instant Sir Magnus had touched her.

Experimentally, Dyan tightened his arms; she shifted within them, but otherwise didn't seem to notice. He raised his brows, and pondered, then grasped her waist and lifted her, ostensibly settling her more comfortably in his lap.

She threw an absentminded frown his way, but didn't even focus on him. She didn't so much as pause for breath—her tirade continued unbroken.

As the weighted heat of her seeped through his breeches, Dyan gritted his teeth. Lady Arctic wasn't freezing him. Far from it.

He let her ramble while he toyed with that discovery. And considered how it fitted with her past. The next time she paused for breath, he asked: "Why didn't you marry?"

Startled, she looked at him.

He raised his brows, his expression as innocent as he could make it. "I was sure you'd accept Rusden."

So sure, he'd gone to India. He'd met Tony, an old and valued friend, in White's; Tony had been bubbling over with his news. He'd come from Coldstream House; he'd made a formal offer for Fiona's hand and was waiting for the summons to return. For Fiona to accept him. No one, least of all Tony, had doubted that she would. He had already succeeded to his father's estate; as a Marquess, he could offer Fiona far more than most others, and she'd made it clear she approved of his company. She'd always had a bright smile for easygoing Tony.

Which was a great deal more than she'd bestowed on Dyan.

He'd been at White's to meet with a merchant trader keen to find a partner to finance a venture in India. The trader had got more than he'd bargained for—a partner, but not a silent one.

He'd left for India on the next tide.

And had never, in his infrequent letters to his brother, asked about Fiona—never asked about the children he imagined she would have with his good friend Tony.

Fiona shrugged and looked down at her hands, loosely clasped in her lap. With Dyan so close, it was easy to re-

member those lonely days in London, when she'd finally
closed the door on her youthful hopes. Witnessing him and
his ladies, she'd been forced to concede she had no future
with him. So she'd done the right thing and considered her
earnest suitors—Anthony, Marquess of Rusden, had been
the outstanding candidate. Remembering Tony, and his easy
smile, Fiona shook her head. "He was too nice."

"Too nice?"

Too nice for her to marry—to let him give her his heart,
without having anything to give in return. That had been
the definitive moment when she'd finally accepted the truth.
She'd given her heart away long ago—it was no longer hers
to give. She hadn't been able to offer any softer emotion,
not even sincere wifely duty. Her unfailing reaction to any
man touching her, especially with amorous intent, had made
marrying a man who required an heir an impossibility. So
she'd refused Tony as gently as she could, turned her back
on marriage, and come home to be her brother's chatelaine.
Fiona shrugged. "My parents died soon after, so I had Coldstream to manage—you know Edmund couldn't do it on his
own."

His gaze locked on her face, Dyan drew a slow, even
breath. Edmund was going to have to learn.

Fiona drew breath and straightened, then leaned back
against his shoulder. After an instant's hiatus, she softened,
and sank against it. Against him. Dyan only just squashed
the impulse to close his arms fully about her. Her fingers
trailed across his arms; he forced himself to remain still.

From their long-ago past in London, he let his mind roll
forward through the years, through the inglorious, notorious
events of his life. Through all the loneliness. All sprang
from the loss of Fiona from his life. Even his characteristic
wildness was driven by a sense of incompleteness—a void
that had come into being fifteen years ago.

And now? Now he was jaded—he'd drunk of life's well

until it was dry. He no longer felt anything—unless it be a mild distaste—for the perfumed bodies so readily offered him. He could walk away from it all—from the women, the adventures—without a backward glance. Indeed, he'd already done so, which was why he was here.

Here—searching for his elusive something. Who he'd discovered in the Brookes' front hall. And who was presently warming his lap.

He focused on Fiona, although he couldn't see her face; his senses reached for her, wrapped around her. In glee, in joy, in a giddy rush of lust—and something far more powerful. His feelings for her were not jaded at all; they sprang from a different well.

She was different. She'd always occupied a special place in his life, the only woman of his generation he'd dealt with person to person, intellect to intellect, heart to heart. She'd been the only woman in his life fifteen years ago— she was still the only one.

Dyan felt her topmost curls, soft as down, against his jaw. And wondered how to tell her.

The fact that she was sitting on a man's lap, his thighs hard beneath her, his arms loosely but quite definitely about her, his shoulder and chest a pillow behind her, took some time to seep into Fiona's mind. And when it did, along with a nagging niggle that she really should stand up—Sir Magnus was long gone and there was no overt danger to excuse her seeking shelter in Dyan's arms—she promptly dismissed it. The man in question was, after all, Dyan—and she was still in Harriet's drawing room, a place she no longer considered safe without close escort.

Besides, she felt comfortable—safe, secure, and pleasantly warm.

Precisely how warm she felt, how relaxed and at ease, how much she was luxuriating in the sense of rightness that held them—that knowledge unfurled slowly, a dawning revelation.

And when it finally burst upon her that she was not rigid, not frigid, that the vise that normally locked her every muscle was simply not active, the answer seemed obvious. This was Dyan, her one and only love, although she'd never acknowledged that except in her heart. She never reacted that way when he touched her. Through the years, they'd wrestled, fought, shared saddles—she'd never frozen at his touch, as she did with every man but him.

Her senses, fully alive, it seemed, for the first time in fifteen years, registered the heat of him, the steely strength surrounding her, the subtle scent of sandalwood. Without conscious thought, she shifted, sinking deeper into his light embrace. The swell of her hip slid over his thighs; her leaping senses registered the hard ridge now pressed against her.

Her breath caught; for an instant, she thought she might freeze. Instead, a warm flush spread through her, insinuating heat just beneath her skin. A tingle of excitement skittered along awakening nerves. Her lungs abruptly resumed their proper function, a little faster than before.

Fiona blinked. And considered an unexpected prospect.

Despite the fact she'd stopped listening, she was aware that the tone of the evening's entertainment had turned overtly salacious. Bordering on the shocking. Then again, none of the guests knew who she was. And Dyan was here, holding her in his lap, holding everyone else at bay.

The unlooked-for prospect teased and tantalized. Dyan hadn't married; the county grapevine had already spread that news. Was she game to seize opportunity and, even if only for one night, take what she'd always felt should be hers?

She took precisely one minute to make up her mind.

Lips firming, Fiona sat up and twisted about to face Dyan. Halfway through the maneuver, punctuated by a *sotto voce* curse from him, a familiar shriek made her glance up.

She froze.

With shock.

"*My God*! Just *look* at Harriet!" Fiona's eyes flew wide. "Great heavens! How *can* she? And where's—"

Dyan kissed her—much as he'd kissed her fifteen years before. His lips closed over hers—more confident, perhaps, more assured; Fiona felt a funny lick of heat unfurl and flick in her belly.

Then he drew back.

"—Henry got to?" Fiona frowned at Dyan. "Why did you do that?" Had her thoughts somehow shown in her face?

His expression studiously innocent, his eyes veiled by his long lashes, Dyan answered truthfully. "To see if you tasted the same." Did sweet innocence have a taste? He rather thought it did.

Fiona frowned harder. "And did I?"

Dyan smiled. "Yes, and no. Just as fresh, but . . ." His lids lifted; he trapped her gaze with his. "Sweeter." He leaned closer, his gaze dropping to her lips. "Riper."

When his lips closed over hers again, Fiona fought down a shivery sigh. It was surprisingly easy to sink into his arms, into his kiss—then again, she'd long ago given up physically fighting Dyan. He was too strong; right now, she reveled in that strength, discovered a whole new aspect of the characteristic as he drew her deeper. Deeper into his arms, until they locked, steel bands, about her; deeper into his kiss, so that she forgot where she was, forgot who she was, forgot everything beyond the subtle pressure of his lips, the artful caress of his tongue as it swept her lower lip.

She had no idea why she parted her lips; it simply seemed the right thing to do. When he surged within, she stilled, then quivered as excitement gripped her. He slowed, but his languid possession never faltered; deep inside her, embers glowed. Caught in the game, she tentatively returned the caress—and felt, unmistakably, the rush of desire that surged through him.

Muscles that were already hard became harder; he shifted, turning and drawing her down beside him, so they were locked together in the chair, breast to chest, his hips to her thighs. Fiona wasn't about to protest. This time, she wasn't going to ask him if he loved her. This time, she wriggled her arms free, twined them about his neck and kissed him back with a fervor no wanton scullery maid could possibly command.

Dyan took all she had to give, drank it in—wallowed in the heady taste of her. Her flagrant encouragement prompted him to deepen the kiss; a minute later, he swept one hand up her side, then closed it gently over her breast. And felt the jolt of passion that rocked her, heard her soft moan. Her nipple hardened to a pebble against his palm; he felt confident in interpreting that, too, as incitement.

So he stroked, and fondled.

She responded with an ardency that nearly stole his mind.

His fingers were drifting to the closures of her gown, eager to release her abundant charms to all his senses, before he recalled precisely where they were. Although he'd swung her around so she was shielded from the room by his body—and the room was shielded from her—Harriet's drawing room was no place for a seduction.

At least, not this seduction.

Intent on removing to a place of greater privacy, he drew back.

At precisely that instant Harriet's unrestrained shriek lanced through the room.

It startled them both. He, however, recognizing the tone, knew better than to look. Unfortunately, before he could stop her, Fiona, eyes wide, peeked over his shoulder.

Her jaw dropped; her eyes grew even wider—then

wider still. Glued to the spectacle, she tried to speak—but no words came out.

Reluctantly, Dyan glanced over his shoulder; it was, if anything, even worse than he'd expected. With a not-so-muffled curse, he shoved the ottoman aside, stood, then scooped Fiona up into his arms.

She clung to him readily, twining her arms about his neck. She was still too shocked to speak, her face blank, as if she hadn't yet decided on her expression. Dyan didn't wait for her decision; he strode to the door to the terrace, mercifully ajar. Shouldering it fully open, he swung Fiona through and headed around the house to the library.

As he'd expected, that room had been prepared for the use of guests; its French doors stood wide. Fiona's breasts swelled mightily as he pushed into the room. *"Did you see . . . ?"* Her expression was horrified.

"Unfortunately, yes." Dyan's jaw set. "Just forget it." He crossed the candlelit room swiftly, pausing in the shadows of the open main door to scan the front hall. It was empty.

"Forget? How can I possibly forget seeing Harriet like that?"

An unanswerable question. "Sssh." His eyes on the drawing-room door, through which the sounds of the orgy they'd just escaped clearly permeated, Dyan strode, as silently as his bootheels allowed, across the tiled hall. To his relief, Fiona held her fire until he'd climbed the stairs.

"And where the devil was Henry?" she demanded.

Up the redhead. Thankfully, engrossed with Harriet's misdemeanors, Fiona had missed seeing that.

"How *could* they?" she asked—and looked at him as if he ought to know.

Dyan narrowed his eyes. "Strange to tell," he said, as he swung down the long corridor leading to their rooms, "there's a certain code of behavior us rakes-of-the-first-order abide by.'' The scene he'd glimpsed before they'd left the drawing room replayed in his mind; jaw firming, he shot Fiona an affronted glare. ''If you're harboring any notion that I ever behaved like that, forget it. I may have indulged in my share of wild antics, but my standards preclude public performances.''

She humphed, but seemed to accept his reassurance, just as she'd accepted him carrying her all this way. Knowing Fiona, it was safer to carry her—that way, she could only argue, not try to elude him and mount any action on her own. He couldn't see any reason to put her down. Yet.

''They're married,'' she stated as they neared their rooms. Her tone rang with matriarchal disapprobation—it would have done credit to his great-aunt Augusta. ''They've two beautiful children asleep in the nursery.'' A gesture indicated the floor above. ''How *can* they behave like that— consorting with others openly? Don't they have any pride?''

When he made no answer, she humphed, and tightened her hold about his neck. ''I can't understand it.''

Dyan decided she was right—he couldn't understand it either. But he was no longer concerned with Henry, or Harriet, or what they were getting up to in the drawing room. His predator's soul had finally sighted his ultimate target— he was about to seize it.

Fiona was the solution to all his problems—his relatives, his great-aunt Augusta—and even more importantly, the wild restlessness in his soul. She'd filled that need before—provided an anchor, a focus for his passions. She would do so again.

It was time—past time—he melted Lady Arctic.

''Hypothetically speaking,'' he said, ''if we married, would you be faithful?''

The wary frown Fiona slanted him was not what he'd expected. ''I'd consider it,'' she eventually replied.

Stopping outside her door, Dyan frowned back. "What's to consider?"

"If," Fiona said, sticking her nose in the air, "you would reciprocate in like vein."

"And if I would?"

She smiled and lightly shrugged. "What's to consider?"

Dyan grinned. Wolfishly. "So will you?"

Fiona's frown returned. "Will I what?"

"Marry me."

Her heart leapt; Fiona fought to calm it. He was teasing her—he couldn't possibly be serious. Not here. Not now. Not like this. She narrowed her eyes at him. "Dyan, I am not going to marry you just so you can get your great-aunt Augusta out of your house."

He sighed. Deeply. She felt it all the way to her toes. "All right." He juggled her in his arms. "But you will remember I asked, won't you?"

With that, he walked on—to the door next to hers. His. Fiona's frown dissolved into blank astonishment. "What are you doing?"

Dyan opened the door, walked in, then kicked it shut behind them. He looked down at her. "Seducing you."

THREE

"Dyan—" Beyond that, Fiona couldn't think what to say. Her earlier thoughts of claiming her due returned with a vengeance, but *she'd* intended to direct the enterprise, not the other way about. She'd run in his harness too often not to know how dangerous that could be. She tried a frown. "Stop funning."

His brows rose. "Funning?" He held her gaze for an instant, then hefted her in his arms and strode forward. "The fun, Lady Arctic, has not yet begun."

Lady Arctic? "What—?" Alerted by the glint in his dark eyes, Fiona looked ahead. The room was lit by a single candle, helpfully left on the beside table. Its flickering flame only partially illuminated the quilted expanse of satin coverlet spread over the massive bed. With said bed drawing rapidly nearer, she didn't look further. "Dyan—this is silly. You don't want to seduce me."

"I've wanted to seduce you for fifteen years."

Fiona stared at him. "Rubbish! You went to India, remember?"

Fleetingly, his eyes met hers. "I left on the day your engagement to Tony was supposed to be announced."

Fiona blinked. "You left . . ." She studied the harsh, tanned planes of his face. "But I didn't accept Tony."

Dyan stopped by the side of the bed. His heavy lids lifted; the expression in his eyes stole her breath. "When I think of the tortures I endured, imagining you in his arms, in his bed . . . swollen with his child."

The planes of his face shifted as he grimaced. "I should have known better."

He tossed her on the bed.

Fiona shrieked. Dyan followed her down, landing half beside her, half over her. Fiona struggled, totally ineffectually, to hold him back. He ignored her efforts; one hard thigh trapped hers. Deliberately, he leaned into her, his weight pressing her into the bed, anchoring her beneath him. He didn't bother with her hands but instead framed her face.

And kissed her.

No gently savoring kiss, but a commanding, demanding incitement—a ravishing challenge—tempting in the fire it offered, tantalizing in its sensual promise. His lips were hard, hungry, ruthlessly insistent. It took no more than two heartbeats for Fiona to react. Winding her arms about his neck, she kissed him back.

Fervently. With all the long-denied ardor in her soul.

She wanted him—she could hardly miss the fact that he wanted her. For now—for tonight—that was enough. He'd spoken already of marriage; she wasn't so innocent she didn't know they hadn't reached the end of that discussion. But such matters—and all others—could be left until the morrow.

Tonight she would be what she'd always longed to be. His.

Dyan didn't wait for any further encouragement. Drawing his hands from her face, he deepened the kiss, locking her lips apart so he could plunder unrestricted. His weight held her immobile; he had no intention of doing the gentlemanly thing and easing back. Instead, he set his hands skimming over the smooth skin of her upper arms to her delicately molded shoulders, partially covered by the tiny silk sleeves of her dress. The interference registered, but he wasn't yet ready to deal with that; his first priority was to fully appreciate the sensation of her silk-clad body, all soft womanly curves, trapped and yielding beneath him.

Sensual gratification was a wondrous thing.

He let his mind absorb the impact of her lush breasts, soft stomach, rounded hips, and delightfully firm thighs, as well as the length of her long, slender legs. Only then did he set his hands moving again, deliberately tracing those selfsame curves.

Her breasts filled his hands—and more. Their softness firmed at his touch. He kneaded, then went searching, capturing each nipple, rolling them to tight, aching buds.

Her breath hitched; she pressed her head back into the bed, breaking their kiss. Dyan shifted his attention to the long curve of her throat, exposed like an offering. Her breathing stuttered as his roving tongue found one pounding pulsepoint; he laved it, then sucked lightly and felt her melt—just slightly—beneath him.

Inwardly, he grinned devilishly. She was going to melt a great deal more. He released her breasts and let his hands quest further, fingers widespread, tracing her ribs, then the sides of her waist, his thumbs following her midline. When his thumbs reached her navel, she arched lightly beneath him, her hips lifting wantonly against him.

Dyan grinned in earnest; he let his lips drift lower, to pay homage to the ripe swell of her breasts exposed above her low neckline. Simultaneously, he slid both hands lower—and lower—tracing her body all the way to her knees. Then he reversed direction.

His thumbs came to rest in the hollow between her thighs; he rotated them, one just above the other.

Fiona's startled gasp filled the room. Driven by the sound, Dyan caught the fine silk of her neckline with his

teeth and tugged it down; one tightly furled nipple slipped
free of the confining bodice. He fell on it—hotly—swirling
his tongue about the ruched peak, then drawing it into his
mouth to taste, to suckle, to torment.

The muted scream Fiona gave was music to his ears.
Her fingers, on his shoulders, flexed, then sank deep. She
arched, offering herself to him in flagrant invitation.

Dyan tormented her some more.

Long before he dragged the silk from her other breast,
and tortured that nipple as he had its mate, Fiona was convinced she would soon lose her mind. Surely women didn't
normally have to withstand this . . . this heated torture—not
every time they mated. How could they?

Her wits were whirling, her mind awash with sensations: from the hardness of his hands locked about the tops
of her thighs, to the heavy weight of him—so peculiarly
welcome—to the heat that welled within her, washing
through her, in response to the heat of his lips, his mouth,
his tongue. He was hot, too—she could feel the heat of him
wherever they touched. His clothes muted the sensation; if
they were removed, his skin would scald her.

The thought made her shiver; his rotating thumbs
pressed deeper and she shuddered, then gasped. Of its own
volition, her body arched, offering. One thumb slid still
deeper and pressed, then caressed—her breathing stopped,
then started on a fractured, shuddering, almost silent moan.

His hands left her, his weight anchoring her completely
once more as he lifted his head and recaptured her lips.

His fingers busy with the closures of her gown, Dyan
spared a moment to consider the next phase. Still kissing
her, he opened his eyes and checked the light—it wasn't
good. When he bared her, he wanted to see her clearly. Half
shadows would not suffice. Evocatively plundering her soft
mouth, tempting her to match him and meet him, he skated

through his recent memories; there were candlesticks on the mantelpiece.

Accepting the inevitable—given he was not about to accept anything less than the ultimate experience tonight—he drew back from their kiss.

He looked down at her—she was panting only slightly. When he saw her eyes gleam beneath her lashes, he trapped her gaze in his. "I'm going to get up for a moment. *Don't move.*"

Enforcing his edict with a warning look, he levered away from her, then sat up and got to his feet.

There was another single candlestick and a three-armed candelabra on the mantelpiece. Dyan lit the candles, then quickly positioned furniture about the bed. One single candle on either side and the candelabra at the end threw an acceptable amount of light upon the coverlet. Upon Fiona, still lying as he'd left her, a dazed expression in her hazel eyes, her lips swollen from his kisses.

The sight sent a surge of sheer lust through him; Dyan shackled it, trapped it—he'd let it loose later. First, he was going to sate his senses—all his senses—in enjoyment, in the sheer pleasure of enjoying her.

Shrugging off his coat, he flung it on a chair and returned to the bed.

Sitting on its edge, he removed his boots and stripped off his stockings. Turning his head, he caught Fiona frowning at the candelabra. Inwardly grinning, he clambered back on the bed.

As he settled beside her, one hand going to her waist, then sliding around to the laces along her side, Fiona transferred her frown to him. "Is this to be some kind of exhibition?"

Dyan toyed with various replies while his fingers loosened her laces; he finally settled for: "More like a demonstration." Flicking the last knot undone, he trapped her gaze. "Consider it a learning experience."

He was going to learn her—all there was to know of her. Tonight he'd know her on every possible plane.

Fiona studied the dark blue of his eyes, and could see nothing beyond brutal candor. He might be teasing her, just a little, but . . . Then he shifted, his weight trapping her again, his hands rising to tug the tiny puffed sleeves of her gown down—and she saw the reason for the light. "Dyan, I don't think the candles are such a good idea."

She tried to catch the sleeves, but her dress, which she'd surreptitiously hiked back up, was steadily moving down.

"First lesson," Dyan said, his gaze fastening on her freed breasts, concealed only by her tissue-thin chemise. "You don't think. That's my role—you stick to yours and we'll get on just fine."

The gravelly note in his voice, the heat in his eyes, roaming her barely veiled body as he drew her gown down, set desire coiling insidiously through Fiona. She caught her breath—and wasn't at all sure she'd done the right thing in not resisting. She'd remained on the bed because she hadn't believed her legs would support her, because she'd known Dyan's reflexes were lightning fast and he would catch her long before she reached the door. And because she'd wanted, beyond anything else, to be his tonight.

She suddenly realized she didn't have any real idea of what being his entailed. Not to him. "Ah—" She had to moisten her lips before she could ask, "My role—what's that?"

The answer came back so quickly her head whirled. "To *feel*." The deep purr of his voice slid under her skin and vibrated through her bones. Drawing her gown free of her legs, he tossed it aside and turned to her, his hands sliding up her body, his touch laden with possessiveness, his eyes no less so. He cupped her breasts; Fiona lost her breath.

"To lose every inhibition you ever had."

His eyes glinted darkly as he surveyed what he held, then they flicked up to hers. Deliberately, holding her gaze, he lowered his head—and licked; first one aching nipple, then the other; long, slow licks that dampened the thin silk and left it clinging. He observed the effect with transparent satisfaction.

Then, lowering his long body to hers, he kissed her deeply, until her head spun and her senses whirled. He ended the kiss and waited, his lips a mere whisker from hers, his breath another form of caress. When Fiona caught up with reality, his hands had left her breasts to slide beneath her, cupping her bottom. As she made that discovery, he gripped her and lifted her, tilting her into intimate contact with the rigid length of his staff.

Deliberately, he rocked against her, the heavy fullness riding between her thighs, over her mound and across her taut belly.

"To do everything I ask," he breathed against her parted lips. "To be *everything* to me."

Fiona hauled in a desperate breath. "Dyan—"

"Stop arguing."

She had to, because he was kissing her. Quite when it was she gave up all resistance, Fiona couldn't have said— the whirling, swirling maelstrom Dyan called forth was beyond her strength to fight. It came from him—it also came from her. A deep, compelling desire to be one, to shed the outer, peripheral trappings that society placed between them—not just their clothes, but their inhibitions as well— to lose themselves in the vortex, each holding the other fast, relying on the other to give all that they needed, to assuage the driving, inchoate desire—the desire to know and be known.

As simple as that, and even more powerful.

When Dyan drew her chemise from her, Fiona was

ready to let it go. She was a-simmer, her skin heated and skittering, aching for his touch. When it came, bare hand to bare skin, she gasped and held him closer. Their lips met as his hands roamed—and he learned all he would.

Naked on the satin coverlet, her hair loose, a silk pillow about her head, she wantonly let him touch her—as he would, where he would. She parted her thighs and let him stroke her, probe her, tease her. Until her body ached with urgent longing, a mass of overheated skin and straining, overstretched nerves—of slick heat fueled by some inner furnace his relentless caresses ignited. And when his knowing fingers called the constellations crashing down upon her, leaving her waltzing with the stars, her body arched, bowed, and ached—for him.

He left her only briefly; when he returned, she'd regained enough wit to register his nakedness. Enthralled, she would have stopped him, held him back so she could admire the lean length of him, the heavy muscles banding his chest, the taut, ridged abdomen, narrow hips, and long, strong legs. And the flagrant maleness gilded in the candles' golden light—fiercely strong, rampantly male, urgently possessive.

She would have taken time to absorb it all, but he was in no mood to dally. His face hard, set, the dark planes etched with desire, he brushed her questing hands aside and came to her, lowering his body directly upon hers, nudging her parted thighs wider so his hips settled between. As she slid her arms about him, reaching as far as she could to hold him close, Fiona understood. She tipped her head back and he took her lips, her mouth, instantly; he was ravenous.

He felt as hot as the sun, and as loaded with primal energy, his every muscle heavy with it, sinews taut and tight.

Pressing beneath her, his hands slid down the long planes of her back, down over her hips, then fastened, his grip firm and strong, fingers sinking into the softness of her bottom.

Again, he lifted her, tilted her. This time when he rocked, he pressed into her.

Fiona tried to gasp but couldn't; as she felt the thick, steely strength of him invade her, stretch her, she tried to pull back from their kiss.

Dyan wouldn't let her. He held her trapped with his kiss, held her immobile with his hands—and relentlessly, inch by steady inch, claimed her.

Fiona shuddered, and gave herself to him—opened her arms and held him tight, opened her body and let him come in, opened her heart and let him take possession of what had, for so long, been his.

She was so hot, so slick, so *tight*—Dyan had to devote every last ounce of his considerable control to holding himself back. He felt the resistance of her maidenhead; a second later, it vanished. She remained so softly pliant beneath him, so welcoming, he wasn't sure she'd even felt it. He surged deeper—and felt her instinctively rise. He pushed deeper still, then slowly withdrew, then returned, more strongly, more forcefully. Filling her.

She took him—took him in, scalding him with her wet heat, with the inner furnace of her desire. Beneath him, she rose to each thrust, her breasts caressing his chest, her thighs cradling his hips, her long legs tangling with his. He set a slow rhythm—he saw no need to rush; her body was a heaven he wanted to savor for all time. He used his tongue to teach her the beat; once she caught it, he drew back from their kiss and, straightening his arms, held himself over her.

So he could see her—see her in all her glory, totally, wantonly his. See her breasts rock with his thrusts, the sheening ivory skin delicately flushed, rose-red nipples engorged, erect. See her hands, clutching spasmodically, fingers sinking into his forearms as he plunged deeper and pushed her higher. See, looking down, the gentle swell of her belly, taut with desire as he filled her deeply, completely. See the fine thatch of bronzy hair that veiled her soft center merge with his darker curls.

See the ridged length of him, slick and gleaming with her wetness, thick and heavy and hard as oak, slide, again and again, into the hot heaven that was her.

And, at the last, see the mindless wonder infuse her face as her body clenched around him and ecstasy took her.

The gentle ripples of her climax gradually died; her breathing slowed. Her features relaxed; her hands fell from his arms as she drifted into paradise.

Dyan looked his fill, then closed his eyes, let his head fall back, and, with three deep thrusts and a long, shuddering sigh, joined her.

She was his.

She woke to the sensation of the sheet sliding away, to the cool caress of night air on recently flushed skin. Lifting her weighted lids was an effort; the candles had guttered—the room was in darkness, except for the wide swath of moonlight lancing in through the uncurtained window. It fell across the bottom half of the bed, illuminating the rumpled sheets, sheening the folds of the crumpled satin coverlet, and revealing two pairs of legs.

Hers, skin white and pearlescent in the silvery glow; and his, darker, rougher, long muscles etched in shadow. As she watched, his legs shifted, sliding over hers.

In the same instant, the sheet whisked away completely, slithering over the side of the bed. Hard hands replaced it—hot, urgent, and demanding—roving her skin, every curve of her body, possessively claiming, stroking, stoking her furnace again.

He shifted her onto her back and surged over her, covering her; his body, hard, rigid, taut with sexual promise, settled heavily on hers. His lips captured hers in the same moment; the embers of their earlier passion flared, then caught flame.

She felt the fire rise, felt the conflagration take her, cindering the last remnants of inhibition, leaving her heated and panting—wantonly, recklessly his. As his lips left hers, streaking fire down her throat before moving on to her naked breasts, to her nipples tight with yearning, she gasped—the only thought her reeling mind could grasp. "Again?"

"And again." He took one aching nipple deep into his mouth; when he released it, it ached even more. "You've melted for me—now I want to see you *burn*."

She struggled to blink, struggled to catch his eyes—but he wasn't interested in conversation. He surged over her again, taking her lips, her mouth, devouring greedily. In the same movement, he took her, pressing into her again, relentlessly surging inward until he filled her.

Until she thought she would fracture from the sheer joy of feeling him a part of her. She tilted her hips and took him in; he pressed deep, then withdrew, and returned. This time, he didn't lift from her, but remained, moving heavily, erotically, upon her. The friction, the seductive rasp of his hard, ridged, hair-dusted body over her soft flesh, quickly set her afire. She wrapped her arms about him, locking his hard frame to her; she squirmed beneath him, seeking to assuage the heat spreading beneath her skin, flowing through her veins, flooding her belly, flaming where they joined.

For one crazed moment, she thought she'd never get enough of him. Then she felt the tingling, tightening sensation—the coalescing of her heat—the first heralds of that volcanic sensation that had rocked her twice before. She felt her body tighten, straining to capture his; she gave herself up to the deep rhythmic rocking, the steady, relentless possession.

His. Only his. His and no other's.

The refrain filled her—her mind, her heart, her soul. He impressed it upon her with every slow, deliberate, harnessed thrust, with every urgently ravenous kiss. Their lips melded, parted, and melded again. And the fever built.

Panting, her mind awash with glorious anticipation, her body striving for that magnificent surcease, she reached for it—

Abruptly, he drew back. Lifting from her, he sat back on his ankles, hands on his thighs. Stunned, she stared at him. He was breathing hard, his chest rising and falling dramatically, his eyes dark pools glinting in the faint light. The moonlight fell across him; he was flagrantly aroused—as aroused as she.

She blinked—he reached out and caught her hands.

"Come." He hauled her up. "Like this."

He dragged her to her knees, then positioned her, kneeling in the moonlight facing the end of the bed. The bed end was a high one, carved oak, its knurled top not quite level with her waist.

"Hold the bed end."

Dazed, heated, aroused to her toes, she obeyed; his hands, locked about her hips, prevented her from shifting her knees—to grasp the bed end, she had to lean forward.

Immediately her fingers clamped around the cool wood, she felt him behind her.

The next second he was inside her.

She gasped; he withdrew and slowly, deliberately, speared her again.

She shuddered and looked down; bracing her arms against the driving thrusts, she struggled to think—but her mind, her senses, refused to focus on anything beyond his relentless possession. He held her hips—his grip like a vise—and repeatedly penetrated her, each thrust deliberate, probing, complete.

Her senses locked on the continual invasion, on the

hard, hot strength that claimed her again and again. She gave up all effort to think and instead surrendered—to the compulsion to let herself enjoy this intimate pleasure and the deep driving joy of feeling him sink into her.

She was open to him, flagrantly, wantonly, without any pretense of restraint. Her breaths coming in panting gasps, she heard again the refrain, louder now, each syllable emphasized by the leashed force behind every steely invasion.

His. Only his. His and no other's.

She had known that all her life; he was demonstrating it now, in a way she would never forget.

As if sensing her acceptance, he shifted slightly, and released her hips. The steady, regular penetration continued, but his hands now roamed, at first lightly, tracing the curves of her bottom and hips, the sensitive sides of her torso, the bountiful fullness of her breasts, the quivering tautness of her belly. Then his touch turned hot, and more sensual—his hands sculpted, then possessed, even as he continued to fill her.

Increasingly intimately, he caressed, fondled, and probed; she gasped and threw back her head, hands gripping the bed end tightly.

Behind her, he shifted, then she felt his chest against her back, his thighs and knees more definitely against hers. He drew her up and back slightly, and closed his hands over her breasts, greedily filling his palms, fingers kneading.

His hips still thrust against her bottom as he held her, trapped, before him.

"Open your eyes." His voice, so low and gravelly she could hardly make out the words, grated beside her ear. "Look across the room."

She did—and saw them reflected in the large mirror on the dresser. The sight stole the last of her breath.

Her body was all shimmering ivory, her hair a tousled swatch of pale silk hanging over one shoulder. Her head was high, thrown slightly back, her lids heavy, her lips parted. Her breasts, swollen and aching, sumptuously filled his hands. Her thighs were widespread, knees sinking into the bed. Her hips rocked suggestively, then rotated, slowly, heavily, as, buried inside her, he ground his hips against her.

Then he withdrew and resumed his steady rhythm. He was a dark presence behind her, his tanned hands and fingers clearly visible as they kneaded her breasts. Dark head bent, he concentrated on each thrust, each deep penetration; what she could see of his face was all hard angles, harsh planes etched with passion. He didn't look up.

The sight that held him so enthralled slowly filled her mind—of his staff, hard and hot, passing between her thighs, between the twin hemispheres of her bottom, claiming her. Possessing her.

His. Only his. His and no other's.

He was her lover, her rightful lord, the phantom of her secret dreams—dreams she had not allowed her waking self to know.

He filled her—over and over—and she was his. Completely. Wantonly. Irrevocably his.

The refrain swelled and filled her, even as he did. Caught in the relentless repetition, she gasped and closed her eyes.

And felt the vortex grab her.

It lifted her; she felt her body tense and tighten, closing intimately about his.

With his next thrust, he pressed deep, holding her to him, then withdrew from her.

Her eyes flew wide—but before she could speak, a fat pillow appeared before her. Followed by another. And another.

He flipped her around and tumbled her onto them, then, scooping her to him, drew her and the pillows up the bed, away from its end. Releasing her, leaving her heated, frantic, and thoroughly dazed on her back in the middle of the bed, he rearranged the pillows, piling them beneath her hips.

"The bed end—hold onto the railings."

She blinked and looked up and back at the wooden fretwork at the end of the bed. Her hands were reaching, slim fingers sliding between the slats in the woodwork and gripping tight, before the thought had formed in her mind. As her hands fisted about the cool wood, she felt his hands on her thighs, felt him grip them and spread them wide.

With a gasp, she looked back and saw him—on his knees between her thighs, hard hands anchoring her hips—slide into her. He surged in, and in, until he was embedded in her softness. Then he leaned forward, into her. She gasped and arched, feeling him deep within her. She felt him groan, the sound harsh and deep.

"Oh, yes—there's more."

The pillows held her hips high against him; reaching back, he lifted her legs and wound them about his waist. Then, planting his hands flat on the bed, one beside each of her shoulders, he braced his arms and, still leaning heavily into her, started to move.

She was frantic from the first, already tight and tense—each deep, impaling stroke drove her relentlessly on. On into a land of selfless passion, where nothing existed beyond the wild heat that gripped them, the wild force that filled them, where their writhing, panting bodies became mere vessels for their greedy senses.

A wild cry escaped her; she lifted against him, head back, fingers tight about the wooden rails. He lowered his head and laved her breasts, his tongue a burning brand. Then he trapped one nipple and suckled—fire arced through her; she cried again and tried to draw back, away from the forcefully intimate probing of his body sunk so deeply into hers.

Before she moved an inch, he caught her, coming down

on his elbows to grasp her shoulders and anchor her beneath him. The sudden movement brought his weight more fully upon her, forcing him even more deeply into her.

His next compelling thrust drove the air from her lungs.

She gasped desperately, and felt him surge powerfully again. Her eyes flickered open; his heavy lids lifted and he met her gaze. Of their own volition, she felt their bodies ease, then forcefully fuse; lost in his midnight gaze, she felt the flames rise.

"Now burn," he said. "And take me with you."

He surged again; she closed her eyes and heard the flames roar.

She let go and let them take her, and him, burning away all the past, all the barriers, all their pride, their vulnerabilities—everything that had ever stood between them. Burnt, too, were the wild, stubborn children they'd once been; the trappings of their youthful love caught fire and exploded, then rained down, ashes on the forest floor.

Leaving only their naked selves, locked intimately together in the moonlight, clasping each other as the flames roared on.

Their lips met, parched, dry, and hungry; they drank from each other and clung closer still.

And then it was upon them, a bright pinnacle of ecstasy that flared like the sun, then fractured, hurling them into a heated darkness where the only sound was that of two thundering hearts.

She screamed, a gasping, keening cry, as the moment shattered about them; she felt him gather her closer still, felt the final powerful fusion, the ultimate joining of his life and hers.

And then it was past. The moment slowly died, the ecstasy faded, yet neither moved. They lay locked together; the moon shone softly upon them, a gentle benediction.

Nothing any longer lay between them; there was nothing to interfere with the selfless, compulsive communion of their bodies, and their souls.

She heard the refrain as she slid into sleep, his breath a gentle caress against her throat.

His. Only his. His and no other's.

Dyan awoke to find the muted light of dawn sliding into the room. In his arms, Fiona slept, her back curved against his side. He'd fallen asleep with the sound of her ecstasy ringing in his ears.

The memory warmed him.

He turned on his side and gathered her close, letting her silken warmth fill his senses. The result was inevitable; he was long beyond fighting it. He wanted her, needed her—and the ache was too new, too fresh, too excruciatingly sensitive to let it go unassuaged. And after last night, when her maturity had entirely overwhelmed her innocence, he felt no compunction in gently easing her upper thigh high, and sliding his fingers into her hot softness.

He had loved her well, stretched her well, yet she was still very tight. He found the bud of her desire and stroked, caressed. Soon she was slick and swollen, his fingers sliding easily into her soft channel.

It was the work of a moment to withdraw his fingers and, easing over her, replace them with his throbbing staff. Gently, very gently, he eased himself into her.

All abandoned innocence, she was fully open to him; luscious and hot, her soft flesh closed about him. Dyan closed his eyes tight and held back a groan as he sank deeper into her heat.

And felt her awaken, felt that single moment of shock—then she melted about him.

Fiona awoke to the indescribable sensation of being intimately invaded—of feeling Dyan's body, hard and strong, surround her—of feeling him, hard and strong, fill her completely. She felt every inch of his slow slide, of the steady, relentless invasion.

And felt within her a glorious well of feeling rise up and swamp her. She closed her eyes, as if to hold it in, and felt his arms close about her. Felt his chest against her back, felt his jaw brush her shoulder.

"All right?"

She smiled and nodded. And felt his spine flex, felt him move within her.

She said nothing more, did nothing more, but simply lay there—his—and let him love her. Let him fondle her breasts, each caress gentle, long-drawn, heavy with wondrous feeling. Let him fill her gently, riding slow and easy, with no hint of the mindless urgency that had overtaken them in the night.

After last night, she had no doubt that her body would satisfy him. When, at the last, he'd collapsed in her arms, he'd been beyond words, thought, or deed. He'd been sated so deeply he'd not moved for ages; she'd felt the difference in his muscles—the complete loss of tension.

The same tension that was slowly coiling within him now; he pressed closer, tightening his arms around her, splaying one hand across her belly, under the sheet. Holding her steady as he moved more forcefully, but still with the same lazy rhythm.

His jaw rasped her shoulder; his breath tickled her ear. "The others—the wanton scullery maids?"

"Hmm?" Eyes closed, Fiona smiled, concentrating more on his movements than his words.

"They were just practice—all of them."

Her smile deepened. "Practice?"

"Practice," he averred, and rocked deep. "For this."

"Ah." Eyes still closed, Fiona felt the shudder that passed through him. She concentrated on the feel of him, slickly sliding within her.

"Practice for *you*." He nipped her ear, as if aware she wasn't listening. Fiona giggled, and tightened about him. And heard the hiss of his indrawn breath.

He gripped her more tightly. "No man likes to come to his love inexperienced, unprepared." He shifted within her, then sank deep. "I wanted to be able to give you . . . *this*."

This was a slow, rolling climax that washed over her like gentle sunshine, a flush of heat that spread from where they joined through every vein, every limb—leaving her weighted with the most delicious languor, her senses spinning with delirious joy, and her heart filled with a heady rush of emotion.

Tears sprang to her eyes as the sensations peaked. She felt Dyan stiffen behind her, then felt the warmth as he flooded her.

Fiona closed her eyes; her smile slowly deepened. Regardless of what he thought, Dyan had given her much more than *this*.

FOUR

F ive minutes later, or so it seemed, Dyan hauled her from the bed.

"Come on." He pulled her up to sit on the bed's edge, then bullied her into her chemise.

Yawning, Fiona frowned. "I'm sleepy."

"You can sleep later—at home."

"Home?" She yawned again. Her bag had miraculously appeared in the room; Dyan, fully dressed, was rummaging in it.

He turned, with her carriage dress in his hands. "Here—put this on." He pulled it over her head.

Emerging somewhat irritated, Fiona, left with little choice, pushed her arms through the sleeves. "What's the time?" she grumbled.

"Late enough."

Fastening the dress, Fiona looked up, and saw Dyan cram her turquoise silk evening gown into the bag. "Dyan! You'll crush it!"

She started forward; scowling, he pushed her back. "Never mind about your gown—we've got to get moving. Where are your stockings?"

They found them under the bed. Still dazed, half-asleep, Fiona pulled them on. "But what—?"

"Here." Dyan bent and slipped her shoes on. Then he stood and scanned the room. "That's it. Let's go."

He hefted her bag, grabbed her hand and towed her to the door.

"Where are we—"

"*Sssh!*" Opening the door, he glanced out, then hauled her through.

Swiftly, he strode along the corridor. Muttering direfully under her breath, Fiona hurried beside him, too occupied with making sure she didn't stumble to utter any further protest.

They tiptoed down the stairs. Reaching the bottom, Dyan paused to peer through the open drawing-room door; behind him, perched on the last step, Fiona whispered in his ear, "Why are we acting like a pair of thieves?"

He turned his head and glowered at her—and didn't answer. Instead, with long, swift strides, he towed her across the front hall, down the side corridor and into the garden room. A male guest, collapsed in a state of considerable disarray in a garden chair, snored noisily; Dyan tugged Fiona past, shielding her from the sight.

The next instant, they were out of the house and striding for the stables. Long inured to Dyan's method of covering ground—and his habit of hauling her along with him—Fiona valiantly scurried to keep up. If she didn't, he'd been known to toss her over his shoulder; she didn't think India had changed him all that much.

As they rounded the corner of the house, she caught a glimpse of his face—grimly set. "Do you always wake up in such a delightful mood?"

The glance he sent her was fathomless. "Only after orgies."

"Oh." Fiona glanced back at the house. "Was that what that was?"

"Take my word for it."

Dyan's bootheels rang on the stable cobbles. Sleepy grooms blinked wearily; Dyan waved them away. "I'll get my own horse."

The grooms turned back to their duties, glad to be spared, but remained too close for Fiona to question Dyan further.

Left holding the head of a magnificent gray hunter while Dyan saddled the beast, Fiona gradually woke up, gradually recalled all that had taken place in the night. Grateful for the crisp morning air, and its cooling effect on her red cheeks, she gradually remembered all that had passed between them—and all that had not.

By then, Dyan had the saddle on, and had tied her bag behind it. He mounted, then, urging the gray forward, managing the beast with his knees, reached down and plucked her from the cobbles. The next instant, she was crammed between him and the pommel.

She immediately wriggled; he stiffened and hissed, "Sit still, dammit!"

"I used to fit," Fiona grumbled, still wriggling.

Cursing fluently, Dyan lifted her, and resettled her with one knee about the pommel. "That was years ago—there's rather more of you now."

Fiona sniffed; there was rather more of him, too. The most interesting part was pressing into the small of her back. Ignoring it, she clung to the arm that wrapped about her waist. He clicked the reins and the gray clattered out of the stable yard. Dyan turned him toward the forest, and the track that led to her home.

Yawning again, Fiona sank back against him. "Was it really necessary to sneak out like that?"

"What did you plan to do—stay for breakfast?"

Fiona raised her brows. "Do they serve breakfast after orgies?"

Dyan humphed and didn't answer.

Comfortable enough, and secretly glad to be safely on her way home, Fiona relaxed in his arms, smiling softly as the familiar scenery slipped by. She felt a twinge or three, but that was a small price to pay for the glorious sensation of fulfilment suffusing her. She was going to enjoy reveling in it, studying it from all angles—and managing what came next.

She was deep in plans when the roof of Coldstream House rose through the trees. She sighed, and straightened. "You can drop me off by the shrubbery—I'll walk in from there."

She felt Dyan's glance, then he looked ahead again. "I'm coming in."

Fiona blinked, then she turned and looked into his face. "Why?"

His glance was so brief she couldn't read it. "I want to talk to Edmund, of course."

"Of *course*?" A dreadful, not-at-all appealing suspicion unfurled in Fiona's mind. "Which course is that?"

"The course I intend to follow—to wit, to ask for your hand."

"My hand?"

"In marriage."

"Marriage?"

"I did ask, remember?"

"But I didn't agree!" Fiona glared at him. She could see his direction now—it didn't fit with her plans.

Turning into the drive, Dyan glanced down at her, the set of his jaw all too familiar. "As far as I'm concerned," he growled, "you agreed—a *number* of times—last night."

"Rubbish!" Fiona ignored her blush—this was definitely no time for maidenly modesty. "You seduced me!"

"And you allowed yourself to be seduced. *Very* enthusiastically."

Glancing ahead, at the stables drawing rapidly nearer,

Fiona grimaced. "But that was just . . ." She gestured vaguely. "*That*! It wasn't about marriage."

"It was as far as I'm concerned—and I suspect Edmund will agree."

Fiona set her jaw. "He won't be up."

"He's always up at cockcrow. Buried in a book, maybe, but he'll see me."

Fiona drew in a deep, very determined, breath. "I am *not* marrying you." Not yet. Not until he'd answered the question she'd asked fifteen years ago. Fifteen years was a *hell* of a long time to wait for an answer; she'd be damned if she let him wriggle out of giving her that answer now.

And, oh, she knew him well. If she gave any sign of agreement, of being ready to countenance any announcement of their betrothal *before* she'd convinced him to say the words, she'd never hear them! Given last night, this was her last chance; avoiding him physically would be impossible—the only thing she had left to bargain with was her agreement to their marriage.

The stable arch loomed before them; Dyan slowed the gray to a walk. "Fiona, if I ask, and Edmund gives his blessing, what are you going to do? Refuse?"

"*Yes!*" She was quite definite about that.

Dyan snorted derisively. "Of all the *buffleheaded* females!"

"I am *not* buffleheaded!" Fiona swung to face him as they entered the stable yard. "It's *you* who can't think straight!"

His face set, Dyan looked past her, at the groom who came running. "Where's his lordship?"

"He's unavailable!" Fiona informed him.

Dyan kept his gaze on the groom. "In the library?"

Fiona swung about and, ominously narrow-eyed, stared at the groom, who cravenly kept his gaze fixed on Dyan's face—and nodded.

Damn, damn, *damn*! Inwardly seething, Fiona swallowed the vitriolic words that burnt her tongue—she might swear at Dyan, but she would not curse before her brother's servants.

She had to wait while Dyan dismounted. She tried not to notice the fluid grace, so redolent of harnessed masculine power, with which he accomplished that deed, tried not to notice how easily he lifted her—no mere lightweight—from the saddle. Lips shut, she allowed him to tow her, her hand clasped firmly in his, out of the stables.

Just like him to race ahead, to recklessly cram his fences. But she'd hauled on his reins before; she was determined to do so again. To hold him back, until they got things straight—clearly stated—between them.

There was no way she'd wait another fifteen years to hear what she wanted—*needed*—to hear.

She had to wait until they gained the relative privacy of the gravelled walk up to the house before she could reassert her intransigence.

"Why all this rush over marrying me?" She darted a glance at his set face, and tried to slow her steps. "You've waited fifteen years and now you can't wait another day?"

His grip on her hand tightened warningly; if anything, he strode faster. "One, I seduced you." He flicked a measuring, too-arrogant-by-half glance at her face. "Quite thoroughly, if I do say so myself."

He looked ahead, neatly avoiding her dagger glance. "Two, you need someone to ride rein on you—Edmund demonstrably can't. Three, my great-aunt Augusta will approve of you and consequently take herself, and all the rest of the family, off home. And four—" He drew her relentlessly up the terrace steps. "I've grown exceedingly tired of my cold ducal bed—you can come and warm it. Particularly as the exercise appears to meet with your approval and you don't seem to have anything better to do with your life.''

As a proposal, it lacked a certain something. From Fiona's point of view, it lacked a great deal. Jaw set, teeth clenched, she set about demolishing it. ''For your information, *Your Grace*,'' she uttered the title with relish—she didn't even need to look to know it brought a scowl to his face. ''At my age, I do not consider a quick tumble—even three long tumbles—to be sufficient reason to tie myself up in matrimony.''

''More fool you,'' Dyan growled, and dragged her through the open morning-room French doors. ''I know you've always been stubborn, but don't you think this is overdoing it—even for you?''

''Furthermore,'' Fiona said, rolling over his interruption with positively awe-inspiring dignity, ''as I have survived the past fifteen years quite comfortably without anyone riding rein on me, I can't see that your assistance in that sphere is of any particular advantage.''

''Yes—but has anyone else been comfortable? What glib lie did you feed Edmund for your absence last night? Do you imagine he believed it?''

It was an effort not to answer that, but Fiona ignored her blush, stuck her nose in the air and forged on: ''And I do not at all see that the notion of saving you from your just deserts—to wit the attention of your great-aunt Augusta—should in any way influence me in such an important decision.''

''That's because you haven't recently met her.'' Dyan ruthlessly towed her down the corridor to the library. ''When I tell her I want to marry you, she'll be over here in a flash—you'll marry me quick enough to be rid of my great-aunt Augusta.''

Fiona's eyes kindled at the thinly veiled threat. ''And as for your last inducement to marriage, while last night was enjoyable enough in its way, I do not feel any overpowering urge to repeat the exercise anytime soon.''

To her surprise, Dyan halted; the closed door to the library was two steps away. Slightly behind him, Fiona stepped up, intending to peer into his face. He turned in the same instant.

And the wall was at her back—and his lips were on hers.

One hand framing her jaw, holding her trapped, he voraciously plundered her mouth. He leaned into her, letting her feel his muscled weight, letting her sense her vulnerability, her helplessness. Letting her sense the instant desire that raged through him—and her.

His chest crushed her breasts—they promptly swelled and ached. She felt her body soften, felt her limbs weaken, felt all resistance melt away. Felt his other hand press between their bodies, sliding down to evocatively cup her, felt his hard fingers search, and find her. Felt the skittering thrill that raced through her as he stroked, even though his touch was muted by her skirt.

And felt, within seconds, the slick wetness he drew forth. For one aching instant, he pressed more firmly against her; his tongue probed the wet softness of her mouth with a now familiar, deliciously deliberate rhythm while through her skirts, he stroked the wet softness between her thighs, probing her to the same evocative beat.

Then he drew back from the kiss.

Dyan continued to stroke her, feeling her heat scorch through the cambric, sinking one fingertip between the luscious, slippery folds. He looked down at her face and waited for her lids to rise. When they did, revealing her eyes, all stunned hazel and gold, he cursed softly; driven, he took her mouth in a last, ravenous kiss—then drew back. ''You'll melt for me, Lady Arctic—anytime, anywhere. Believe it.'' He growled the words against her lips—then forced himself to release her. He took a step back, supporting her against the wall. The instant he judged her legs capable of holding her upright, he caught one of her hands; flinging the library door wide, he tugged her over the threshold.

The room was a large one, rolling away down the wing. Edmund's desk stood at this end, perpendicular to the door. A massive, dusty-looking tome lay open upon the desk; Edmund—a large, heavily built gentleman in a soft tweed jacket—was poring over it. He looked up as they entered. His expression mild—deceptively vague—he smiled gently and sat back, removing the thick-lensed pince-nez balanced on his nose.

Dragging in a quick breath, her eyes wild, her hair still loose about her shoulders, Fiona wrenched her hand from Dyan's. He let her go; she threw him a mutinous look, then marched across the room.

Dyan closed the door—and remained in front of it.

Brows lifting slightly, Edmund shifted his mildly bemused gaze from Dyan to his sister, now pacing furiously before the fireplace.

Color high, Fiona swung to face him. "Edmund—I do not wish you to listen to a single word Dyan says—not one!"

"Oh?" Looking even more bemused—in fact, faintly amused—Edmund looked back at Dyan. "Good morning, Darke. What was it you wished to say to me?"

"*No!*" Fiona wailed.

"By your leave, Edmund, I wish to—"

"*Don't* listen to him!"

"—Apply for Fiona's hand—"

"Edmund—he's entirely out of order. I don't want you to pay any attention—"

"—In marriage." Eyes locked with Edmund's, Dyan ignored the seething glare Fiona hurled his way.

Edmund blinked owlishly, then looked at Fiona. "Why shouldn't he ask me that?"

Still pacing, Fiona folded her arms beneath her breasts. "Because I don't wish to consider the matter at present."

"Why not?"

"Because it's too soon."

Edmund blinked—very slowly—again. "Too soon after what?" His gaze slid back to Dyan; he raised a quizzical brow.

"I suspect she means too soon after last night, which she spent in my bed."

"It *wasn't* your bed!" Fiona hotly declared.

Across the room, Dyan met her gaze levelly; he could still see the last remnants of the gloriously distracted look that had filled her golden eyes in the corridor. And last night. "The bed I was then inhabiting." He glanced at Edmund. "At Brooke Hall."

Edmund met his gaze and nodded once, in understanding. Still utterly unperturbed, he again looked at Fiona, now pacing even more furiously. It was Dyan's firm opinion that Edmund, ten full years Fiona's senior, had been born unflappable—which, given his sister's propensities and the adventures he himself had led her into, was probably just as well.

After a long moment, Edmund asked, still in the most reasonable of tones, "How long should Darke and I wait before we discuss this matter?"

Fiona stopped. Lifting her head, she stared at Edmund. Then her eyes blazed. "I don't want you discussing it *at all!* Not until I give my leave. I don't want you to discuss *anything* with Dyan—if he has anything to discuss he can discuss it with me."

Edmund merely opened his eyes wider. "And how long are these discussions between you likely to take?"

Fiona flung her hands in the air. "How the hell should

I know?'' She threw a furious glance at Dyan. ''Given his progress to date, it might well be another fifteen years!''

Uttering a barely smothered, distinctly unladylike sound, she whirled on her heel and stalked down the long room to another door to the corridor. She flung it open and left, slamming it shut behind her. The sound rang in the silence of the library. Both men stared at the door.

''Hmm,'' Edmund said, and reached for his pince-nez.

Dyan blinked. He watched as Edmund settled his spectacles back in place and refocused on his dusty tome. Dyan frowned. ''You don't seem overly concerned. Or surprised.''

Edmund's brows rose; he continued to scan his page. ''Why should I be concerned? I'm sure you'll sort it out. Never was wise to get in the way of either of you—and as for getting *between* you—a fool's errand, that.'' Reaching for a ruler, Edmund aligned it on the page. ''And as for surprise—well, that's hardly likely, is it? The entire county's been waiting for years for the two of you to come to your senses.''

Dyan stared. Oblivious, Edmund went on, ''Only real surprise is that it's taken you so long. Fiona's the only one who's ever hauled on your reins—and you're the only one who's ever rattled her.'' He shrugged. ''Obvious, really. Of course, with you in India, no one liked to *say* anything . . .'' His voice was fading, as if he was sinking back into his tome. ''Presuming you don't actually *want* to wait another fifteen years, she's probably taken refuge in her office—it's the room that used to be Mama's parlor.''

Dyan continued to stare at Edmund's bent head for all of thirty seconds—then shook his head, shook himself, opened the door and went off to track down his obviously fated bride.

Who obviously hadn't expected to be found. The stunned look on her face when he walked in the door was proof enough of that. Coldstream House was a rambling mansion; she should have been safe for hours. Realizing Edmund had betrayed her, she stiffened, lifted her chin, and edged behind a chaise.

His eyes on her, Dyan closed the door. Noting the tilt of her chin, the flash of ire in her eyes, he turned the key in the lock, and calmly removed it. He hefted the key in his palm, watched her gaze lock on it—then slid it into his waistcoat pocket.

And started toward her.

"Dyan—" Fiona lifted her gaze to his face, and retreated fully behind the chaise. She frowned at him. "What do you think you're doing?"

"I'm about to get your agreement to a wedding— ours."

Not entirely under her breath, Fiona swore. He was going to avoid saying the words—she *knew* it. But she'd be damned if she married him after all this time without that— without a clear, straightforward declaration.

"I'm not simply going to agree to marry you." She fixed her gaze on his face, on his eyes, waiting to read his direction.

"That much, I'd gathered." His gaze lifted; his eyes, deep midnight blue, locked on hers. "What I don't yet know is what's going to change your mind."

Snapping free of his visual hold, Fiona, suddenly breathless, realized he was rounding the end of the chaise. With a half-smothered shriek, she turned and raced around the other end. "Words," she said, and glanced over her shoulder.

He followed in her wake, unhurriedly stalking her. "Which particular words would you like?"

"Reasons," Fiona declared. "Your reasons for marrying me." She scuttled behind the second chaise, facing the first on the other side of the fireplace. As long as he didn't pounce, they could go around and around for hours.

Something changed in his face; he looked up and again caught her eye. Fiona fought not to let him mesmerize her. "I don't want you to marry me for any stupid, chivalrous reason—like saving my reputation."

His brows rose; his eyes glinted wickedly. "I didn't know your reputation needed saving." His lips quirked. "Other than from me, of course."

Fiona glared, and slipped around the second chaise. "I *meant* because of attending what I have on excellent authority was an orgy at Brooke Hall."

"I think," Dyan said, head to one side as if considering the matter, "that you'll discover you didn't attend any orgy—in fact, I seriously doubt anyone will remember seeing you there at all. But," he said, steadily tracking her, "if that's what you're bothered about, you may put it from your head. I'm not marrying you to save your reputation."

"Good. So why, then?" Fiona returned to the safety of the first chaise. "And if you tell me it's to get rid of your great-aunt Augusta, I'll scream."

"Ah, well." Dyan surreptitiously closed the gap between them. "You are going to get rid of great-aunt Augusta for me—there's no doubt whatsoever of that. However," he conceded, swiftly lengthening his stride as he neared the *chaise*, "that's not, I admit, why I want to marry you."

"So why?" Safe behind the *chaise*, Fiona turned; Dyan caught her and hauled her into his arms. "Dyan!" She struggled furiously, but he'd trapped her arms instantly. Furious, she looked up, a blistering tirade on her tongue—

He kissed her, and kept kissing her, until she couldn't remember her name. She couldn't think at all; she could only feel—feel the ardor in his kiss, the deep, long-buried yearning, the soul-stealing invitation that she'd first tasted fifteen years before.

And her answer was there—all she needed to know of

why he wished to marry her—it was all there in his kiss. He laid himself bare—showed her what was in his heart. Not simply passion, though there were clouds of that aplenty; not just desire, though the hot waves lapped about them. And not just need, either, although she could sense that, too, like a towering mountain planted at the core of his being.

It was the emotion that rose like a sun over it all, over the landscape of their bound lives.

That was why he would marry her.

The heat of that sun warmed her through and through; Fiona shed her icy armor. Softening in his arms, she wriggled her own free and draped them about his neck. He instantly drew her closer, deepening the kiss, letting the feelings intensify—the passion, the desire, the need—and that other. Fiona gloried in it. Dyan shifted; she didn't realize he was backing her until her hips hit the edge of her desk. He gripped her waist and lifted her, balancing her bottom on the very edge of the desk.

Almost instantly, she felt the cool caress of the air as he lifted her skirts—pushed them up to her waist and tucked the folds behind her. Then he slipped one hand under the front edge of her chemise. Balanced as she was, with his hard thighs between hers, she was open to him; within seconds she was shuddering.

Dyan broke their kiss and trailed his lips down the long curve of her throat. Fiona let her head fall back, her fingers sinking into his shoulders as he slid one long finger past the slick, swollen, pouting flesh throbbing between her thighs, and reached deep. He stroked; she moaned.

Satisfied, Dyan withdrew his hand and went to work on the buttons of his breeches.

"And," he whispered. Fiona lifted her head and their parched lips brushed, then parted. "If you haven't yet got the message—or you've suddenly been struck blind and

can't read it—how about I'm marrying you because . . ."
Even now, he couldn't resist teasing her. Dyan studied her
face, her gloriously distracted expression; his lips twitched.
"You might, even now, be pregnant with my heir."

Her lids flickered; beneath her lashes, her eyes glinted.
Her lips started to firm—Dyan kissed them. "And," he
murmured, wrestling with a button, "if you aren't, I fully
intend to come to you, day and night, and fill you at every
opportunity—until you swell and ripen with my child."

Her lips parted—he immediately covered them. "How
about," he said, the instant he released them, "that I'm marrying you because, without you, the rest of my life will be
as empty as the last fifteen years."

That, he could tell from her eyes, was almost acceptable.

The last button refused to budge; he was so aroused he
was almost in pain. Dyan bit back a groan. Fiona, noticing
his problem, reached down to help. Her smaller fingers dealt
deftly with the recalcitrant button; his staff, engorged, erect,
sprang forth, into her hands.

Dyan groaned again—louder—as her fingers closed
about him. "How about," he ground out, quickly pushing
her hands away, "that I'm marrying you because I need to
be inside you—you and no other—or I'll go insane."

She looked up and, one brow rising quizzically, caught
his eye—he was clearly getting very close to achieving his
goal. He was also getting very close to—

"Dammit, woman, *I love you*! I've loved you forever,
and I'll love you forever. Are *those* the words you want to
hear?"

"*Yes!*" Fiona's face turned radiant. She flung her arms
about his neck and kissed him passionately. She broke off
as he grasped her hips, anchoring her on the very edge of
the desk. "Anyone would think," she said, wriggling a little
as he pressed between her thighs, his staff urgently seeking

her entrance, "that saying those words was painful."

Dyan knew what was painful—he found the source of her slick heat and thrust deep. She gasped, clung tight, and melted—not an iceberg but a volcano, all hot heat, around him. He wrapped his arms about her and, with an aching shudder, sank deep. "Am I to take it that's acceptable? That you can accept that as a suitable reason for our marriage?" He knew she loved him—had known it for confirmed fact the first time she'd parted her thighs for him; she was, after all, Lady Arctic—and he was the only one who'd ever melted her ice.

All he got in answer was a sigh as he embedded himself fully within her. "For God's sake, woman—say yes!"

Fiona tipped back her head; a glorious smile curved her lips. She met his dark eyes, almost black with leashed passion; deliberately she arched, and drew him deeper still. *"Yes."*

She said it, panted it, screamed the word at least six times more, before all fell silent in the office.

He took her in his arms and filled her heart, gave her life purpose, completed her. She took him in her arms and held him, filled the aching void within him, and anchored his wild and reckless soul.

They were married two weeks later; Dyan's heir was born a bare nine months after that. His great-aunt Augusta, for quite the first time in his life, was pleased to approve.